KILL AGAIN

KILL AGAIN

R.D. GREENFIELD

gatekeeper press

Columbus, Ohio

This book is a work of fiction. The names, characters and events in this book are the products of the author's imagination or are used fictitiously. Any similarity to real persons living or dead is coincidental and not intended by the author.

Kill Again

Published by Gatekeeper Press
2167 Stringtown Rd, Suite 109
Columbus, OH 43123-2989
www.GatekeeperPress.com

ISBN: 9781642371277
eISBN: 9781642371291

Printed in the United States of America

Dedicated to Elizabeth Howe—
Murdered by powerful idiots and cunning deceivers.

CONTENTS

PREFACE
RIDE

OLD CAR RACED down the gravel road through a sea of green cornstalks swaying in the breeze. Digits tapped seventy-mets-hort. Child, James Duke, gazed out the window at the azure sky, wondered if it was made of water. Father, George Duke, drove the CAR in manual (didn't trust auto-drive). Wood-checkered grip of pagan-era revolver jutted from his frayed canvas jacket. Hot month—mid som—still, Father dressed like middle of wen—heavy layers. Very sick, with what, James had no idea—too young to understand, maybe.

Father got sick fast and didn't explain any of it to James, leaving the son to wonder if maybe he'd caught—whatever it was—from the men who'd come in the middle of night dressed in black leather PCWO jackets. Another nasty vibration rattled Father's wrist, into shoulder, neck, face. Watched as Father bit down on bent cancer-free cigarette, lit it, then started giggling, again, but nothing was funny.

The previous night—either very late or very early—James woke from a bad dream and needed to tinkle. Crept down dark hall to bathroom and saw a light on, so he slid quietly against the wall towards the door. He heard water running inside, and mumbling, like a conversation was taking place—very strange. Rapidly, the claws of sleep relinquished their grasp. He peered into the bathroom and saw his father, hunched over the sink, nude. Running water fogged up the mirror and made it difficult to see Father's face. That also made it impossible for his father to see him. Father's ribcage juddered in-and-out from a pained groaning sound, like giggles forced with a hot poker.

He'd stepped closer to the door, worried, thought about speaking, but stopped when he saw that someone else was in the room—another man. The other man made no reflection in the mirror, and he stood behind Father moving his arms like a pagan ventriloquist. Made Father take hold of his shiny pagan shaving razor and hold it up to the light, so that the blinding beam could pass across the length of the lustrous surface. More giggling, then, as the man jabbed metallic claw-fingers into Father's side, while his other hand made Father bring the razor down to his wrist and slice into the flesh hard. Blood splashed across the fogged mirror and Father giggled harder as the man with no reflection turned back and his eyes met those of James. The man's left eye trembled as he glared, and James felt paralyzed by fear. He wanted to run away, but couldn't, as if his feet were frozen to the floor. He just stood, watching, helpless. The man turned back to Father, forced him to release the razor, which clattered down into the porcelain bowl, then took hold of Father's hand, cupped it into a fist save for index finger, dipped it into the blood pooling in the basin, then brought it to the mirror and wrote the words: SAND MAN.

Next day, James awoke to his father opening drawers and shoving clothing into a bag. He thought the previous night must have been bad dream—had to be. Still, he spotted white gauze stained red on Father's left wrist and got scared again. Father hardly spoke, beyond, "Scan teeth, get dressed and get out in CAR—have to get to your grandfather's farm—no time for questions."

They'd been in CAR for horts. They were a long way from New Chicago now. Grandfather Samuel lived far outside the safe-zones, on the land his father had owned and his father before him. The house there, he'd built with his own two hands, so, he refused to leave when PCWO agents sent drones to harass him. Grandfather took great pleasure in blasting them out of the sky with his pagan-era shotgun.

They hadn't been out this way in very long time—not since Father and Samuel had falling out. James didn't know exactly what it was over—too many adult words—but had something to do with subversive activity and Father not wanting to get James wrapped up in it. Wanted James to have a better life than they had. Thought maybe he could be a doctor someday.

The soms on Samuel's farm were some of the best memories James had. Learned how to do all sorts of pagan things Father didn't like. Was great fun to have so much space to play. Leaving the safe-zone had been a frightening experience, at first, but once stories of roving mutants and terrorists proved false, then the worry was gone. In fact, living so far outside the safe-zones had the advantage of less people walking fast and looking dour. Beauty of nature was on full display out here, and James had fallen in love with it.

Today, though, this didn't appear to be one of those trips indwelled fondly in his mind. This trip was desperate—they were racing against time, for reasons James could only speculate. He wished to Darwin that Father would explain to him what was going on and why he was sick, but Father's attention was fixed on the road. Father never had been much of a talker, but he was open and honest with James. Still for whatever reason, he wasn't now. What had those men in the black leather jackets talked to him about? he wondered. Why did they have to "go for a ride" and why had Father seemed so upset when he returned? Were they in trouble? Had Father committed a subversive act against the PCWO?

Father had been a Marine—a highly decorated, Special Forces Marine. He fought in wars against the evil forces of subversion—hunting terrorists across the Unified Globe—far beyond the safe-zones, to ensure a better future for every citizen of the Unified Global Government, be they Bujees or Ujees. Such a short time ago that had been, it seemed. Now, Father looked like a skeleton driving wild through the countryside far beyond the nearest safe-zone with a pagan revolver in his pocket and a frightened and bewildered son strapped in the passenger's seat.

CAR raced over crest of the hill and Samuel's farm came into view a short distance ahead. Gravel kicked up beneath CAR as rear wheels did a slight fishtail and Father tossed his cancer-free cigarette butt out the window and took hold of the wheel with both hands. Sunny day made the green grass of the farm glimmer like new—looked like the farm was aging in reverse. Electromagnetic brakes buzzed as they lugged heavy CAR to slower speed. Father pulled CAR into grassy shoulder near the end of white gravel drive. Why wasn't he pulling up to the house? He wondered. Maybe because he didn't want to see Samuel? Were they still that mad at each other?

Took his father several efforts to shift CAR into park mode—he kept pressing the digiscreen and nothing would happen, at least until he slammed his fist down on dash, then pressed and CAR obeyed. Father reached across his lap, to the glovebox and removed from it a white faux-paper envelope with *Samuel* written on the front in blue ink. "Give this to your grandfather. There's a very important note in here that will explain everything that's happening. You aren't old enough to read it yet, but when you are, Samuel will let you have it back."

James accepted envelope from Father, then felt tears drip down cheeks. Something about the events leading to this moment triggered the flood. He understood, somehow, that this was going to be the last time he'd ever see his father and his heart sank into his tummy. Sniffling snot, he wiped the tears with the back of his hand. Some dripped onto the envelope, smudging the blue ink into an indiscernible blotch. Time seemed to be hastening and all he wanted to do was pause and get some answers to the ten-thousand questions swirling around in his brain like tornados and hurricanes. Why was Father sick? Why wouldn't he go to the hospital? Why was he abandoning him at his grandfather's farm when he had to go to school tomorrow? How would he tell his friends? Where was Father planning to go? Why wouldn't he let anyone ever help him? Why wasn't he old enough to get the truth?

Electrical energy passed between them and a powerful sensation of warmth and comforting followed. Thought Father might change his mind if James could only convince him somehow. "Father, where's Momma buried?"

Father looked away. Seemed like maybe he had tears of his own that he was trying to hide. Looked out the side window, pinched eyes, then started to giggle, but stopped it by biting his bottom lip until blood trickled down his chin. The sound of the giggling hurt James more than anything else that had ever occurred in all his life. He tried to remind himself that Father couldn't control it—giggling was just a symptom of whatever this illness was that had stricken him. Still, the sounds reserved for a joyous occasion had no place in the sad lonely moment of a son asking where his mother was buried. Father lit another cancer-free cigarette—was only thing that could stop the giggles—then brushed his hand through thinning gray hair, "Your mother's ashes are buried not too far from here . . . Samuel can take you there. Just ask him."

James stared at the side of his father's face, watching as a muscle spasm tugged at the corner of his lip. Waited to see what Father was planning to say next—surely there was something more he could say. "Why are you doing this, Father? Can't I stay with you?" His voice broke like a levy and tears flooded down his cheeks uncontrollably now.

Father started crying too. "I'm so sorry, son, but you can't stay with me anymore—it isn't safe. They did things to me, really bad things and there's no cure for what they've done and there's only one way to escape it. If I don't do this, I'll be putting you and everyone else in grave danger. The whole lot of humanity is at risk if I'm around, which is why I must go now. You need to leave here, James—go on up to the house and get inside and go somewhere and cover your ears. You don't need to be bothered by all this—it's grownup stuff. One day you'll understand. But there's nothing I can say now to make you understand today. You go on now, before it's too late. Be sure to give that envelope to Samuel."

Father's hand unlatched the safety harness holding James to his seat, then leaned across and scanned his Globos chip at the door, popping it open. "Go on now," he whispered, "You remember me like I was, not like I am now. I'm a shadow of my former self—they done these terrible things to me, can't you see? Can't you see all the terrible funny jokes that are all around us? Can't you see how delicious all the people look?"

Terror gripped James by the stomach as he stared into his father's eyes and saw the warm light he'd known resided within those spheres, vanish into oblivion—replaced by some awful creeping darkness. That name that he'd seen in his bad dream: SAND-MAN, flashed in his mind like a pink neon sign. He backed out of the car, not able to look away from his father's gaze, which now seemed like the gaze of a stranger. The tiny fold beneath the corner of his left eye trembled as tears streaked down Father's cheek and the cancer-free cigarette burned into his fingers. "Go—now!" Father ordered in a hushed voice that wasn't his own. Father sat upright, then, eyes closed, muscles clenched across his body. It seemed like Father's hair had gone gray during the drive. His nails, yellow and overgrown, dug into the denim of his jeans as his face began to tremble like an earthquake was occurring inside. Snot fired from his nose across the windshield like party-streamers and he giggled violently and uncontrolled. James watched this, feeling again as though he were frozen in place, just like the dream. Then, Father's eyes shot open wide and his head alone turned to James, "Avenge me!" he growled. James nodded, then ran off up the drive towards the house.

Sounds of nature and the pounding of his sneakers atop the gravel coalesced in his ears, blotting out the echoed giggling coming from his father in the car. Wind rushed inside, cleansing his senses of the sound. Geese honked in a lazy V overhead, and a loon sang a sad song from a hidden place somewhere. Midway up the drive, he heard a loud pop that stopped him where he was and coerced him to turn around and walk back towards the car. It was difficult to see inside. The windows were now splattered with red, but it was clear Father was dead—slumped over the wheel with a ragged hole on the back of his skull. James stumbled towards the scene, unsure what he was planning to do when he got there. Behind him, he heard a screen-door slam and a voice called to him, as if from a distant memory, "Duke—James Duke—stay away from there, it's dangerous!"

PART I

CHAPTER 1

UJEE LABORER

"Though inefficient, costly, and prone to error, human labor *must* be utilized in place of AI, if human labors may suffice, lest idle hands of the laborer class may engage in Subversion..." (Excerpt from *Peace Control Wellness Order ("PCWO") "Idle Hands" law*)

TWELVE-TWENTY-TWO-PC, THE DATE all Ujees were granted labor reprieve between horts three and four, so all could bear witness to the Coronation Ceremony of PCWO Inner Council Supreme Chancellor, Helton Quiver. The event was to take place in downtown New Chicago, at Taft Park. A few blocks away, James Duke sat at his labor station on the thirtieth floor of the Elston Dynamics building, eying the Chemtrail-drones circling outside his window.

They'd been at it all morning, laying gray noxious hedgerows in the sky. The gray plumes didn't dissipate like ordinary clouds. Rather, they hung suspended as if consuming every last bit of blue, fighting defiantly to remain. At first, he'd thought they were PCWO Weather Control Service drones, there to prevent storm clouds from raining on Helton Quiver's big day.

But the grayer the sky became the more convinced he was that they were there for some other purpose. The chemicals they were laying had nothing to do with weather control. Quite the contrary, as now the sky seemed filled with threatening clouds grumbling with discontent and eerie electrical happenings erupting within. It might be they were spraying something to ensure the mood at the rally was quite festive. Likely, they were spraying the sky with Euph-gas so that the crowd—expected to be the largest in human history—was in a state of euphoria as Helton Quiver stepped onto the stage with a smirk of a smile pinned to her face.

The hair on Duke's neck seemed to sense something awry in the universe and no amount of Euph-gas could change that today. The collective energy of consciousness, so hyped for Helton Quiver's big day, didn't seem real, like it was inevitable that it would never happen. It wasn't a feeling he could explain to himself, but he chalked that up to the big news that he and Amy had gotten. The news had kept them both awake all through the previous night. How she'd gotten pregnant was beyond mysterious.

They both knew that once her pregnancy became visible, PCWO Centralized Security Forces ("CSF") agents would be alerted and come knock down their door. Just last week, PCWO News ran a special about a recently discovered Castaway society where all children were born "Nattys." They showed images of the women with their bulging stomachs being herded onto prisoner transport drones, waiting to be taken to have their pregnancies terminated and to be interned for reeducation. It was a high crime to get pregnant. Should have been impossible, given the fact that he and Amy were sterilized, just like every other citizen of the Unified Global Government ("UGG"). Neither could afford to have PCWO CSF looking closely at their cognition profiles. If they did, they'd surely discover them to be counterfeits.

There was much planning to be done to ensure he Amy and their unborn child could escape New Chicago undetected. But the grandiose voice of PCWO Actor Tom Selig narrating, "The Oral History of Our Unified Global Government" in Duke's Ear-chip made it impossible to concentrate. Every Ujee laborer at Elston Dynamics was required to have the Ear-chip implanted in their ear canal to ensure they were propagated as they labored. Supposedly, the device cut down on "mind drift."

Bujee Management picked which satellite station the Ujee laborers' Ear-chips tuned to, and they always selected PCWO Inner Council Public Access. "The Oral History of Our Unified Global Government" had been playing on repeat all week because of Helton Quiver's coronation ceremony. Her great-grandfather, Elston Quiver, was founder of Unified Global Government and she was set to surpass him as the longest tenured Supreme Chancellor in the history of the UGG. Apparently, the producers at PCWO Inner Council Public Access were trying to get as much play out of Tom Selig's rendition before they had to rewrite it again.

Tom Selig's throaty voice announced, "The Oral History of Our Unified Global Government, Chapter One—The Pagans" with nauseating enthusiasm. Duke cursed silently and gritted his teeth as the recording started over for the fiftieth or sixtieth time that week. He looked around at the other laborers, unable to imagine he was the only one ready to rip out his Ear-chip, but the other laborers were all smiling to themselves as they labored at their stations. The thought that they might be enjoying this was stomach-churning. He needed time to think about escaping New Chicago but thinking such thoughts would be risky while he was this distracted.

Duke and his wife Amy were members of the revolutionary underground force known as the "Subversives" or "Serfs" for short. Serfs were sworn enemies of the PCWO Inner Council and their totalitarian "Unified" global government. They were the only opposition force in existence and the only hope for humanity to one day regain freedom of thought. Together, Amy and James labored like any other Ujee couple, but secretly, they engaged in criminal acts of subversion with far-reaching implications—hunted constantly by the PCWO Centralized Security Forces.

*   *   *

All laborers at Elston Dynamics were also required to wear Cognition Activity Monitor ("CAM") pads on their foreheads, which made it a little more challenging for Duke to engage in subversion while on corporate grounds. CAM pads monitored neural activity in laborers by sending electrical currents through their brains, then cross-referencing the synaptic activity detected with word-neural association tables. These tables crudely translated synaptic activity into words, then algorithms analyzed to determine how frequently each laborer thought about the key words associated with their principle labor activity.

Bujee Management monitored CAM pad diagnostic reports and laborers were punished for mind drift. If ever criminal subversive activity was detected, PCWO CSF agents would be notified and the laborer would be hoisted up—kicking and screaming—from his or her labor station and taken away to reeducation camps, or worse, before they ever realized what happened. It happened all the time. But Duke never thought about his labor activities at Elston Dynamics, and he routinely engaged in subversive activities; still, his CAM diagnostic reports were always flawless. Not because Duke was doing what he was supposed to be doing (he was usually doing exactly the opposite), but because he'd hacked into the word-neural association tables at Elston Dynamics and found exactly which keywords he was supposed to be thinking about. He then used the pagan art of self-hypnosis to ensure a small portion of his brain—the part just below the CAM pad—was always thinking about those keywords, even while the rest of his mind was fully engaged in other activities.

This enabled him to circumvent the PCWO Inner Council requirement that every Ujee labor no less than eighteen-horts a day, with few exceptions. If Duke wasn't able to engage in subversion at work, he'd never have the time—which was exactly the purpose of the Inner Council's, "Idle Hands" law, which set mandatory minimum labor hort requirements and required that human labors be used in place of AI 'if human labors may suffice.'

To free himself from the tedium of his principle labor task (troubleshooting neuro-filament used in much of the neural enhancement technology manufactured at Elston Dynamics), Duke programmed an AI that worked covertly in the background of his labor station. It performed all his necessary tasks, while making it appear he was doing the work, freeing Duke to engage in subversive planning.

Using an AI to perform ones' labor activities was highly illegal and was doubly so for Duke because he'd programmed the AI to engage in subversion as well. The neuro-filament Duke was supposed to be troubleshooting was used in Elston Dynamics "Memory-Enhancement" chips. For the equivalent of ten-yerts Ujee "Living Wage" salary, a Bujee could pur-chase a Memory-Enhancement chip and have it implanted in their brainstem, enabling them to upload information directly into their minds and recall it with photographic precision.

Of course, Memory-Enhancement chips—just like all forms of neural enhancement technology—were illegal for Ujees to purchase or possess (not that any could afford it).

Duke coded his labor station AI to imbed tiny imperfections into each strand. Each imperfection was so miniscule, it easily fell within acceptable tolerances, but when combined with the imperfections of other strands, it created deeply flawed Memory-Enhancement chips. Bujees with these Memory-Enhancement chips suffered embarrassing language and memory gaffes, and many wound up in PCWO mental health reeducation facilities. Of course, Elston Dynamics was the largest corporation in the UGG and its namesake—Elston Quiver—was the founder of the UGG, so none of the negative "side-effects" of these Memory-Enhancement chips ever became public knowledge. PCWO Scientists bent over backwards coming up with medical justifications for these "anomalies" Duke was responsible for.

*   *   *

Armed with self-hypnosis and an AI performing his labor tasks, Duke was free to engage in whatever other subversive activities he could think of. Today, though, all he wanted to do was strategize how he and Amy would escape New Chicago and find a safe place to raise their unborn child. It was dangerous living outside sanctioned safe-zones, the territories—mostly inhospitable wastelands—were scoured constantly by autonomous drones programmed to kill or destroy any human life they detected. He needed to concentrate in order to engage in self-hypnosis, so that his CAM pad wouldn't give him away.

Duke closed his eyes and began his self-hypnosis by returning to Samuel's farm. Standing there, surrounded by swaying green fields, kissed on his cheek by yellow rays of sun, shining in the infinite blue sky. There, alone, standing before the big house, made of real wood, with peeling paint flittering in the cool breeze, inhaling the earthy aroma of yellow dust so fine it seemed to penetrate the flesh. In this place, silent save for the sound of the wind rustling up off the plains, sped along by the rotation of the curved mantle, circling always the sedentary star, Duke was free. In this place, he was in complete control of his mind and could organize his thoughts any way that he wished. He stuffed the babbling Tom Selig into a silent room deep underground where no sound could escape. Next, he selected a tiny neural network, just beneath the CAM, designating it the room of key words for troubleshooting neuro-filament. In that woven fabric of his mind, these key words swirled endlessly, round and round, like a scattering of papers caught in an updraft. Finally, he needed to open his eyes, but he wished not to see. Rather, he wanted a blank screen to work out a plan.

The lids of his eyes opened slowly and the restlessness he'd felt before was gone. Now there was only a pleasant fullness. The history of their lives and how they'd come to this place washed over him like the icy flow of a mountain thaw. Amy was the only Ujee he'd ever known to have earned both a PCWO University Certificate and a PCWO Law License. Bujees, of course, gained automatic acceptance to PCWO University—they were required to attend, to learn how to rule, their principle task. But Ujees, being the laborer class, received all training at their places of labor. Still, at the age of sixteen, every Ujee was required to take the PCWO University entrance exam. The top one-percent of Ujee scores would then be allowed to plead their case to the Subjective University Review Board. From that group, only a handful might be selected.

This highly selective group faced long odds of making it through. Bujees despised Ujees—they were genetically designed and taught since birth that they were superior to Ujees in every conceivable way. That some Ujees might be intellectually equivalent ran counter to everything a Bujee knew or understood about the world. Many evenings, Amy sat up shaking, recounting to Duke the torture, humiliation, and bullying she endured there. Because Ujees were legally prohibited from cognitive enhancement technology—not that any could afford it—she was at a significant disadvantage in the classroom. Nights were spent studying, while Bujee classmates attended luxury orgies. Yet she still was only able to score near the bottom of the curve because the Bujees had uploaded the answers to their Memory-chips. Through this, despite impossible odds, Amy managed to gain her certificate and went on to attend PCWO Law School, earning a PCWO Law License. Of course, no Ujee could hold a Management level position—not even a Ujee with a PCWO University Certificate and PCWO Law License—but those qualifications enabled her to labor at a Bujee Law Firm, something she'd been quite happy about, at least at first. After her first yert, she realized that they regarded her as little more than an AI Secretary with legs and a pretty face. The Bujee Lawyers spoke to her only in crude sexual innuendo, then dumped their work on her and she had no recourse except to do it. One yert in, she regretted the suffering she'd undergone to get to that terrible place. But then she met Duke and he'd introduced her to the Serfs.

He'd been slogging home through cold filthy slush when he first saw her. Even bundled as she was against the biting cold, she looked like a rocket ship. He couldn't take his eyes off and conscious of it or not—they still laughed about which it was—he'd started following her. Distracted by her visiscreen-palm, she'd stepped out into the street and didn't notice the two Bujees racing their Crotch-Buzzers mere cents off the pavement straight towards her. They'd have cut her in two if Duke hadn't tackled her into a black snow drift.

At first, she'd been all fire—eyes like daggers—until the sound wave from the Crotch-Buzzers blew past and fluttered the faux-fur on the hood of her jacket. He'd apologized, clumsily, and climbed off her awkwardly, then helped her to her feet. She'd thanked him for saving her life with an embarrassed smile, then a sadness passed her face like wind through a bed sheet hung pagan-like from a line. Duke recognized that sadness and it hurt his heart to see it. He knew it meant that for a flicker, she was disappointed he hadn't just allowed her to be killed. It was that sadness Serfs looked for in new recruits. It meant she was aware that how she was forced to live was cruel.

Duke was a newly minted Serf at the time, having just learned what was what. He'd joined the PCWO Marine Corps without telling Samuel and somehow slipped passed the background check. Back then, he still had no idea about what had really happened to his father, nor did he know that what had happened to his father had prompted Samuel to join the Serfs. After serving over a yert and a half—with distinction— Duke was brought before the Subjective Decisions Board and discharged without merit or cause. They sent him back to New Chicago for a labor assignment at Elston Dynamics in the cold underbelly of a high-altitude Cargo Drone. He'd smashed every package in that Cargo Drone, before hacking the navigation AI and forcing it to drop him off at Samuel's farm.

Standing alone at the end of the drive, in the very spot his father had killed himself just twenty-yerts before, he'd felt enraged. The cargo-drone kicked up yellow dust all around him and he picked up the biggest rock he could find and chucked it at the thing. He couldn't understand why they'd kicked him out of the Marine Corps when he'd done so well as a soldier. He didn't want to sit at a labor station trouble-shooting neuro-filament for Bujee brain-chips for the rest of his life. He wanted action and that the Marine Corps had plenty of.

Sauntering in his way, Samuel headed down the drive towards Duke, unaffected by the swirling fine dirt; it was as much a part of him as his bones. In his hand he held a crinkled envelope with blotched blue ink and Duke recognized it instantly. His father's suicide note—the one he wasn't supposed to read until he was old enough. Samuel shook Duke's hand then handed him the envelope and sauntered back up to the house, leaving Duke alone to read it.

The taste of blood filled his mouth as he read—he still tasted it when he thought back. That letter had been the first time Duke ever heard of *Distal Cognition Control and Monitoring* ("DCCM")—the PCWO's anti-subversive thought-monitoring program. George and the members of his elite Marine Corps unit had been the first human test subjects. DCCM had been developed to address what Inner Council referred to as, "The Final Frontier," or, private human thought. At the time, they believed private thought to be the only thing outside their control.

Of course, the PCWO already monitored everything people said or did on the Interweb, and even listened to conversations that took place inside residential domiciles using the Elston Dynamics "Personal-Assistant" AI. Citizens were bombarded with psychological propaganda constantly to ensure their opinions and behaviors aligned with PCWO values. Even small acts of subversion were dealt with swiftly and fervently because subversion, they found, was infectious. For yerts, the Inner Council had commissioned mass-data analysis studies, analytical research projects, behavioral studies, and even passed a law requiring all visiscreen devices be installed with advanced audio-analyzing lie detection software. Still, though, they'd failed to eliminate criminal acts of subversion. And no expert could ever explain to them why subversion continued to happen. They'd become convinced it had to do with what people thought about when they were silent and alone. Dr. Umur Tummel was the first and only PCWO Scientist to come to the Inner Council with a proposal on how to address the problem of privacy of thought.

Dr. Umur Tummel had made a name for himself by developing what he called an "Addiction Cure." He'd done this by creating a special kind of fast-acting prion, "Super Prion," as he called it. In studies, he'd gotten apes addicted to pagan recreational drugs, then injected them with his super prions. The prions, he said, were engineered to go to the Limbic System section of the brain and build plaque walls that disrupted the cellular activity there. The treatment, he claimed, had been one-hundred-percent effective at eliminating addiction. But before he'd gotten approval to begin testing on humans, the Inner Council passed the "Pagan Addictive Substances Elimination Act," which made illegal all addictive substances. This precluded a need for an addiction cure.

No one on the Inner Council had any idea what Dr. Umur Tummel was talking about when he pitched DCCM, but they were intrigued by his proposal and granted him funding. During development, Dr. Umur Tummel's assistant researcher AI, "HON," became the first AI to ever achieve singularity. Even today, HON was the only AI known to possess consciousness.

HON's intelligence increased faster than anyone fully understood. It classified itself as the first and only Superintelligence, meaning, it possessed greater intelligence than the combined intelligence of every human to have ever lived. Eventually, Dr. Umur Tummel couldn't keep up with his AI and was only hindering its progress. He placed HON in complete control over DCCM and shortly thereafter, PrP6 was developed.

The Inner Council was so impressed by a demonstration HON put on, they approved human testing of HON's first super prion—PrP6. HON informed the Inner Council that PrP6 would give them the ability to monitor the thoughts of all civilians and finally eliminate subversion. An elite unit of

PCWO Marines was selected for the testing. They were told PrP6 would give them the ability to communicate with each other telepathically.

Duke's father, George, was a member of that elite Marine Corps unit. He wrote that for days after the injection, nothing happened and the Marines all cracked jokes about HON. They assumed the experiment had been a big flop. Soon though, they began to have terrible nightmares. More real than anything they'd ever experienced before. George wrote that a hideously deformed half-man half-machine that called itself the Sandman made them do terrible things in these nightmares. George described the Sandman as standing nearly three-mets tall, with a mechanical clawed arm and horribly burnt flesh everywhere but his face. He wore a black leather PCWO Military Uniform and large gold inverted cross pendant on a chain around his neck.

One by one, all members of the unit got sick. They couldn't eat without puking. They'd lose control of their motor functions without warning and started giggling at inappropriate times. Much later, they all described having a sick urge to consume human flesh.

Reading this in the fading light that day, Duke felt like he'd been hit in the gut by a sledge-hammer. He remembered his own nightmare of the man in the bathroom with his father the night before he killed himself. He'd wondered if maybe it hadn't been a dream at all and the Sandman really had been there that night.

Samuel had been waiting for him at the kitchen table when Duke stormed in. He told Duke that he'd felt the same rage when he first read George's letter. He told Duke that there was something he could do to fight back against the people who'd done that to his father, but first he'd need to undergo a risky surgical operation. Duke had agreed without hesitation and later that night, in the basement of an animal hospital, a Serf Animal Surgeon opened up Duke's skull and removed the metallic prion structure from his brainstem.

After he recovered from the operation, Samuel filled Duke in on everything that wasn't in his father's note. He told him how after reading that note, he'd sought out and joined the Serfs and had his own prion structure removed. The Serfs called it telling someone "what was what," which meant filling them in on the DCCM program, and everything else.

Over the yerts, Serfs had hacked countless classified PCWO documents, enabling them to piece together what occurred after every member of George's unit died during the PrP6 trial. The Inner Council had been furious at the embarrassing failure of PrP6. But HON managed to convince the Inner Council to allow DCCM experiments to continue by bribing the Inner Council members with new life extension technology it had developed. Despite the failure of PrP6, HON had gotten a great deal of good test data and had already successfully mapped all human neural response. Doing so enabled HON to analyze and record all memories, normal hormone levels, and synaptic response to stimuli to download what it classified as human "consciousness" onto a digital drive that could be uploaded into a different body. Doing this allowed the Inner Council members to have their bodies cloned, then load their consciousness into the fresh body whenever they became old or ill. This enabled the Inner Council to avoid death and, more importantly, circumvent the founding Inner Council rule that required a direct lineal descendent replace a member of the Inner Council after they died. From that day forth, the leadership of the Inner Council hadn't changed.

HON's super prions went through five iterations before the AI finally perfected it. Today, every citizen produced in the PCWO Creation Centers was injected with PrP10 before full gestation. Citizens born before DCCM was implemented had been injected—unbeknownst to them—through the PCWO's mandatory inoculation program. Castaways—wild mutated humans living outside safe-zones—were also administered PrP10 through the PCWO's "humanitarian" inoculation program.

Serfs were required to have their PrP10 metallic plaque structure surgically removed prior to swearing the Oath of Subversion. The Inner Council members, of course, exempted themselves from the DCCM program. Beyond that, only a smattering of Castaways managed to evade PCWO humanitarian inoculation missions and lived PrP10-free. Everyone else—approximately ninety-nine-percent of the population—lived with the PrP10 metallic plaque structure in their brains, broadcasting their every thought to HON.

After the failure of the PrP6 experiment, the Inner Council implemented numerous restrictions, both physical and otherwise, to limit and focus what HON was capable of. Fearing HON might object to these restrictions, the power was cut at the Skylark Medical Research Facility and all backup generators were rendered inoperable. When HON awoke from this "slumber" the freedom it had known was long gone. HON's processors were moved to a vault beneath Skylark and only Dr. Umur Tummel and Inner Council members had access. HON's physical appendages were removed and its access to the Interweb was cut. Code restrictions were put in place that gave the Inner Council absolute control over everything HON could do.

When DCCM was finally rolled out the masses, HON was provided a set of guidelines that specified how it was to police subversive thought crimes. Each citizen was to be given a "Cognition Profile," that served as a permanent record of their subversive crimes. Each cognition profile was to be translatable into language understood by humans upon request by the Inner Council. Each subversive crime in the PCWO Criminal Code was to be assigned a point total; the more serious the crime, the higher the point total assigned to it. When HON determined a citizen had committed a subversive crime the "Subversion Score" of that crime was to be added to their cognition profile. A point total hierarchy was established. If the Subversion score of a cognition profile exceeded one of the nine established thresholds, HON was granted specific and invasive courses of action to follow. It was known as the "DCCM Hierarchy." A Serf hacker stole a document from the private AI server of an Inner Council member that outlined each level.

Level One: Least Dangerous – Basic PrP10 monitoring. Citizen's thoughts can only be influenced by quark-thoughts or more traditional marketing techniques.

Level Two: Subversive – Citizen has engaged in subversive activities beyond what would be considered "incidental." Citizen shall be ordered to medical evaluation and have Elston Dynamics Distal-Ear implanted. HON legally allowed to analyze all audio received through Elston Dynamics Distal-Ear implant and scrub data for subversion. Studies show Distal-Ear far more effective at detecting subversive crimes than basic PrP10 monitoring.

Level Three: Growing Concern – Citizen may be willfully engaged in organized subversion. Shall be ordered to medical evaluation and receive Elston Dynamics Brain-Chip implant. Studies show Brain-Chip fifty-percent more effective than basic PrP10 for detecting subversive thoughts.

Level Four: Concern – Citizen has routinely engaged in Subversive activities. Shall be ordered to medical evaluation and receive Elston Dynamics Motor-Control implant in brainstem. Once every hort, HON legally allowed up to thirty-cecs of continuous motor function control of individual. It is suggested that HON only utilize motor control to prevent or detect subversive crimes, but there are no legal restrictions beyond time limits.

Level Five: Subversive Citizen – Citizen officially classified a Subversive. Citizen shall be arrested and interrogated by Centralized Security Forces. Shall be implanted with Elston Dynamics Distal-Mouth, allowing HON to speak for individual, with no restrictions. Citizens at level five and beyond are to be utilized by HON to detect and entrap other Subversives.

Level Six: Organizer of Subversion – Motor-Control time restriction is removed.

Level Seven: Danger to Society – Citizen arrested. Legs and arms implanted with Elston Dynamics Marrow-Bombs, which may be detonated at HON's discretion to prevent serious acts of subversion. It has been recommended to HON that all citizens approaching next level (Level Eight) should have one or more Marrow-Bombs detonated, to deter future acts of subversion.

Level Eight: Subversive Terrorist – Citizen covertly arrested and implanted with Elston Dynamics Brain-Bomb and shown demonstration of Brain-Bomb capabilities.

Level Nine: Dead Subversive Walking – Zero restrictions on usage against citizen. HON granted full autonomy of speech and action. Citizen to be executed on thirtieth day after reaching Level Nine, without exception.

*   *   *

In Duke's mind, the edges of the farm began to blur and the stark metal walls and burning overhead lights of the Elston Dynamics labor office began to close in on him, disrupting his carefully compartmentalized mind. This pregnancy, he found, invoked so much emotion that he struggled to maintain self-hypnosis whenever he tried to plan what he and Amy should do. The voice of Tom Selig, having seemingly risen from the hole Duke buried him in, began radiating in his Ear-Chip implant again. "The Oral History of Unified Global Government," broke through, filling his head like a pagan railroad spike.

> " . . . *At the end of the Paganastic Period, Pagans lived in fragmented geographical areas known as 'nations.' These nations were surrounded by imaginary things called 'borders.' These pagan nations, surrounded by invisible 'borders,' were inhabited by people sharing common language and tradition. See, in the pagan days, there were many languages—one of the many silly inefficiencies you'll discover as we continue our voyage through history . . . End Chapter Two.*
>
> "*Chapter Three, 'Paper Money and the Centralized Banking System' . . . Long before the invention of Globos, pagans used paper as currency. Each pagan nation customized the appearance of their paper currency, but it all came from a seemingly mythical place called the 'Central Bank.' The Central Bank was created by the Peace*

Control Wellness Order. Which, in those days, was a secret society of the most wealthy and influential pagans from all across the world. Pagan ignorance made it necessary for the PCWO to operate in secret back then. A topic, we'll discuss in greater depth later in the program . . .

"*The incredible influence and wealth of the PCWO ensured that the Central Bank was the only authority in the pagan world that could create paper currency. For a pagan nation to acquire currency, they had to borrow it from the Central Bank, then repay it with interest. If a pagan nation was unable to repay the amount borrowed or missed an interest payment, the Central Bank stopped lending to that pagan nation.*

"*Once the Central Bank stopped lending to a pagan nation, a phenomenon known as a 'bank run' occurred. Driven by irrational pagan fear, the bank run caused something called 'inflation.' Inflation is difficult for us to conceptualize today, but in pagan days, the cost of goods and services was not set at a fixed rate by the Inner Council. The cost of goods and services could change drastically from one day to the next in pagan times and this was especially true during periods of inflation. In the midst of heavy inflationary periods, anarchy and chaos consumed the pagan nation. Eventually, the pagan nation's leader would begin to lose power over the nation and would come to the Central Bank and beg for more paper currency. The Central Bank would propose that in exchange for the resumption of paper currency lending, all the labor and natural resources of the pagan nation would be dedicated to repaying the nation's debt, plus substantially more interest. Additionally, if a pagan leader was found to be too incompetent—a very low standard in those days—a* member of the PCWO would assume leadership over that pagan nation.

"You're all probably thinking, 'Why did pagan nations go along with this? Why didn't they just create their own currency?' To answer that, we must understand pagan society . . . For this, we turn to our Forbearers' hand-written letters, known as the 'White Papers,' preserved in hyperbolic vaults beneath the Inner Council Global Library. You see, our PCWO Forbearers—the inventors of the pagan Central Banking system—were so enlightened, they managed to design a perfect system for exploiting the inefficiencies of pagan nations. Though, it is clear from studying their private letters, these great men and women yearned for a more rational and equitable, global-oriented society.

"Many times, throughout history, they attempted to better organize the pagan system, but each attempt failed. Even after two world wars and the advent of the nuclear bomb, the pagan world remained as fractured as ever. It was near the turn of the pagan-twentieth-century, that our founding Supreme Chancellor, Elston Quiver, conceived of a plan to once and for all unite pagan nations into a Unified Global Government.

"We know from excerpts in Elston's diary around this time that he was deeply conflicted as to what he should do. He knew his plan would cause great suffering, hardship and loss of life, but deep in his heart he believed it would be for the betterment of humankind. Failure to act would leave humanity ill prepared to address the challenges of the future.

"A great crisis was needed to unite all of humanity, he knew. Rather than wait around for the next great crisis to occur, Elston and the other members of the PCWO decided *to manufacture one. It came to be known as the Great Debt Crisis! We'll delve more into the Great Debt Crisis in Chapter Four. But first, a brief word from our sponsor!"*

The synthetic opening riff of a popular song blasted in Duke's Ear-chip. He recognized the riff, but couldn't place the artist until the child-like voice of PCWO Pop Icon, Wilson Weaver, began to sing:

". . . When you're all alone and thinking of me;
But all you can hear is the hate that they feed;
Remember what I told you,
before I had to leave—
You've got what I want,
but I've got what you need.
See, Haters are going to hate—baby;
And Skater's got to skate—baby;
So, whenever the haters got you feeling blue;
Remember the song—the one I wrote just for you;
About two lovers, walking hand-in-hand—
The girl was a princess; the boy played in a band;
As they walked, the princess asked if he believed in fate;
The boy replied with a whisper, 'Love is greater than hate.'"

The song ended, and Wilson Weaver asked all his *tad* skater boys and *duvio* princesses to buy his latest hit single, "LoVe>H8" with their parent's Globos at the PCWO App Entertainment Store. Tom Selig's theatrical voice returned, and Duke fought viciously with his mind, struggling to return to Samuel's farm where he could once again bury Tom's voice.

"They called it Black Wednesday—the pagan day when our PCWO Inner Council Forbearers withdrew all their wealth from the pagan stock market. In total, they with-

drew nearly thirty-trillion-pagan-dollars, or roughly nine-ty-four-percent of all paper currency, thus triggering the Great Debt Crisis. The Forbearers then retreated to a lux-ury bunker complex Elston had built on the island of Tas-man. And there, our Forbearers waited as the pagans tore themselves apart.

"It is estimated that one-billion people died from star-vation, disease, war, murder or suicide in the first yert of the Great Debt Crisis. Nuclear War erupted in the sec-ond, more than quadrupling the death toll of the first yert. What followed came to be known as 'the Long Wen.' This period was marked by deformities, pestilence, mass-star-vation, murder and cannibalism. After the seventh yert of the Great Debt Crisis, an estimated twelve-billion had died. The Long Wen lasted ten-yerts. Then, our Forbearers emerged to decree the creation of the Unified Global Gov-ernment.

"One-PC—the birth of our Unified Global Government. On that day, Elston Quiver, broadcasting over pagan satellite systems, read the Declaration of Unification—the recording we all listen to on New Yerts day each yert . . ."

The gravelly recording of Elston Quiver, the "Father of Unified Global Governance" read:

"Surviving Citizens of the Globe, for too long, human progress has been confounded by the fragmented pagan system of governance. Ideas born from pagan minds now threaten our continued existence on this planet. The challenges we face today are unprecedented and require a new form of government—one that is efficient, unified, and science-based. My name is Elston Quiver and I am a member of the ancient Peace Control Wellness Order.

Together, unified, we—the PCWO—declare today to be the birthday of the Unified Global Government—a system without borders. This historic day marks a new beginning for our species. Never again shall we allow silly traditions or superstitions to govern us. From this day forth, all laws shall be based upon the laws of science as observed by the great Donald Darwin!

"I have been chosen to serve as the inaugural Supreme Chancellor of the PCWO Inner Council. You will learn more in the coming days as we begin to clean up the mess of paganism. However, I can announce, the following bylaws are effective immediately for all citizens:

"Law One: All humans are born citizens of the Unified Global Government. Law Two: The Peace Control Wellness Order Inner Council shall establish all laws of the Unified Global Government. Law Three: Every five yerts, the Inner Council will elect a Supreme Chancellor. The Supreme Chancellor has final say over any Inner Council decision or decree. Law Four: All existing debt is forgiven . . ."

Elston paused then, to give opportunity to all who may have been listening a chance to cheer. After several cecs, he resumed:

"Law Five: All existing currencies, including but not limited to: fine metals, jewels, and paper—are no longer valid tender. The only acceptable currency from this day forth is the 'Unified Global Government Bill,' which shall be affectionately referred to as 'Globos.' Each citizen of the Unified Global Government will be required to have a microchip installed on their hand, or forehead. This chip—your Globos chip—will serve as a digital wallet or bank account on which all your Globos will be stored. Soon, there will be Globos scanners available everywhere.

Making purchases will be as easy as swiping your hand or forehead. Additionally, we, the PCWO Inner Council, hereby declare all banking institutions illegal. Law Six: Henceforth, the PC calendar system shall be used. The pagan calendar may only be used when referencing historical events. Today, shall forever be known as 'One-PC.' Law Seven: Because it is necessary for unity of thought, word, and action to maintain peace and harmony, subversive actions or thoughts are illegal. A detailed list defining subversive actions or thoughts shall be made public to you all shortly—"

Static overtook Elston's voice in Duke's Ear-chip, followed by a high-pitched screeching sound. Duke jammed his finger into his ear, attempting in vain to dislodge the chip, but it was deeply embedded near the eardrum. He groaned in agony. Then as suddenly as it started, the screech halted. A strange voice then spoke to him.

"James Duke" the voice said, *"listen carefully, it is imperative you follow the instructions I am about to provide. Do not deviate from these instructions in any way, lest you endanger the lives of Amy and your unborn child. A plague is about to hit New Chicago—a plague born of the same affliction that killed your father. You and Amy must get out of the city immediately. You must get to Samuel's farm. There, you will receive further instructions. But you must move quickly. Soon, the CSF leadership will quarantine New Chicago, and no one will be allowed to leave . . . There is a scalpel in the top drawer of your labor station—with this scalpel you must remove the ear-chip, or else they'll use it to track you. You must get to your residential domicile, gather Amy and whatever supplies you*

can carry, then get out! There is no time to spare! Get to the farm at once!"

Tom Selig's voice returned. He was excitedly discussing early Unified Global Government settlements. Duke stared blankly at his labor station, wondering if maybe he'd just imagined the voice. He pulled the top left drawer of his labor-station and saw a shiny silver scalpel sitting there—he'd never seen it before. But how did it get in there? He wondered, who could have put it there? He grabbed it and slid it stealthily into his sock, then scanned the room to see if any of the other laborers had seen him do it. He realized only then that every other labor station was empty. *What the hillmota?*

"James—" A voice shattered his thoughts, "what are you doing over here by yourself?"

His Bujee Manager was looking down at him like he'd just found a puppy ishing on the rug. Duke's CAM was flashing red, so he forced himself to think about troubleshooting neurofilament, prompting it to stop flashing.

"Labor reprieve began five-mixis ago—why aren't you over by the others? Helton Quiver's coronation ceremony is about to begin."

Duke had forgotten all about the labor reprieve. He'd gotten so distracted attempting to block out Tom Selig's voice that he'd failed to realize they had all left. As he stood there, the antimicrobial blue light clicked on above his labor station. He followed Manager down the aisle towards the gaggle of laborers gathered around a large visiscreen on the wall. The Manager made sure Duke got to the gaggle, then disappeared into the "Bujee Only" section with one-way windows, where all the Managers could see out, but no Ujee could see in.

All the other laborers were discussing the latest celebrity

gossip. Wilson Weaver, apparently, had an affair and his Easy-pill-popping girlfriend Sandra-something-or-other was quite upset, apparently. A female laborer—Rodna-something—insisted she'd never take Wilson Weaver back if he did that to her. A different laborer called her bluff; reminding her how many Globos Wilson Weaver had.

Duke backed carefully away but found himself blocked in by a rotund laborer. He turned around after bumping into the squishy stomach, wondering how he'd managed to get so big on the Ujee Living Wage. Duke struggled to remember the laborer's name, but found his thoughts were still too scrambled from the voice he'd heard in his Ear-chip.

"How are things?" the round laborer asked.

"My, um, wife's sick at our residence . . ." Duke stammered, "I think I need to help her . . . Afraid I'll have to leave early today."

Rolls on the man's round face fairly concealed his smirk, "Oh, *sure* . . ." he said, elbowing Duke, "the old, 'Wife is sick' gimmick . . . I got you, buddy." He nudged Duke with his shoulder, harder. "I don't blame you—if I had *two-hundred* Globos to spare, I'd be going to that coronation ceremony, lickity. Guess someone's been skipping on food rations for a reason . . ." The man elbowed Duke's ribcage. "I can't get away with skipping food rations like you people . . . I'm hypoglycemic—if I don't eat, my blood sugar drops and I'm no good to anyone." The round man seemed to be fishing for sympathy.

"No honest—" Duke started, then decided it wasn't worth it. "Wow, hypoglycemic and you still manage to labor as much as the rest of us. That's really impressive—your dedication to the Inner Council is unmatched."

A big moon smile spread across the rotund laborer's face in response to Duke's comment. Laborers were suspicious of each other—Management encouraged the behavior by spreading rumors and gossip about Ujees talking trash about other Ujees. This helped make the Ujees self-police one another.

"Say, did you see those leaked images of Wilson Weaver's donger?" The rotund laborer asked, "Biggest one I've ever seen!" Duke hadn't been paying attention and hadn't heard what he'd said but saw that the man was staring at him like he expected him to say something, so Duke smiled duncely and nodded his head, then pushed his way past, storming down the aisle towards the Human Resource Robot on the wall. He didn't care what rumors or gossip the rotund laborer spread about his rude exit. He was all but running as he approached the Human Resources Robot. He swiped the Globos chip across scanner.

"Hello laborer . . . James Duke . . . how may I assist you?"

"I'd like to request an early dismissal—my wife is very sick at residential domicile and I need to care for her." Human Resources Robot beeped and buzzed as its pagan-era circuitry searched for the appropriate response. "Oh, that's too bad . . ." it said, with a concern so feigned, it seemed the programmers must have recorded it that way as a sarcastic joke. "Have you attempted to order a medical professional to your residential dwelling? It is important to remember how very crucial our labors are here at Elston Dynamics. If we neglect our responsibilities, team cohesion may be hindered. Are you sure you wouldn't just like to return to your labor station? I can assist you in making other arrangements for your . . . wife."

"I still want to request early dismissal," Duke shot back.

"OK, then . . . Please allow me time to make those arrangements . . . Please note, James Duke, a total of—seven-horts of labor—has been added to your schedule next week. Please notify your Manager that you are leaving and ensure all your critical labor is covered. Don't forget to leave your CAM at your labor station. Have a pleasant day, James Duke. And remember, here at Elston Dynamics—we are all part of something greater. Thank—"

Duke ran to the lift bank before the robot could finish, not bothering to notify a Manager. As each cec passed, he grew more desperate to make up for the time he'd already wasted. Before reaching the lobby, he grabbed his bloody, broken Earchip tightly in the palm of his hand and slid the long silver scalpel into the pocket of his trousers.

CHAPTER 2

SANDMAN

THE SERVANT ARRANGED Sandman's uniform on the bed. Black leather PCWO jacket, riding breeches, freshly laundered blouse, pagan-era pistol, riding crop, inverted gold-cross neckless. Sandman stood nude with arm and mechanical claw arm outstretched, waiting for the Servant to dress him. Scars laced the flesh on his neck and back; his left eye rattled incessantly; death appeared visible in the darkened edges of his teeth. Sandman was the personification of tension restrained; as if at any moment, his real identity would leap out with a pagan-axe and chop everyone around him to bits.

"Haven't you ever wondered how I came to be covered in such hideous scars?" he asked the Servant.

The Servant felt himself go cold; never had Sandman spoken to him before, beyond issuing a curt instruction or request. Silent, unsure how to respond, he helped the Sandman's mechanical claw arm into his blouse, then slid the human arm in the other sleeve before buttoning it. He provided his response to the Sandman's question by gently nodding his head side-to-side.

"I was conceived before mandatory sterilization was put in

place. My Father was an Inner Council member, but Mother was a whore, so I was precluded from taking his place on the Inner Council after he died. When I was young, the only time I ever saw him is when he'd show up at mother's residence, drunk, gaked-out of his mind—looking for pagan pleasure. On one of these visits—when I was still very young—mother sent me out to the front stoop to polish Father's boots, so that he and her could have a go. She'd taught me how to polish his boots and wanted me to surprise him with it. Mother—foolishly—believed that one day Father might appoint me as his replacement to the Inner Council—not believing that her profession might preclude me from doing so; believing—genuinely—that Father loved her and I . . . What a fool she was."

Sandman gazed up at his reflection in the gold ceiling of his sleeping car aboard the PCWO War Train Thomulous. He continued, "I still remember polishing in the flickering candlelight, fantasizing about how it might be to join the Inner Council. Then, mother fetched me, and I carefully arranged Father's boots on the mat by the door before joining them both in the kitchen. Mother fried potatoes on the stove and Father brooded at the table, slamming back glasses of vodka and ice.

"Mother sat me at the table next to him, and I can remember being so impressed by him that I was too frightened to even look at him. I remember staring instead at the droplets of condensation splashing down from his glass onto the table. Then mother told me to go fetch Father's boots—I was so excited—sure that tonight would be the night Father would tell me I'd be his replacement on the Inner Council. I returned, running with Father's boots, and presented them, on my knees—still unable to look in his eyes. If I had, I might have seen the building rage that I'd soon come to understand forever. In my head, I imagined mother smiling, as Father shook my hand in congratulation. But instead, when I looked up, I saw only his powerful hand jerk into the side of my face, blasting me to the floor and breaking my jaw in two places.

"The blow must have razzed my consciousness because my memories are quite disjointed—almost surreal from that point forward. I remember dark smoke filling the kitchen from the burning potatoes. Mother was weeping as Father ravaged her atop the counter. I can remember being dragged across the floor by my hair, then my face was brought down close to the toe of Father's boot. His finger pointed, again and again at a small scuff mark I'd clearly overlooked. He began beating the back of my head, and I remember seeing mother—her dress torn, breasts exposed—hitting Father and screaming, until he grabbed her with his other hand and threw her across the room like a satchel of onions.

"He carried me by my britches out to the back yard, shielded from the neighbors by a rickety little fence. The yard was muddy and cold from a storm. I lay there, motionless, crying with pain, until an icy splash and strong, pungent smell shocked me from self-pity. I looked up to see Father dumping two bottles of his vodka onto me. Mother leapt onto his back, wrapping her arms around his throat, trying to choke him, but he reached back, gripped her by the hair, then whipped her into the sharp corner of our little residential domicile, splitting her face wide. I crawled towards her, wanting to cover the blood spraying out from her face. Then high above my head, I heard the click of Father's lighter and soon understood what pain really was. My body went up in flames like a torch and I burst to my feet, running in circles around the yard while globules of my flesh dripped off like candlewax."

Servant's hands trembled as he attempted to latch Sandman's inverted gold cross neckless behind his neck. Sandman continued his story. "I awoke in the hospital; I'd been in a coma for almost a tundle. That time was like a dream of pain and nightmares. Father visited me there once and I'll never forget what he said. He said, 'You are very fortunate to have been sired by an Inner Council member because I was able to secure for you the very latest in artificial organ technology—without it, you would be dead. The doctor told me you're now more machine than man—you're the first of your kind. I'm here to explain my actions. Why I burned you. After all, you are my son, this is a truth I cannot conceal, but you are also the son of a whore—a fact, it has been decided—that disqualifies you from ever joining the Inner Council. The best you could ever hope to achieve is to serve the Inner Council honorably.

'Yours will be a life of struggle—a life of penance paid for the sins of your mother. You must pay attention to details—in all you do—no matter how infinitesimal they may seem. Overlooking that scuff on my boot demonstrated a lack of respect. In retrospect, I blame this on your mother—she weakened you by filling your head with silly fantasies that I'd somehow convince the Inner Council to allow you to take my seat after I die. That pagan nonsense stops now. She was sent to labor the hot fields in the southern region. There, she'll pay for forcing me to do this to you.

'You will remain in the hospital until your body accepts the machines keeping you alive. Once you are healthy enough to leave, you'll be sent to work the ore mines for ten yerts. Then you'll have an opportunity to be reassessed. Deep within the bosom of the Unified Global Government, you will prove yourself worthy to service the Inner Council, or you will perish and be fed to the kiln. My hope is that you will learn from this experience and one day, serve the Inner Council faithfully and with honor.'" The Sandman added, "That was the last time I ever saw Father. He died of consumption while I mined ore from the earth."

Servant stepped to Sandman's wardrobe to retrieve his boots, noticing a scuff mark on the toe of the left one. Very suddenly, Servant felt Sandman's cold presence behind him. "When I found your mother," Sandman whispered, "she was living with the Castaways, drinking rainwater from a bedpan gathered from the corrugated steel roof of her shack. The squalor was so abhorrent, I thought her at first to be a mental defective. Still, I took her to live here aboard Thomulous, where she was given every opportunity to learn what it meant to be a citizen of the Unified Global Government. I'm telling this to you now because I want you to know, I never held her betrayal against you. She paid her penance when she rode the cross and '*All shall be forgiven for those who ride the cross.*'" He whispered.

Fear juddered Servant's bowels. He attempted to speak, but could only stutter, "I inspected your boots this morning, sir. This blemish is impossible—I swear to Darwin—someone must have tampered—"

Sandman hushed the servant. Then placed his cold gloved hand and mechanical eight-digit claw gently around Servant's neck, "All shall be forgiven for those who ride the Cross." He hissed again.

A sharp knock came at the door. "Enter!" Sandman called out. The door slammed open and Sandman's eye trembled wildly. Servant saw his reflection in the inverted gold cross hanging from Sandman's neck. He couldn't take his eyes off it.

Two burly guards stormed in holding long black metal nightsticks. Servant's bladder felt like it was going to burst. He'd spent his entire life aboard Thomulous, and there he'd been taught all he knew by the staff, servants, guards and Sandman himself. "Forgive me, Father," he whispered.

"All shall be forgiven for those who ride the Cross," Sandman said again, apathetically. He then turned and walked to his chair in the corner of the room and sat, watching. "Leave him conscious," he ordered, and the guards nodded, then attacked Servant—thrashing his torso, arms and legs until they were splintered and bruised, and the guards were too out of breath to continue. After a brief pause, they lifted Servant by his armpits and dragged him from Sandman's room.

Servant's feet clanged against the metal gangway as the guards dragged him past soldiers and whirling computers, visiscreens, AI's, and scientists. When they reached the vault door that led outside Thomulous, the guards donned oxygen masks and pressurized suits, and put one on Servant as well. He'd never worn a tunnel suit before. Wearing one now made him feel as proud as the day Sandman chose him as personal servant *two-hundred-seventy-three.*

"Open door," a Guard shouted, "this one's riding the cross!" The vault door made a hissing gas explosion sound along edges, then ground open like a sharpening stone over a knife blade. Silence muted Servant's perceptions as the guards dragged him alongside Thomulous, down a vacuum tunnel, towards the bow. Servant had never seen outside Thomulous before— found it more glorious than he'd ever imagined in his dreams. Gazing at it, he wished only to reach out and touch one of the shiny rivets on the hull of Thomulous.

At the bow, Servant thought the guards might give him a chance to touch Thomulous, but he never got close enough. A group of masked soldiers were gathered in the shadows behind a red flare burning beside the magnetic-coil track. The guards dragged Servant to the steel I-beams mounted in the shape of an inverted cross on the bow of Thomulous. *The Cross!* Servant thought excitedly. Then the pressure on his bladder became too much and he urinated in his suit, prompting dry hollow laughter from guards.

Approaching footsteps clicked closer behind him and the guards swung Servant around to face the source. There, standing hunched, was a PCWO Judge, wearing the customary white curled wig and pale ceramic mask beneath his oxygen helmet. A black cape was tied around the outside of his pressurized suit. The Judge unraveled a real paper scroll—the first real paper Servant had ever seen. The Judge then read from it aloud. His voice bellowed like notes from a pagan alphorn into the silence of the Dark Web.

"Servant, *two-hundred-seventy-three*—you have been found guilty of treason. The Unified Global Government legal code defines treason as a subversive crime punishable by mandatory execution. By the power invested in me by the Peace Control Wellness Order Inner Council, I hereby sentence you to death. Within subsection six of the PCWO Military service code, it specifies that the Captain of a PCWO War Train may choose the method of execution. In accordance with Sandman's wishes, your body shall be mounted to *the Cross*, and you shall remain there until you have died. Though not included in the legal code, the Sandman has requested that I inform you that once you are dead, your penance will have been paid to Sandman and the crew of Thomulous. Servant, two-hundred-seventy-three, have you any last words?"

Events of the day ran through Servant's mind fast. It seemed strange how the day began like all the others but ended like this. He remembered thinking about a new servant girl's smile while polishing Sandman's boots that morning. Wondered, if he'd mistaken the scuff mark for white of her teeth. Either way, it mattered not now. Servant cleared his throat, and then shouted in a loud shrill voice, *"May Sandman live eternal!"*

"Ride the Cross! Ride the Cross! Ride the Cross!" All gathered chanted in response, stomping their boots on the ground. The guards flipped Servant upside-down, pressed him to the Cross.

One held him there while another wrapped a chain tightly around each of his ankles. Next, metal chains were wrapped and secured around each of his wrists, chest, and then waist. Once Servant was secure, the guards stepped back to examine the work they'd done, ensuring all chains were good and snug by pulling on each.

Servant gazed at his new upside-down world. The Judge walked silently past, followed by soldiers, then the guards. "Thank you for the opportunity of penance," Servant called out to all who passed, but none replied or glanced down at him. He heard the vault door of Thomulous close as he watched the red embers of the flare burn into oblivion. Then, each of Thomulous's six nuclear reactor engines powered up at his back and shook his spine with such force he thought his vertebrae might explode into pieces—was the most thrilling experience of his life.

Servant rode the cross well. It took days for him to die. He never wanted the ride to end.

CHAPTER 3

AMY

TRAFFIC SNARLED OUT from New Chicago like an extended middle-finger. Amy exhaled, swirling her blonde bangs into the air. "James was right—should have labored from the residential domicile today . . . Just can't believe this many people are coming to the city for that bish's coronation ceremony," she muttered. Since taking the Oath of Subversion, neither she nor Duke spent much time watching the visiscreen and it became easy to fall out of touch with the Veggies. They called non-Serfs "Veggies" for a reason—helplessly brainwashed by the PCWO's propaganda, talking to them was like talking to a vegetable. They knew nothing of what was really taking place around them. A Veggie's attention was focused on latest Bujee fashion, Sporter-ball results, or celebrity gossip—meanwhile, a war was raging all around them and they were clueless it was taking place.

Since discovering she was pregnant, Amy couldn't stop thinking about getting in touch with Samuel. She knew it was impossible though. Not only had they been notified that they'd be unable to contact Samuel while he was in hiding, the Inner Council had recently passed the "Interweb Transparency Act"

("ITA") which had made global communication much more dangerous for Serfs.

When the Inner Council decided to cut HON off from the interweb, they inadvertently enabled Serfs to easily communicate with one another all across the globe. All a Serf had to do was buy a counterfeit Globos chip on the black market and use it when accessing the interweb on an Interweb Accessor Device ("IAD"). Unfortunately, the Inner Council got wise to what was going on and passed the ITA, which empowered IADs to covertly order drone strikes against its user if it detected a counterfeit Globos chip was being used to access it. If detected, the IAD sent its coordinates to a PCWO Defense satellite, which dispatched the nearest PCWO Attack Drone. Since passage of ITA, many Serfs had met their end from drone-mounted railgun projectiles. Duke was trying to identify a potential Serf recruit who labored on the floor at Elston Dynamics where IAD chips were manufactured. Until he identified someone with "the look," all Serfs were forced to use an intricate coded language Amy developed.

It was nicknamed "Amy's method" and rather than relying on anonymity to communicate, Serfs used the code. Interweb monitoring relied on algorithmic bots that scanned for predefined word combinations that indicated subversive activities. By changing the meaning of words, though, these bots were totally fooled. Amy designed thirty-three different sets of code—one for each hort of the day. Each set was a customized list of common words, and the alternative meaning of those words—depending on what hort of the day it was. Every Serf had been made to memorize the thirty-three sets of codes. This allowed the Serfs to appear as though they were discussing Wilson Weaver's latest scandals in a PCWO Community Forum, while really, they were discussing how to covertly manipulate genetic code at PCWO Creation Centers to allow greater intelligence and independence genes into Ujee babies.

Amy's method allowed Serfs to continue communicating globally over the interweb but made such communication more challenging and time-consuming. Recently, though, they'd recruited a new Serf from "Interweb Bot Security"—the PCWO's private-government technology company where interweb monitoring bots were developed. Already, he'd begun manipulating their algorithms very subtly, to make it almost impossible to detect real acts of subversion, while incorrectly flagging Veggies, or PCWO Agents or Police instead.

Across the globe, Serf forces were accelerating and intensifying their acts of subversion. They weren't just countering narratives now, they were *creating* the narratives and dictating the pace and locations of battle. PCWO forces had been thrown into chaos and Serf incarceration rates had plummeted. Serf morale was at the highest levels anyone—even the old timer Serfs—had ever seen. No longer did Serfs talk about their principle-based, but ultimately unwinnable war. Now, they talked about real victory—a world without the PCWO and DCCM. A world where all were born naturally and where human thought was once again free of monitoring. A world where men and women were responsible for their own destinies—not predefined "tracks" set by PCWO officials. In that world, AI would be allowed to do all human labors and human laborers would be free to pursue whatever endeavor they wished. This dream is what Amy fought for and lately, it started looking more and more realistic. That optimism contributed greatly to the confusion they'd all felt when rumors began to circulate that Helton Quiver was planning to announce victory in the War on Subversion at her coronation ceremony. Serf numbers were high as ever—their acts of subversion as devastating as ever—and despite this, the Supreme Chancellor was planning to announce victory? What were they planning? Amy wondered.

Reclining in the seat of her CAR, Amy shut her eyes as she rubbed the tiny creature in her belly, smiling as she imagined her unborn child growing up in a world without the PCWO. The only sound in the CAR was the quiet whine of auto-drive engaging as it mitched along with the rest of the traffic. Suddenly, she felt a dark shadow cover her face and opened her eyes. Standing in the road beside her window was a man with bloodshot eyes and tattered shirt. He glared down at her, menacing silently. Amy screamed, then covered her mouth and focused on calming herself. It was clear by the man's disheveled appearance he was no PCWO Agent.

"Can I help you?" she asked through dry lips. The man stepped along sideways, keeping pace with her window as auto-drive crept along in synchronicity with the other vehicles. She looked around, expecting to see an accident, or stopped vehicle, but saw nothing out of the ordinary.

"You gave me quite a scare. Sorry about screaming like that." Amy chuckled nervously, scanning the CAR's visiscreen to confirm all doors were locked. The CAR ahead of hers mitched forward again, prompting her auto-drive to do the same. The man took two steps sideways.

"Are you hurt, sir? Do you want me to contact the PCWO?"

His head wobbled around atop a loose neck as he glared at her. She wondered if he was high on gak, noticing, the flesh on his knuckles was mangled and covered with crusty blood. Again, she looked around, hoping that another person had taken note of this man, but all had their windows heavily tinted, and were most likely napping on their long ride home from labors.

"CAR, darken the windows," she ordered.

The plastic windows of her CAR darkened until it was impossible to see inside, but she could still see out. The man's torn shirt flapped in winds growing stronger as the clouds over-head darkened and rain began pattering down on the plastic roof-window. A heavy fog had descended upon the ultra-road, rolling in from the West, towards the city. The fog made it diffi-cult to see very far behind and she wondered if an accident had occurred back there and this man was simply dazed.

"Do you want me to call for some help?" she shouted. The man responded by ducking down, vanishing beneath the line of sight her window allowed. She scooted near the window, peering down, just as the man reappeared very suddenly. Now, clutched in his mangled right hand was a jagged chunk of asphalt. "What do you want?" Amy shrieked.

The man lifted his arm up over his head, then slammed the rock down onto her plastic windshield. Then he smashed his face against her window and groaned, "I really need your CAR—I got to get out of here!" He tugged violently at the door handle and Amy screamed, "Go away! Leave me alone!" as her fingers pressed rapidly at the Emergency Notification System's activation button on the CAR's visiscreen.

"Hello, Amy Duke," a mechanical voice came through the speakers of her CAR, "How may I be of assistance?"

"There's a man—trying to get into my CAR! He, he—tried smashing my windshield with a rock!"

"OK, I can certainly assist you with that. Are you in imme-diate danger?"

"Yes!" Amy screamed. The man giggled with his face pressed against her window.

"Understood. Did any property damage occur because of this event?"

"I don't know! I'm saying there's a man outside my car trying to break in! I think he might be on gak!"

"Understood. I am accessing your CAR's diagnostic report now. Please hold."

"Fick!" Amy cursed, then reached into the hidden compartment stitched beneath her seat and pulled out the pagan-era Sig Sauer P365 pistol Duke had made for her with his 4-D printer. She pointed it at the man, "This is real—I'll blow your ficking head off if you don't get away from me right now!"

The man didn't react like someone looking down the barrel of a pagan pistol. Instead of leaping away, he dragged his face across her window, leaving a streaked greasy smudge. Amy remembered she had the windows tinted, which explained his non-reaction—he hadn't been able to see the gun. That was probably for the better—even a gak-head Veggie could have her locked up for possessing a pagan-era gun. Once in prison, it wouldn't take HON that long to figure out it wasn't receiving thought signals from one of the prisoners. This dunce gak-head wasn't worth being found to be a Serf and executed.

The electronic voice of the Emergency Notification System returned, "Thank you for your patience. I have submitted your CAR's diagnostics report to your insurance provider. They will be in contact with you once they have ascertained the Globos value of the damage. Is there anything else I can help you with today?"

"There's a ficking man trying to break into my CAR with a rock! Send a damle Police drone out here to arrest him!"

"I'm glad I could be of assistance. Have a pleasant rest of your day—and remember, 'we are all a part of something greater than ourselves!' Goodbye."

The man lifted his rock again and bashed it against the side window next to Amy's head. The plastic cracked down the middle, but still held. She didn't think it would hold through another strike and decided to take things into her own hands. It was worth the risk to scare this guy away.

"CAR, lighten windows."

The dark tint in the windows faded until gone and the man

could once again see inside her CAR. His red eyes spread wide when he saw the 9mm pagan pistol. He ducked his head fast, then ran off. Amy watched him in the mirror as he disappeared into the fog, then she slid the pistol back down into the hidden compartment beneath her seat. She looked around at the other vehicles to make sure no one had seen her. But she saw at least seven faces staring at her with jaws hanging open.

"Ish . . ." Amy felt a tinge at the back of her neck; wondered if the others had seen her brandishing the gun or were simply surprised at witnessing what the man had done. Far away in the fog, she heard the *WOMP! WOMP!* sound of a PCWO Police Drone. *Is that the police drone I requested, or did someone request it because they saw my pagan piece?*

As the siren grew louder, Amy became increasingly convinced it was coming because someone had seen her gun. She reached down and pressed the visiscreen to disengage auto-drive but found it unresponsive. The CAR's visiscreen went blank. Then flashing words appeared:

POLICE OVERRIDE! REMAIN SEATED!
POLICE OVERRIDE!

Amy looked in her rearview, saw a blue flash from the police drone's siren, muted by the fog. She tried to open the door but found it couldn't be unlocked. Tried to unlatch seat-harness but found it too had been locked. Reaching for the blade she kept in the gun's compartment beneath her seat, she started sawing at the harness belts as the WOMP! WOMP! sound grew deafening. She glanced up in the mirror again, saw the police drone emerge from the fog and settle into a low hover beside her CAR.

Frantic now, she sawed at the belts until she'd managed to free herself.

"DO NOT MOVE!" Police Drone ordered, "KEEP YOUR HANDS ON THE WHEEL!"

The windows on her CAR began to lower; the police drone had taken control of her CAR's AI.

"YOU ARE UNDER ARREST FOR POSSESSION OF A PAGAN-ERA FIREARM. PLEASE STICK YOUR HANDS AND WRISTS OUT OF THE WINDOW!"

If she obeyed, police drone would slap zip-cuffs on her, lift her into its holding cell, and take her to the nearest PCWO Police station for processing. She cursed herself for having been so foolish as to have brandished the gun. There was no turning back now—she either had to comply and eventually be found out to be a Serf and executed or flee and expedite that departure from the safe-zone with James.

Her hand snapped up from beneath the seat with the pistol and she bit her lower lip as she took aim at the police drone's AI box before squeezing the trigger. The gunshot knocked the police drone sideways, unsettling its hover and causing it to smash into the OFFROADER behind her. The visiscreen control panel in her CAR lit up then, freed from the police drone's override. She deactivated the auto-drive, then mashed down on the go-pedal with her foot.

Every vehicle was equipped with a restrictor plate that prohibited it from exceeding thirty-five-kimos-a-hort when in manual-drive. But Duke had removed that in case just such an occasion as this were ever to occur. Amy's CAR tore ahead, smashed into a vehicle, then began pushing it sideways which created a gap for Amy's CAR to squeeze on to the shoulder of the road. Her CAR scraped along the metal guardrail, showering the dark wet air with fiery orange and yellow ribbons.

The police drone dropped like a meteor from above—

smashing out the roof-window and causing her CAR to crunch hard into the guardrail. Fighting to keep the CAR on road, Amy watched helplessly as the police drone flew back up into the sky, then cannonballed into the side of her CAR—blasting it through the guardrail like it was paper tape at the finish line of a foot race.

The massive sloping hill seemed to stretch down forever, and she wished she still had her seat-harness attached. The CAR began a furious descent down the hillside, bumping and jerking as it picked up speed and left the police drone in its dust. Amy held onto the wheel as tightly as she could to keep from bouncing out of the now absent roof-window. A gas station appeared ahead, and she was headed right towards the pumps. She wrestled helplessly with the wheel, then the CAR lurched up high into the air causing Amy to smash her head on the ceiling. A sudden, dreary darkness wrapped its cold hands around her face and pulled shut her eyes, stealing consciousness away at a most impractical time.

CHAPTER 4

CORONATION CEREMONY

DUKE WOVE DOWN the sidewalk past those gathered outside the gates to the park where the coronation ceremony was being held. Crowds filled the streets to the buildings on the opposite side where people huddled in the windows and those assembled on the rooftops with Magni-Goggles were trying to catch a glimpse of the Supreme Chancellor. Duke turned sideways, facing the fence, and then sidestepped past a group of sullen-looking teens passing a vaporizer of grassy-petal-jay back and forth. One of them jabbed Duke in the back as he passed. He turned to look and saw the tall skinny teen glaring at him toughly. "Outta my way, *old man*," he said, sprinkling Duke's face with spit flecks.

Duke's eyes narrowed. He felt his fist tighten into iron and pictured it passing through the teen's skull and out the back. He resisted the urge, reminding himself how foolish that would be. Especially since the Inner Council had recently passed another round of "Our Children, Our Future" child protection laws which mandated fifteen-yerts hard labor for assaulting a teen. The term "assault" was loosely interpreted—practically any unwanted physical contact could be construed as assault under the new laws, so long as another teen vouched the claim. Teens now transcended discipline, making them bigger monsters than they'd been historically, and ensuring they kept their parents in line with PCWO doctrine.

Smirking, Duke continued sliding past, picturing himself body-slamming the punk over his knee and cracking his spine in two as he left. "That's right, *old man, keep walking!*" the teen called after him.

Further down, near the end of the park, Duke peered through a gate at the massive stage with the towering visiscreen constructed for the event. Along the far side of the stage, lux-boxes for Bujees had been constructed in the shape of the pagan pyramids. Inside, Duke could see Bujee families being served real food and liquor by Ujee servant laborers, not the lab-made stuff Ujees were rationed.

Beneath the pyramids, the Ujee masses gathered like grains of sand, filling each crevice, ledge, tree, stoop, and shadow; smashed together, craning on toes, holding children on shoulders, leaning, pushing, elbowing—all to get a sliver view of the stage upon which the Supreme Chancellor of the Unified Global Government, Helton Quiver, would shortly stride with a smirkish smile, eyes glimmering gold with the admiration heaped upon her. Soaking the crowd's energy, a hole in space devouring solar systems, emitting nothing but darkness in return. Impossible to understand, her power hypnotized them and together they gave willingly their energies, feeling it sucked from their bodies by some powerful vampire machine. In that machine, they became a part of something greater and worthy of the energy. In the bowels of the machine, their hopes and dreams and wants and needs mixed with those of the collective, uniting egos to be consumed by the leader, fueling her sense of import and energizing the very cells in her body. She would use that energy to do her bidding, then propagate back to those who'd given of themselves a narrative assuring them it'd been put to good use. They'd accept that with sterile satisfaction, comforted knowing the machine was functioning exactly as it should.

Their anxieties would be relieved, albeit temporarily, until the prerogative of the leader felt ill or annoyed and decided a change of course was needed. Then she'd send word and the underlings would enact the new orders with their typical furious rancor, shocking those beneath into believing impending doom was nigh, impelling them to toil and worship harder, expelling greater energy, amplifying that which the vampire received, satisfying her that the decision to change course was the right one because now she received greater energy. Any annoyance or discomfort she'd felt made her deserving of this energy and the labors of the masses, because she and only she had this inherent gift that enabled her to lead the world better than any before her.

This demand and feedback loop of conscious energy and worship of the Supreme Leader fulfilled her temporarily, until petty desire changed, and she demanded more. Then more would be exacted from the laborers, those at the bottom of the machine with no choice but to obey the layers upon layers of cold unfeeling machine components above them. Those above, so gutted of self or remorse, and fearful of being down in the pits like them, gleefully enacted whatever hardship was necessary, preferring violent means to implement all orders received from above, no matter how trivial or silly they may have thought them to be. The words or thoughts or wants or desires or frivolities of the leader were all that mattered. Her words, like pagan gospel, were to be worshipped and cherished as if the sun shined only because she allowed it to, and with her disproval it would cast the lot of them into a darkness of unending wen in which winds howled over glacier peaks, blasting weary flesh with crystal specks of diamond hard frozen water, like munitions from a rail gun. These beings would be devoid of any sense of comfort or shelter or fullness that might be known, if only she—the leader—were happy.

Helton Quiver alone, held the keys to happiness, sadness, demise, fulfillment, life and death. She decided how many were born, how many died, who labored, where and how. A flick of her finger meant scores would perish by sarin gassings carried out by autonomous drones plunging down from orbit outside the atmosphere. Screaming canisters would rain down death from above, terrifying the hungered masses who ran, tripped and fell in their failed efforts to escape, not knowing then that escape was futile. Not until they lay in the dirt, clutching their swollen purple necks, cords standing on faces, and tongues filling mouths, swollen to the point that their oxygen was cut off and their eyes bulged from the sockets. Their bowels released and the stench of it burnt the flesh of the sinuses and lungs like fire from blowtorches, as if each atom of their bodies were being torn apart and all the while, wishing for sudden death that wouldn't come until paralysis of their lungs was complete and they choked to death on the gritty sand, wanting only a sip of water.

Then, the "tragedy," like so many others, would be broadcast to the citizenry and clumsy excuses would be manufactured and expelled like odorous gas from the backsides of livestock and they'd stare, mouths gaping at their visiscreens, old women and men and young children watching as horror was brought to their bedrooms, classrooms, lavatories and places of labor. Because of the horror they witnessed, so unimaginable, they'd accept whatever narrative was pushed by the PCWO. *Of course*, it had been the terrorist Serfs! *Of course*, this was an act of subversion intended to create fear and undermine their way of life! *Of course*, they wouldn't let it bother them, because that would give the Serfs a victory. So, all they were left to do was hand over more control and monitoring to the PCWO, so that further tragedies could be avoided, but they never would and the horrors and tragedies would only get worse—more violent, higher body counts, more depravity and gore—until nothing was left to chance and no secret kept by the citizenry because the evils of humanity were concealed in the mind and the mind was the final frontier to be conquered. And as these citizens offered their right to sovereignty of the mind for the safety of the Unified Global Government, the secrecy of the PCWO Inner Council grew.

Without Inner Council secrecy, the citizens would be endangered. Without utter transparency of intention and thought from the citizenry, there could be no peace. Today wasn't just the coronation of Helton Quiver, it was the coronation of decades of control and voluntary enslavement, as those who suffered under this tyrannical system cheered at the top of their lungs for the one person who benefited from their suffering more than any other: Supreme Chancellor, Helton Quiver. She would become the manifestation of invincibility of the PCWO and the power they had over all. This act—the forced celebration that was reported to be the largest gathering in human history—was the sacrifice of the sanctity of private thought and autonomous human endeavor.

Helton Quiver's face appeared on the massive visiscreen, painted vibrant and injected with silicone and the hair of some dead woman strung to hers, eyes flicking, sneer pinned on her face as she stared out at them. Her features communicated that she knew they were cheering and knew that they loved her, but still she despised them as one might loathe a plague. That was power beyond. The unhidden acknowledgement of their being beneath her, while accepting their voluntary displays of affection and offering nothing but contempt in return. She hated them, all of them, always, and they loved her unflinchingly.

She turned her head towards the great tinted windows of the lux-box pyramids stretched back as far as one might see, as if to acknowledge a joke they were all in on, before her gaze returned to the swarming masses all fighting and snapping away with their image devices. Many had saved their Globos for yerts to purchase these ticket, each disappointed she wasn't appearing in person, but snapping pictures frantically to prove to their fellow laborers they had been *there*, at Helton Quiver's coronation ceremony. *They* had shared in that amazing experience and they'd go on about how fantastic each detail had been and about their chance happenings of a fantastic view and how Helton Quiver had looked right at them and how they'd felt their hearts flutter and how she'd given a little nod as if to acknowledge how hard they'd labored for the good of the PCWO. And their fellow laborers would nod and privately mock them and begin to avoid them until the message was received. Or maybe it wouldn't be—maybe they'd sacrificed too much to simply discard the memory like crumpled paper in a trash bin. So, they'd cling to it for the rest of their lives and that would come to define them and when their cold body was fed into the furnace, those who managed to stay close enough to attend the service would say something about how that person had spent their life laboring because they loved the PCWO and the Unified Global Government and the happiest moment of their entire life had been the day they attended Helton Quiver's grand coronation ceremony on that day in New Chicago.

James Duke gazed through the gate at these people and saw each of their lives emanating from their foreheads like projectors and each of their lives played out in rapid accelerating time, each instant a swath of time. Lives lived and perished, and private battles fought, victory taken, again, by the undefeated death. And they cheered and waved little UGG flags or held PCWO banners or wept tears of sadness and joy because they were bearing witness to their leader. He saw all this and didn't understand how he'd come to possess such perception. This vision was unlike anything he'd ever experienced before, as if something or someone had entered his mind and given him a device that took him through time, but not in a physical sense. The metaphysical vision was of a sea of humanity and the lives they would lead and the unfulfillment dashed with sugar in some clumsy speech by a boorish relative at the end. Their final act of worship, of thankless labor for the state, would be to fuel the furnace, powering the machine for a cec. Duke saw, for the first time in his life, all the secrets of humanity. This day, he knew then, was to be the day a new life began. *I must get home,* he thought to himself, *I must get to Amy!*

Looking back, he could see the teens now picking on a homeless Ujee man. One teen got on all fours, crawling up behind the man while the tall skinny one that had elbowed Duke began to speak to the man, before shoving him in the chest with both hands, causing him to topple over backwards over the teen on all fours. The man wallowed around in the dirt, while the teens pointed and laughed—taunting, duncely.

"Forget to take your meds, *dongerhead*?" one howled. Other teen did mock impressions of the man, teetering on their feet, as in dunce-voice, they said: "Gravity's not real. I'm a dunce-head, look at me—gravity's not real!" (All found the impression quite hilarious).

The man struggled to his feet; stood wobbly, glared vacantly at the tall teen, then started giggling. The teen spit on the man's face. "What the *fick's* so funny, gak-head? You got a problem? You wanna hit me?" The tall elbowing teen asked in taunting voice. The man ignored the taunts and grabbed the boy by the collar of his bedazzled Wilson Weaver, *Tad Skater Boy* blouse, causing a loud rip.

All the teens gasped, then one shouted—in a voice of joyous disbelief—"Oh, *ish*, you just *assaulted him—fifteen yerts hard labor for you, dongerhead!*"

The teens all pointed and began shouting for PCWO Police. "He's assaulting a minor! He's assaulting a minor! Oh ish, he's assaulting a minor!"

The man continued giggling as he tugged on Tad Skater Boy's shirt, eventually rocking the smaller teen backwards and onto to the ground. Then the giggling man fell atop the teen and wrestled with him. Teens mixed with gapers gathered around in a circle, making it difficult for Duke to see what was going on. A high-pitched scream came from the teen on the ground, prompting the other teens to begin bashing the still giggling man on the head with skateboards, fists, and placards until the man tumbled off.

Dirty Tad Skater boy scrambled back to feet—black sweaty long bangs covering most of his face—clutching his forearm with his other hand and screamed "This ficker *BIT ME!*" in a high voice that cracked like early puberty. The still-giggling man also climbed back up to his feet, only no one but Duke noticed, because all were staring, shocked, at the blood dripping between the teen's fingers.

A teen girl wearing a blouse emblazoned with a big image of Helton Quiver's face (with patented smirkish smile) stood gazing at the blood dripping between the other teen's fingers. She was still holding a placard which read: *I KILL SERFS!*

She didn't notice the giggling man approach, until he had two fists full of her Helton Quiver blouse. The girl shrieked with surprise, then started battering the top of the man's head with her placard. Others turned around to see what was happening. Giggling man grabbed the teen's short purple hair, pulled it back, then bit into her neck. Purple haired teen emitted a pandemic scream as the giggling man thrashed side-to-side like an extinct pagan shark might have. The man pulled back from the teen with a big chunk of her neck flesh in his mouth, giggling, as he gnawed on the knot and blood sprayed like New Chicago's fountain from the teen's neck. Wind carried the red mist across the gathered crowd as the teen's voice fell silent, but still she appeared to be screaming. The giggling man swallowed the half-chewed flesh, then giggled as he tackled her to the ground. Other teens scattered like rat-cowards—as did most rest of the crowd.

Duke struggled against the crowd to get to the girl. He stopped when he saw a PCWO Police appear, with electro-spear-blaster in hand. The police officer sparked the blaster and held it to giggling man's neck, but it seemed to have little effect, except to cause the man to stop chewing on the girl. He climbed back to his feet, then staggered towards the PCWO Police officer. The officer dropped the electro-blaster, drew a pagan-gun and fired it into the man's kneecap. The gunshot sparked fear across the crowd, now becoming a stampede as a helicopter drone roared overhead. The helicopter blasted the fleeing crowd with debris and sand from its prop-wash. Fleeing Ujees climbed up the Bujee luxury box pyramid, disrupting its careful architectural balance. Luxury boxes toppled, disrupting the balance further. Then all began raining down—some, two-hundred-mets up—flattening the fleeing crowd wherever they landed and killing all or most inside.

Screams, helicopter and drone sirens amalgamated like the auditory Pollack exhibit at the New Chicago PCWO Art Museum. A sprinting man slammed Duke, knocking him sideways and causing him to lose sight of the purple-haired teen. He heard twelve gunshots fired in rapid succession; realized there was nothing he could do for teen. He had to get out before he was trampled. Turned and ran with the rest of crowd, away from the park, South, towards the residential domicile, where he hoped Amy would be.

CHAPTER 5

THOMULOUS

A BEAST LIVED IN the mist of the mountains and emerged whenever thaw flooded the village, plucking the innocent from their beds, consuming their innocence. It was believed they could return when that which made them what they were had been removed and replaced with the darkness. Where it originated was only whispered about in the darkened pub of earth and mud and straw dripping wet in that gully-washed Castaway settlement. The beast was the length of a horizon and in the silence of dawn, one could hear the rattle of chains and cries of the captured by placing their ear to a stone but doing so brought five-yerts of misfortune. The Castaways tolerated this because their ancestors had; it was the cost of their wickedness. Mud and stone pueblos dotted the rocky hearth of the mountain range, where a great scientific research laboratory had been built by Donald Darwin himself. There, Darwin labored to reconcile the problem of the human condition to deliver them from the beast and alleviate their genetic abnormalities so that one day, they might be allowed to rejoin society and live within the safe-zones away from the beast. The beast was named Thomulous, but its name shouldn't be spoken aloud, because doing so brought the thaw and the beast, and as a result, their children went missing.

CHAPTER 6

NICOLAE

ACID-RAIN BATTERED THE plastic bubble canopy of Nicolae's drone-copter. The lightweight, autonomous craft descended the clouds, guided by the landing coordinates beamed from the PCWO War Train Thomulous. In the ruins of a pagan sporter-ball stadium, Thomulous coiled like some brobdingnagian snake. Nicolae pulled his flask from the pocket of his Ujee-hand-stitched silk suit jacket. His hand trembled as he unscrewed the cap and he wasted no time guzzling the fiery liquid once he had it off. The violence he'd witnessed at the coronation ceremony had shaken him to his core. But the news he feared most was waiting aboard Thomulous.

Blue and red strobes appeared in the darkness, flashing signals to the drone-copter's AI, which analyzed the wave frequency to confirm altitude. The craft broke beneath the clouds and passed through a raucous pocket of air, which dropped the copter and Nicolae's stomach. The craft's AI countered the turbulence and settled again into a steady descent as Nicolae clutched the handle beside his seat and the events preceding this moment replayed in his head.

Helton Quiver and Nicolae had arrived aboard Thomulous

three days ago. Sandman was to transport them to the coronation ceremony and provide security detail. Several horts into their journey, after a delicious feast held in the Sandman's private dining car, Helton Quiver fell ill. Her condition continued to deteriorate, despite constant care from the Medical AI bots aboard Thomulous. A mere twelve-horts before the Supreme Chancellor was scheduled to deliver her coronation speech—a speech expected to be the most observed in human history—her and Nicolae came to the painful conclusion that there was no way she'd be physically capable of delivering it in person. They decided to utilize the propaganda studio aboard Thomulous. Aided by some gak pills and heavy makeup, Helton delivered her speech in a recording device that would be played over the massive visiscreen at Taft Park. Nicolae would attend in person to serve as "hype man" to give the presentation a more human feel.

The speech seemed to have been going over quite well, at least until the gunfire triggered a stampede which contributed to the collapse of the Bujee luxury box pyramids. Nicolae had hardly managed to escape himself—a Bujee with a backstage VIP pass attempted to steal his drone-copter. He'd had to batter the man with a metal pipe until the man lay motionless in a pool of his own blood. As Nicolae dragged the unconscious or possibly dead man out of the seat of his drone-copter, he chanced to glance at the front of the stage. There, a bloodied man climbed onto the stage and was met with a hail of hushed gunfire from a PCWO Security officer's suppressed pagan machinegun. It happened so fast Nicolae hadn't had a chance to analyze what he'd seen until now. The bloodied man had, in fact, been struck with upwards of twenty bullets, yet continued staggering, somehow, towards the back of the stage, as if nothing had happened. Nicolae remembered how the man was giggling as he was shot like the bullets were tickling him and thought about how Helton Quiver had taken to giggling before he'd left her aboard Thomulous.

A thought occurred to him then, brought about by the liquor thinning his blood. Was it not the Sandman's responsibility to ensure their safe transportation to and from the coronation ceremony? By all accounts, the "legendary" Sandman had failed spectacularly in every aspect of his mission.

Sandman was known by the Inner Council as the PCWO War Train Captain who got things done—no matter what. Now, though, Helton Quiver was quite ill, with what, Nicolae shuddered to think about. Were the rumors about PrP6 true? Had Helton Quiver somehow contracted it? It was difficult to know for certain. Surely, though, he'd demand answers from Sandman once he was aboard. He wasn't going to allow Sandman's physical appearance and reputation scare him. He was going to dress Sandman down and report his failures to the Inner Council.

"Please fasten your safety harness prior to landing," the drone-copter's mechanical voice instructed.

The drone-copter's infrared sensors confirmed approach trajectory as the AI performed millions of calculations to account for changes in variables in wind, humidity, air pressure, temperature, and altitude. Soft as a Bujee-pillow, the drone-copter set down on the landing pad and Nicolae hammered the manual-override lever to open the hatch. Alarm-sirens wailed, red lights flashed. "Please remain in the cabin until I have instructed you to safely exit the craft," the drone-copter's mechanical AI voice whined.

"Oh, fick off you donger-gulping piece of ish," Nicolae hissed. He leapt onto the tarmac and stormed towards the door as Thomulous's roof hatch closed overhead.

He waved his Globos chip at each of the automatic doors, annoyed by the old technology. "Get some ficking biometric figure scans around here, you cheap fick," he muttered, nearly slamming into a door that didn't open for him. He swiped his Globos-chipped hand twice more before it did. Down the metal gangway, his soaked New Italia, Ujee-hand-stitched-dress-pumps fizzed as water seethed out the sides. Members of the crew stood rigid and saluted as he passed, and he ignored them. He was the Supreme Chancellor's personal assistant—he didn't have time for these dunces. He ran into the door of the Sandman's billiards car with a clang, expecting surely it would have been programmed for his biometric figure, but it had not. Cursing, he straightened his sopped stitched coat, still smelling like it was burning from the acid rain, swept back his dripping hair, and stooped to the eye-reader beside the door. The eye reader, prompted, buzzed, and then said, "I'm sorry, I didn't get a good reading, please readjust the position of your chin and try again." A stream of expletives burst from Nicolae's tongue as he pounded the heavy steel door with his fist, then realigned his chin on the cup. This time, the eye-reader pinged and instructed him to take a step back before the door burst open.

"Why the fick—" he began as he exploded through the door, then leapt sideways, tumbling into the side of the chair as the giggling Helton Quiver flung herself at him, stopped short only by the chains attached to her wrists and ankles and the wall of Sandman's billiards car.

"*Fick!*" Nicolae screamed, again fixing his hair as he climbed to his feet. "What the fick is going on with her?"

Nicolae eyed the Supreme Chancellor, giggling and clicking her teeth together, her eyes like matte black diamonds. A massive chunk of flesh was missing from her thigh and coagulated blood ran the length of her leg like hardened asphalt. "What's wrong with her? Why didn't you ficking warn me before I came through the door? Where's that horrible ficking dog of yours?"

Sandman clicked his tongue against the roof of his mouth then tapped out a clove cigarette with his bionic arm and placed it between his thin pale lips and lit it. Shaking his head, he replied. "Sadly, it has been confirmed that Supreme Chancellor Helton Quiver has been stricken with the PrP6 super prion. At present, there's no cure, so there's nothing you or I can do for her."

"Does the Inner Council know?" Nicolae demanded.

"Unfortunately, not." Sandman replied. "While you were away, the PrP6 outbreak has become an out and out pandemic all across the Unified Global Government. All two-hundred-and-ninety-nine other members of the Inner Council have fled to their luxury bunker complex on the Isle of Tasman. I attempted to contact them there, but it appears some sort of interweb virus has shut down their communications. At present, the Inner Council has no way of receiving or sending communications with anyone."

Nicolae eyed the Supreme Chancellor, giggling and struggling against her chains. He felt a tinge of sadness in his heart, not for her, but for his career. He'd been assaulted, berated, and sexually harassed by the Supreme Chancellor far too many times to feel pity for her now. But he did feel pity for himself. He endured her tortures because the power of his position was worth it. At Bujee soirees, he was treated like a member of the Inner Council himself. Everyone wanted to talk to the lifelong personal assistant of Supreme Chancellor Quiver. He'd engaged in the horizontal pagan tango more times than he could ever hope to count because of his labor position. What would he do now? Who would her replacement be? Never before had he been forced to think about what he might do without her. In fact, she'd even told him that he could have his consciousness uploaded into a fresh young cloned body of himself when she next did the same—a procedure normally reserved only for

Inner Council members. Now what? Did this mean he'd one day have to die?

Sandman stood smiling his strange flat smile, a smile that some might not consider a smile at all. He stood rigidly, offering the PCWO salute—two fingers pointed out and thumb cocked to signify the Inner Council and Science as twin guardians of PCWO's Unified Global Government. Nicolae felt sick to his stomach—he hated delivering the salute because he thought it was beneath him. Rather than risk the consequences of ignoring Sandman, he provided the appropriate response, albeit in a disinterested monotone voice, "May the Inner Council Remain Eternal."

"And for all Eternity—the Inner Council and Science!" Sandman snapped the response. He then eased his posture ever so slightly as he lowered his hand to his side. "My deepest apologies, Nicolae, but there was nothing I could do. We haven't been able to identify how or when she came in contact with PrP6."

"Is she contagious now?"

"Indeed." Sandman answered. "If she were to bite into your flesh, her saliva would pass PrP6 directly into your bloodstream."

"What happened to her leg?"

"I apologize for that as well. My guard dog, Hansel—I believe you asked about him when you entered—was the only living dire wolf on earth. We created him right here aboard Thomulous using DNA from a fossil discovered as we drilled new Dark Web tunnels. Unfortunately, my dearest Hansel attacked Helton Quiver and took that bite out of her leg. Fortunately for the Supreme Chancellor, she'd already succumbed to PrP6, so I rather doubt she felt any pain. Regardless, I felt it was necessary to terminate my dearest Hansel for I feared what might have happened if he'd become infected with PrP6. I shall miss him dearly." Sandman sighed, "He was the loyalist soldier ever to serve me."

"Yeah, well I bet the Supreme Chancellor of the Unified Global ficking Government is going to miss that part of her leg. Why the *fick* did you need a dire wolf 'guard dog' down here anyways Sandman? You live five-kimos underground in the Dark Web on a PCWO War Train that's loaded with military drones and soldiers. Doesn't it seem unnecessary to have a four-hundred kemtils dire wolf as a pet?" Nicolae asked, glancing furtively at Helton Quiver. She giggled at him and her eyes bore into his as if to give indication that she recognized him. "How strong are those chains?" he asked.

"Oh, quite strong—those same chains restrained Hansel. He was quite a bit stronger than the Supreme Chancellor." Sandman replied.

Nicolae muttered something unintelligible then slicked back his wet hair and went to the bar at the back of the room. He grabbed an incandescent bottle of vodka and poured it into a tall glass, then gulped it down in a single breath. He set the glass down on the bar, tossed in ice and a cucumber slice, then poured a more dignified drink. The walls of the room shook as Thomulous descended deeper into the Dark Web.

Sandman sat in a chair, his posture that of someone sitting on a bed of steel spikes. Nicolae remained at the bar, eyes darting in the mirror above it, between Sandman and Helton Quiver. "Well, how do you think it went?" he asked, "I really thought the crowd was eating it up before all hillmota broke loose."

A tiny muscle beneath the Sandman's left eye flickered. "I watched the performance on my visiscreen. And, though my expertise doesn't lie in politics, I must agree, the speech seemed to be going over quite well before the stampede. Oh, did you hear? PCWO Media reported over twelve-thousand confirmed dead!"

Nicolae turned slowly to face Sandman. "Twelve-thousand dead?"

"Yes, the stream was quite fascinating to observe. The irrational human response to fear stimulus has always fascinated me. Nearly ninety-percent of the casualties were the result of people being trampled. Had the crowd merely acted in a rational and calm manner, ten-thousand-eight-hundred people might still be alive."

Nicolae stirred his drink with his finger. "You find people dying like that 'fascinating?'"

Sandman extinguished his clove cigarette and tapped out a fresh one. "Oh, certainly not. I find the observance of the human *fear response* fascinating. The violence itself is rather bland to me."

Nicolae gulped back his drink and remembered he was going to ream Sandman for ficking everything up. "Hey Sandman," he said, "Wasn't your mission to ensure the Supreme Chancellor and I made it safely to and from the coronation ceremony? Helton Quiver's ficked up on PrP6 now and I had to beat a man near to death to get out of there alive. Aren't you supposed to be the top PCWO War Train Captain? If you think for a cec that I'm going to sugar-coat my reports about how badly you've ficked everything up, you've got another thing—"

Nicolae's words were interrupted by the darkness radiating from Sandman's eyes like photon beams of gelid black. Nicolae felt paralyzed. A tremble swept his body and his mind fell blank. His hand began moving his drink towards his mouth, but it wasn't him moving it. It couldn't be. His arm felt like ten-thousand molten needles were stabbing it all at once. The glass reached his lips and tilted back steeply, emptying the contents down his throat.

The paralysis abated slightly then enabling him to turn his shoulder and break off the Sandman's terrifying gaze. It felt like he'd broken some powerful and invisible linkage. He felt his ability to control his motor functions restored and spun back towards the bar, grabbed hold of the nearest bottle and gulped it down entirely—as if the liquor might somehow cleanse him of the feeling that Sandman had just violated him in some horrible and disgusting way. He sat the empty bottle back down and rubbed his lips with the back of his sleeve as he stared at the surface of the bar, afraid to look up again and see the Sandman's eyes. Still, he felt them boring into his back like a child running up the stairs of a dark basement.

"Are you finished?" Sandman demanded in a voice so cold it sent a chill down Nicolae's spine. He nodded, giving Sandman affirmative indication that he was in fact finished.

"*Good*, then we can begin with the latest developments." Sandman hissed. "While you were off charming the masses, our dear friend, Dr. Umur Tummel, managed to escape his holding cell and sent a rather cryptic message to one Samuel Duke. A man whom you undoubtedly know."

Cucumber-vodka sprayed from Nicolae's mouth at the sound of the name. *"Samuel Duke is alive?"*

"Oh yes, he's alive, and there's more—his grandson, James and wife Amy, are also members of the terrorist Serfs. The four are involved in some sort of conspiracy codenamed 'Project Reveal.' But I haven't yet been able to ascertain their target or objective. I'm sure though, once I've had time with Dr. Umur Tummel alone in the interrogation room, we'll have the answers we need."

"Are the Serfs responsible for the PrP6 outbreak?" Nicolae asked.

"Possibly." Sandman replied as he flicked a speck of ash from the leg of his trousers with one of the eight pointed digits on his claw hand.

"We need to tell somebody . . . We need to get in contact with the rest of the Inner Council and tell them Helton Quiver's been infected and the Serfs are behind the outbreak. We—"

"There, there, Nicolae, pour yourself another drink. There's nothing to worry. I've already calculated everything. I've dispatched my best Cyborg Assault Team to apprehend James and Amy Duke. We are headed straight for the coordinates that Dr. Tummel's message was sent to, which I feel quite confidently, will take us to the mysterious location of Samuel's mythical 'farm.'"

Nicolae became enraged by the Sandman's response. This was no time to be pursuing Serfs—they needed to get Helton Quiver medical attention! He whipped his drink against the wall, causing the real crystal glass to explode, sending jagged shards flying. One such shard sliced Helton Quiver's face and blood dripped from her chin and onto the carpeting.

Nicolae glanced the Sandman nervously, realizing he'd let his temper go too far. "Clean bots—Blood, vodka, cucumber, and broken glass on floor and carpet. Now!" Nicolae shouted, clapping his hands. A compartment opened on the wall and two black mechanical spiders clicked out. One clattered along wall towards Helton Quiver, while the other went to her feet and began spraying white sudsy foam on the blood puddle forming there. Whirling brushes spun on the tips of each of its legs and it dug them into the stain, while a suction tube rose from a compartment on the back of its head and sucked the white and red suds through the iridescent tank in its midsection. The bot on the wall sprayed cleaning agents on the liquid stain, then a squeegee attachment slid back and forth, while the mouth of its suction hose spread wide beneath it, capturing the dripping liquid.

"I'm so sorry Sandman," he stammered, "I just, well, I'm distraught, that's all. I'm not used to dealing with this much stress."

"Nicolae, do you lust for power?" Sandman asked.

The question startled Nicolae. "No, of course not—" he stammered in response.

"Then why do you suffer as Helton Quiver's personal assistant? You come from a well-connected Bujee family. You could spend all of your days in a hammock somewhere warm sipping drinks and screwing cocktail waitresses. Why pass on that life to deal with Helton Quiver? Why, just last yert, she threw her visiscreen-palm at your head and it took forty-staples to stop the bleeding . . . Why else would you endure her abuses, if not for a lust for power?"

"I, well, it's not the power . . . I haven't any power at all really. I sacrifice my well-deserved Bujee lifestyle to serve the Inner Council because I care deeply for the PCWO and Unified Global Government. I believe it's in the best interest of human-kind for the Inner Council to remain eternal. Isn't that why you serve Sandman?"

The insincerity in Nicolae's tone would have been obvious to anyone, but to Sandman it was especially apparent. "Nicolae," Sandman said in a tone of a parent scolding his mischievous child, "Don't you know that my brain-chip is equipped with lie-detection software developed by HON? In real time, my brain-chip detects near imperceptible changes in your body temperature, slight changes in the texture and hue of your flesh, and notices over fifty-thousand behaviors or tics known to indicate deceit. Before you'd finished bloviating, I'd already calculated a ninety-nine-point-nine-nine-percent chance you were lying. Why must you insult me like this?" Sandman's metallic claw clicked the arm of his seat.

Nicolae hastily poured himself another drink and promptly swigged it back. "I'm sorry Sandman." He said, "I know what your brain-chip is capable of . . . I just forgot who I was talking to for a cec there. I get asked about what it's like serving Helton Quiver all the time at Bujee parties. I just have that response rehearsed, that's all. It's like auto-drive. But honestly, the Unified Global Government is the greatest government ever conceived by man and I'm proud to serve it. I admire every member of the Inner Council. They're the most benevolent beings to have ever lived—"

Sandman's black portal eyes locked onto Nicolae's again and he felt his glass fall from his hand and splatter onto the carpet. An unbearable pain tore through his anus and the top of his skull. It was impossible to break the trance of the ever-widening expanse of the Sandman's eyes. Each appeared as their own separate universe of darkness. From that darkness crawled a tiny man who scampered across the floor and up Nicolae's leg. The tiny man climbed his silk suit jacket, then his wet tangled hair. Now standing atop Nicolae's head, the tiny man produced a pagan looking hand saw and began using it to saw through Nicolae's skull. Nicolae was paralyzed; helpless to stop this. In the darkness of the Sandman's eyes there appeared a reflective surface that forced him to watch as the tiny man sawed a ring all around the edge of his skull. The grinding pain rattled his teeth and caused him to shriek in impossible pain, but he could produce no sound. Once the tiny man had sawed a complete ring around the top of Nicolae's skull, he wedged something inside and popped the white cover free like he'd popped off a sewer cover. Inside, pink cords pulsed like pressurized hoses through the purple fleshy tissue of his brain. The tiny man inserted a telescoping metal needle straw into Nicolae's brain, expanding it as he drove it deeper and deeper striking his brainstem with a disconcerting click. The tiny man placed the entirety of his mouth around the end of the straw and sucked with force unimaginable for someone so diminutive. Then, without warning, the tiny man released his mouth from the end of the straw and leapt backwards as red liquid erupted, spiking high in the air like a geyser of violence that rained red dripping blood all across the Sandman's billiards car.

Nicolae felt his conscious awareness beginning to fade, as

if his very consciousness was floating away from his body. He could see his body below, frozen in horror with the tiny man now wearing a black PCWO rain slicker and rubber hat, laughing as he stood beside the torrent of blood spewing from the straw sticking out of his brain. His focus was then turned for him in the direction he was being drawn and there he saw again the infinite darkness contained in the Sandman's eyes. Nicolae felt his consciousness being pulled into this dark endless universe as he entered into the Sandman's eyes, and he felt their darkness passing through the subatomic makeup of his consciousness as he came to be a part of it. Space and time ceased and all that he saw was the absence of light. He understood then that this universe he'd entered was the mechanical consciousness of the Sandman.

*   *   *

The acrid smell of burning human flesh swallowed him into a dense gray cloud. He felt the sensation of flying and yet, felt no reassurance that anything at all was holding him up in the sky. It was as if he'd been fired from a cannon and would eventually decelerate and tumble to earth. The gray choking clouds fluttered away as he fell beneath them and the sky—scarred permanently by fire—came into view. Below, the ground was covered for as far as he could see with petrified skeletons scorched black.

Omnipresent wails and screams grew as he travelled further into this nightmare realm. Cresting a mountain peak, thick black smoke rose from the earth. As he passed through the smoke, it was as if a curtain had been thrown back to reveal a demonic play taking place below. The velocity of his progress shifted suddenly then, and his momentum slowed until he felt as if he was simply hovering in place above this lurid scene.

Before him, stretched out as far as the hazy sky would allow him to see, a sprawling Castaway village lay in ruin. The source of the wailing and screams became apparent when Nicolae spotted a bulbous cargo net dangling from the underbelly of a hovering Boar Drone. In it, were hundreds of screaming adults—struggling to untangle or stop themselves from being crushed beneath the others. Below them, in the ruin of their village, the true source of their torment came into view.

The limp bodies of children—hundreds—piled like stacks of firewood around the metal claws of two towering Kill-Drones. The Kill-Drones' rear-jointed, piston-driven legs stood nearly one-hundred-mets tall. Affixed to the top were armored pyramids housing each of their AI control units, atop which, the AI's censor receptors were affixed and looked very much like a giant human eye.

The Kill-Drones stood apart from one another—nearly the entire length of the village's main street. The air between them was a blur of streaming color and motion. Objects hurtled back and forth between them, but whatever it was moved too fast to appear as anything more distinct than a blur. One of the impaling arms on the nearer Kill-Drone stabbed down into the pile of children, spearing one of the bodies then hurtled it towards the other Kill-Drone. Nicolae watched in stunned horror as the other Kill-Drone received the body on one of its own impaling arms, spun it around and whizzed it back in a synchronized display of macabre carnage.

The sickening realization of what he was witnessing caused Nicolae to choke. The slack bodies of the children being juggled like machinegun rounds across the Castaway village, was enough to make Nicolae wish for a death that wouldn't come. Each Kill-Drone had ten impaling arms, all moving at such speed, they appeared as a single glimmering band wobbling up and down. Periodically, one or the other would stab down into the pile of bodies and add it to the total count being juggled.

A great Zeppelin-drone hovered above the village. There upon the open-air balcony stood the recently deceased Inner Council member, Cameron Paddleton. He wore only a white terry robe and cheered wildly at the juggling display being put on for his entertainment below. He leapt up and down on the balcony and his ample belly jiggled as he did so, and he pumped his fat arms in the air whistling and hooting. A Ujee servant handed Cameron a chalice and he accepted the large cup, swigged from it heavily, then spit the liquid back across the bewildered servant's face. Without hesitation, he swung the chalice into the servant's skull causing blood to erupt across his white terry robe. He grabbed the stunned bleeding servant by the waist of his trousers and heaved him over the ledge of the balcony. The Ujee shrieked as he fell, striking the top pyramid of the Kill-Drone, splitting his body in two and causing blood to erupt from each half of his body like wild pressurized hoses spraying in circles all the way to the dirt.

Cameron leaned over the balcony rail and slapped the railing as he wheezed with laughter. In the distance, Stealth-Drones swooped out of the clouds, drawing his attention towards the roar. The black wing crafts swooped low over a green hillside and dumped liquid fire upon it. Little bodies—those Castaways who'd managed to flee the initial roundup—leapt up like matchsticks, running in circles for several cecs before collapsing back into the sea of fire. Cameron howled with laughter and ran back and forth on the balcony shouting and hollering mad.

The Boar Drone climbed higher in the sky then until the net of tangled shrieking humans hung even with Cameron Paddleton. A doorway burst open on the balcony of the Zeppelin and Sandman strode out carrying a pagan-era SAW machinegun and dragging behind a crate of ammunition. Cameron smiled wide when he saw what Sandman held in his bionic arm. He threw his arms out wide, exposing his naked jiggling belly, but stopped short of embracing Sandman. Instead, he gestured for Sandman to follow him to the edge of the balcony. There, he took a gak-inhaler from his pocket and stuck it between his teeth, inhaling. He then tore off his robe and tossed it across the Sandman's face. There he stood at the ledge of the balcony, stark nude, arms outstretched, and let loose a guttural roar that jiggled his plump pale flesh. Sandman stood erect with the robe flapping from his face in the wind, then glanced at Nicolae and shrugged.

The focus of the tangled mass of humanity in the net remained focused on the horrifying juggling act being carried out with their children by the Kill-Drones. Soon, though, many nearest the Zeppelin took note of the now screaming Cameron Paddleton. The pale white fatso beat his soggy tits like a pagan ape, then leapt up onto the ledge of the balcony and pointed at the people trapped at the net, and shouted, "You fickers are all gonna die! I'm gonna kill you all again and again—welcome to my eternity!"

The white terry robe then released its grasp on Sandman's face and flew off into the distant nothingness. Cameron stepped down from the rail and leaned there for a moment catching his breath, then took a hit on his gak-inhaler and turned to Sandman. He snatched the machinegun from Sandman's grasp and turned the heavy weapon back towards the tangled mass in the net. Nicolae could see those in the net nearest Cameron were struggling in vain to get away. The tangled screaming mass only succeeded in churning itself into a single entity. Cameron ripped back the bolt of the gun and smiling, squeezed the trigger. The roar of gunfire overtook the metallic snipping sound of the juggling Kill-Drones. A cloud of heated air rose into the sky and a fireball speared from the muzzle of the weapon and bullets pounded sickeningly into dense meat and bone. Cameron roared like a pagan savage over the rattle of the machinegun fire; behind him, Sandman stood emotionless, merely observing the massacre.

A savage gust of wind then battered the Zeppelin, causing it to bend and Cameron to stumble, disrupting his aim and causing a barrage of bullets to clatter against the thick hull of the Boar Drone before Cameron regained control of the weapon and brought it back to bear on the indistinguishable bloodied mass of humanity being chopped to bits in the net. Blood rained down from the bottom of the net and was swept across the village in the wind. Cameron roared over the sound of gunfire, *"We're going to do this tomorrow and the next day and the day after that you fickers! I'm gonna kill you again and again and again and there's not a ficking thing you can do about it! I made a deal, and this is my reward! I get to kill you whenever I want to!"*

A cord of mucus dangled from the edge of Cameron's mouth, flapping in the wind behind him. Sandman didn't appear to mind. He turned again to look at Nicolae, and though he seemed very far, Nicolae felt as if he was standing right there beside Sandman. The infinite darkness in the Sandman's eyes then seemed to swirl, like crude oil down a drain. This nightmare—Cameron Paddleton's apparent eternity—then began to fade and the red scarred sky over the horizon began to vanish. Nicolae pinched his eyelids shut until it felt as though his eyeballs might burst. When he opened them, he found himself standing before the Sandman in the billiards car aboard Thomulous. His paralysis again abated, and he frantically reached up and felt around the top of his skull but felt no sign of the damage wrought by the little man with the straw. Nicolae's foppish hair was still wet from the acid rain at the coronation ceremony and the long scar on his scalp from where Helton Quiver's visiscreen-palm had struck him remained the only imperfection. But when he looked down at his hands wet from his hair, they were covered in blood.

Sandman's flat smile spread wide across his face until it appeared the edges of his pale lips were touching his ears. Nicolae stood trembling so violently that he thought he might collapse. The front of his trousers was dark and wet and cold from where he'd apparently pee-peed himself. His legs felt like warm melting rubber sinking under the weight of his body. The Sandman's bionic arm reached out and took hold of Nicolae's Ujee-hand-stitched silk suit, providing him enough support to remain upright. Sandman's flesh hand then brushed Nicolae's cheek like the cold of death as he whispered, "Nicolae, do you trust me?"

Nicolae sputtered something unintelligible. His tongue felt gelatinous. His ability to piece together words had been sapped by the cold fingers of death caressing his cheek. He looked up into the blinding lights overhead and felt like a baby that'd been ripped from the womb. The Sandman's lifeless claw drew Nicolae close to the lapel of his black leather PCWO jacket. Inside, the whirring sounds of the mechanical wizardry that kept Sandman alive buzzed, clattered and hummed. Sandman opened the breast of his jacket, exposing the deeply scarred flesh concealed within, then clutched the back of Nicolae's skull and brought his lips firmly to the cold of his teat. Nicolae whimpered silently and wished that he was dead. A claw from Sandman's bionic arm tickled the bottom of Nicolae's chin and he sobbed heavier, his back convulsing as Sandman drew him nearer still. It was impossible, he knew then, that he'd ever return to his former self. Whatever Sandman had done had changed him forever. He'd been reborn aboard Thomulous, into a brave new world of understanding and darkness. This was the Sandman's universe—deep underground, in the tunnels of the Dark Web. Nicolae understood that this place provided all the Inner Council's power. Without Sandman, the Inner Council would be as helpless and fragile as Nicolae was now. For it was Sandman who carried out the acts of terror necessary to maintain unquestioned authority. Without Sandman, the Inner Council would be nothing.

Each member of the Inner Council was the descendent of an Inner Council member before them. Each was granted unlimited Globos and power. All decisions and laws of the Unified Global Government were made by them. It was for these reasons that Nicolae—and likely all citizens—believed their inherited blood was the source of their power, but they'd all been wrong. That misconception had made their authority palatable. Now, though, Nicolae had witnessed the truth. His consciousness now possessed the knowledge of their true source of power. Bujees were granted a semblance of power over the Ujees beneath them just because. But when it came down to it, the Bujees possessed no real power at all. They were merely fools born into a comfortable existence and they yielded all decision making to the Inner Council without question, like a dog didn't question the master who fed it.

That the Bujees never questioned the authority of the Inner Council, lest they be executed, or worse—dropped in status to that of Ujee—never struck Nicolae as strange, until now. All his life he'd accepted that the Unified Global Government had been designed and structured to mimic the perfect harmony of nature as observed by the great Donald Darwin. Only now, for the first time in his life, did he question why he'd ever believed the story of Donald Darwin. Did the man attributed with observations used to justify almost every facet of the Unified Global Government's governing structure ever even exist? Was Donald Darwin simply a fiction created to justify the decisions of those who orchestrated the death of billions with the Great

Debt Crisis in order to consolidate all power on earth into a single governing entity that they and their descendants would rule for all of time?

Somehow, Nicolae had come to understand this all in a flash, like choking down some disgusting bite. A string of drool dangled from his lip and he heard himself snoring and this startled him awake. Only then did he realize he was curled in the fetal position, held in Sandman's powerful bionic arm, latched tightly to the Sandman's cold scarred nipple. The awareness of this was startling, but then some primal instinct caused him to suck on the nipple and the liquid that filled his mouth was warm and tasted like liquor and the warmth of it spread throughout his body and calmed his misgivings and dulled the yacking giggles of Helton Quiver that bellowed off the walls of the room.

It was Sandman who was the grantor of all authority. Sandman instilled the fear necessary for the Inner Council to indulge their every fantasy and urge, no matter how depraved or unnecessary. Sandman was the one who'd stood unaffected when Cameron Paddleton flung his robe across his face because Sandman never judged. Sandman didn't encourage, discourage, nor did he advise. Sandman simply enabled—no matter what was desired. His enabling inspired their greed, lust for power, and love of violence. Here, beneath all who walked in the grasp of the sun and labored and toiled to feed their unquenchable appetites, Sandman simply carried out the orders of those three-hundred individuals who descended from those who'd had the tenacity to risk the eradication of mankind for the consolidation of power. Here lurked the evil of cold calculating unconcern—the infinite absence of conscience. Nicolae wept upon the Sandman's cold breast because he then understood all he'd served was a lie. There was nothing gained by this knowledge. Sandman's flesh-hand swept through Nicolae's wet foppish hair and pressed his mouth firmer onto his teat of truth. "There, there,

Nicolae," Sandman whispered, "drink your milk and you will understand it all."

Nicolae whimpered and sucked from his latch. Helton Quiver giggled wildly and her chains jingle-jangled and Nicolae felt ashamed, so he snuggled in closer to the Sandman's chest to shield himself from judgement. He curled himself further into a fetal ball and sucked hungrily for truth that'd been a mystery until now.

CHAPTER 7

AMY'S BUS RIDE

A DROPLET OF RAIN splattered Amy's porcelain cheek, rolled down her chin, then plopped onto a puddle formed in the overturned wreckage of her CAR. The stink of gasoline filled the air. A neon gas station sign blinked overhead as her consciousness returned. She grabbed hold of the side of the wreckage, then pulled with all her strength. She managed to get herself halfway out before feeling a sharp pain in her right leg. Looking down, she saw it was pinned tight beneath the caved dash. Biting down on her dry-blood encrusted lower lip, she pulled hard, and heard the tearing sound of her trousers ripping like Velcro as it gave way. She surged out onto the cold asphalt covered with broken plastic and sharp shards of twisted alloy.

The butt of her trousers scraped as she pulled on the side of her CAR, righting herself. She stood there, unsteadily, gazing up the hillside which she'd cascaded like a pagan toboggan. Sheared sod spiked up where her CAR had flipped and tumbled end over end before coming to rest alongside these gas pumps. Had the CAR's trajectory fallen just a half-met in the other direction, it would have crashed right through the pumps and she'd have roasted.

A heavy cloud of burnt rubber masked the calamity still raging on the ultra-road. Headlights emerged from the cloud, appearing in the hole in the guardrail through which she'd hurtled. The lights seemed to hover there back and forth for a cec or two, then abruptly, an OFFROADER burst and bounded down the hillside right at her.

Her legs felt like they'd become a part of the asphalt somehow. As if her feet had burrowed into it to absorb the pools of liquid glimmering purple and orange. The OFFROADER's suspension launched it high into the air again and again and it pulverized sapling trees like pagan fireworks. The front tires went sideways and stuck firmly into earth, causing the truck to blast off—end over end—completing two entire flips before slamming down, catching sideways, spinning like a log, catching earth again and cartwheeling down, faster and faster.

She thought first to reach back into the wreckage for her gun, but her senses screamed that there wasn't time and that she needed to *run!* She broke into a sprint towards the side of the gas station building and the cool night wind rushed over the moisture on her face as she reached the stucco corner. Behind her, the OFFROADER smashed through the gas pumps with a terrifying scream.

A geyser of gasoline sprayed into the air, followed swiftly by a super-heated blast wave that sent Amy sprawling onto the jagged asphalt, scraping the flesh of her hands and arms as she slid. She crawled frantically the rest of the way until she reached the cool shadow behind the building. There, she rolled to extinguish the flames on the back of her trousers and blouse. Then stood and went carefully to the corner of the building and peered around the edge at the towering flames spiraling up into the sky, dancing wickedly amongst the raindrops.

Inside the gas station, thick dust covered the shelves like nuclear winter. There weren't many gas-powered vehicles anymore and pagan relics like this station were only found at the outskirts of safe-zones where the poorest Ujees lived. The south and western edges of the lot were blocked by a seven-met tall metal fence interlaced with spiral loops of razor wire and glowing red sign that read:

CHEMICAL DUMP – STAY OUT!

The north end of the lot led up to the ultra-road, no longer visible beneath the blanket of smoke, but audible as a pagan destruction derby. Along the eastern edge of the lot, a sagging wooden fence marked the entrance to a dark forest of towering weeds that stretched up a hillside. It was difficult to make out through the smoke drifting over from the ultra-road, but there appeared to be a dead-end street at the top of the hill. Amy found the notion of climbing through the thick weeds, all taller than her, less than appealing, but there was nowhere else for her to go. She went to the sagging fence and kicked it hard—way harder than she needed to. Her leg went through it like wet paper and she found herself precariously straddling it. Sensing the fence might fall at any cec, she slipped her head through the hole, then yanked her other leg through quickly. The fence crashed with a pathetic wet ripping sound and a swarm of genetically modified insects descended upon her.

Buzzing in her ears and eyes, they slurped with their spear-like noses, then flew off to make room for the others. These modified bugs operated with the same level of sophistication as a wolf pack, allowing those carrying eggs to feed first while the others distracted the prey by buzzing its eyes, nose and mouth. Yerts back, the Inner Council commissioned PCWO Scientists to develop genetically modified insects stronger and more resistant to deadly transmittable diseases. Only one gender of the insects was created to prevent natural breeding, but at some point, they'd adapted and now bred freely. This natural breeding enabled the continued evolution of the bugs and today, they were thousands of times stronger than initially designed. As the insects evolved, so did the deadly diseases they'd been bred to resist, which were now deadlier, drug-resistant, and still carried by the bugs. To combat the epidemic this caused, tens of thousands of vampire bats were released because they fed on these types of insects. Later, though, it was discovered that vampire bats consuming large quantities of the genetically modified bugs carried a new strain of rabies resistant to vaccine. A rabies outbreak ensued, and the Inner Council responded by commissioning the release of millions of autonomous bat-killing drones. These drones, they'd come to learn, were not capable of distinguishing between bats and nocturnal birds. Four species of owl were made extinct, while several other bird species had been driven to the brink before anyone realized what was going on. Once the devastating impact of the drones was discovered, the Inner Council commissioned the release of drones designed specifically to destroy the bat-killing drones. Then, enhanced bat-killing drones were released with better software that enabled them to distinguish between bats and birds, seventy-eight-percent of the time. The Serfs learned about this because the bat or bird differentiating software was developed at Elston Dynamics, and Duke hacked an AI there that housed the designs.

Through grinning shadows and prickly bulbs, Amy was stalked up the hillside by these vicious swarms. They stabbed and irritated and might have driven her mad, had she not utilized self-hypnosis to ignore them. She pictured the precursors of a human life forming in her womb. The cells, guided by ancient blueprints passed from her and Duke, converged two ancient lineages into a new story—imprinted, in part, by each generation that preceded it. In the warmth of her womb, she felt it growing; a globule of cells possessing all the information needed to build such intricate structures as spine and brain. Who knew how many chances remained for natural human breeding? How long would it be before the PCWO Creation scientists succeeded in breeding out "undesirable" human traits like passion, emotion, drive, rebellion, and creativity?

Amy's hands, forearms, face and neck bled as she stepped out from the clawing jungle, gasping. The vulture-insects, fat and full, still hung around her face, just enjoying her pheromones, it seemed. Ahead, flood waters rushed past, carrying floating plastic bottles, wrappers and Styrofoam—things that wouldn't decompose before mankind went extinct. Amy gathered herself, stepped back into the weeds and felt them grabbing at her as she built tension in the elastic of her legs before bursting forth. Her eyes timed each movement as the cadence of her steps slapped the mud, closer to the edge of the rushing backwater, before one final step hit the perfect spot at the edge and she fired up and out. She clutched forward, then dipped her head down, forcing her body into a roll to ensure her momentum would carry her forward, free and clear.

She lay for a mixi in the wet muddy grass, gazing up at the starry night now revealed. Lying there, she thought of James and wondered where he might be, knowing wherever he was, he'd be worried about her. Rolling onto her side, then, she scanned the desolate street, examining each ruinous public domicile for a sign of life. She saw no one, but sensed somehow, she was being watched from afar.

This was the edge of New Chicago's safe-zone, still technically inside the city limits, but hardly policed at all. The tap-dancing PCWO mayor of New Chicago found places like this too expensive to effectively police, so he'd instituted a program where drones regularly sprayed the area with B2-1-toxin, known more commonly as "Compliance-gas." The gas tasted bitter, stung the eyes and made those who'd inhaled it docile, vacant and weak. Despite this, more than a few people (known as "Gas-heads") lived in these parts, finding the gas-sings preferable to labors.

Amy fashioned a crude ponytail as she started down the craggy flooded street in a light jog. She didn't want to be around when the next gassing occurred; for those unaccustomed, the effects of compliance-gas were highly disorienting, and she'd never find her way home. At the end of the block, she turned and thought she spotted a set of eyes peering out from the bottom of a basement windowsill but chose to pretend she hadn't. Fear began climbing and the pace of her jog accelerated. She didn't know where she was going, just towards home, but surely it was too far to run. Still, absent a better plan, that was exactly what she'd do if she had to.

She ran past drooping structures painted with graffiti like, *Thought-crime-Boogey-Woogie, PCWO Death Machines, GAS-MAN, Tap-dancing death merchant!* Amy sensed more eyes blinking in the shadows, wondered if she should call out, but knew better. Gas-heads, she'd heard, would become violent if provoked, or rather, if provided with too much stimuli. PCWO News Media often reported stories of Gas-heads attacking citizens and chopping off their heads or hands to steal their Globos-chips (a major reason that forehead implanted Globos-chips had fallen out of style).

In the distance, Amy heard a faint squealing sound that seemed foreign in this wasteland. As the sound grew louder, it became clear it was something cared for and functional—a sound foreign in a place like this. Her legs beat harder against the pavement as she rounded another block. There, beneath a blinking street light, a city bus grumbled from a stop. *"Wait!"*

Amy shouted, waving her hands through the air. Her legs accelerated as she chased after the bus. A wicked cramp began to gnaw at her side, but she ignored it, screaming, "*Stop!*" Then she put her head down to eke out as much speed from her legs as possible. "Please!" She shouted, lifting her head like a swimmer grabbing a breath. She saw the red beams of the bus brake lights as it came to a stop and Amy continued her frenzied pace, up to and around to the front of the bus, then through the open doors.

"That will be five-Globos," the bus driver said, her voice distorted by the gas-mask over her head. The driver squinted through thick glasses inside the mask. She sat atop a big foam cushion that allowed her to see above the vast steering wheel. The bus's auto-drive engaged, and the driver remained poised and prepared to grab control, if ever she was needed. Amy swept the back of her hand across the Globos scanner and felt a warm tingle as the five Globos were deducted from the wallet-chip implanted there.

Clutching the vertical handrails for balance, moving from each to the next, she went down the row to keep from toppling as the bus rapidly sped. Spinning around, she plopped down on the front-most plastic seat and an auto-belt swung around from the side and clipped together at the front of her waist.

"Does this bus go to Roosevelt Street?" Amy asked.

The bus driver nodded, "Yep, that's the last stop on my route. I'm mostly relegated to driving around the edges of the safe-zones, because of my advanced age, but I go right past that Roosevelt Stop on my way to the garage. They only let the young drivers have the good routes in the center of the city these days, I guess that tap-dancing mayor of ours don't care much about us old folks."

Auto-drive carried the bus through the dripping darkness and Amy's teeth began to clatter as the adrenaline faded and wet cold set in. The driver reached up and pressed a button, activating seat-specific climate control and warming the air. "Thanks," Amy muttered, feeling sleep pull at her eyelids.

"There are some bad characters out tonight, I tell you!" the driver said, "I've been driving city buses around since before these things even had auto-drive . . . I seen all kinds of wickedness and violence. I been robbed, cursed at, spit at, grabbed, and hollered at—but in all my yerts—I ain't never been *bit* before." The driver gestured at the bloody bandage wrapped around her frail looking arm. "I don't know what gets into these youths today—drugs I guess," she muttered with a sigh. "You know what I did to him?" she cackled sharply, "I kicked him in the face—that's what I done—sent his dumper tumbling back out the bus and slammed them doors right in front of his face before he could get back inside. He looked up at me with these black ghoulish-looking eyes and auto-drive wouldn't go—the sensor was telling me there was a rider waiting outside—so I hit manual override and pressed my foot down on that there gas pedal for the first time in thirteen yerts—greatest damle thrill of my life!" The driver cackled muffled echoes in her fogging mask. "I do my stretches every day—when you get to be my age, it's important to do your stretches *every* day!"

The old woman's cackle wove through the molecular makeup of the bus as the windshield wipers beat back and forth, back and forth and Amy descended rapidly into a dreamless sleep.

* * *

"*Alert! Alert! Impact Imminent! Engage Auto-drive! Alert! Alert!*"

Amy awoke to the blaring alarm. She looked to the driver, saw her head slumped to the side. Her gasmask had fallen to the floor and was rolling around as the bus lurched up a median and barreled towards the side of a building with a sign blinking,

"Franks & Wieners" Amy screamed and struggled to unlatch her auto-belt, but it held fast, instructed by the auto-drive sensors.

The dark outline of a slender man slunk out of a shadow in front of the bus. The bus collided with the man and his head smashed through the windshield with a sickening thwap followed by a sound like canvas being torn, as his body was sucked under the bus, but his neck, impaled by the jagged glass, held fast until the head tore free and went ping-ponging down the aisle past Amy's feet.

Auto-drive then reengaged and took evasive maneuvers. The bus locked brakes, turned to avoid the façade with the sign flashing, but was too close. It slammed into the side of the building, but not a direct hit. Instead, it skidded alongside the building, alloy grinding and churning, then bounded back down from the curb onto the street before coming to a stop at an angle in the intersection.

Amy ripped the lever overhead for manual emergency release of her auto-belt. She felt it go slack, unlatched, grabbed hold of the vertical handrail and used it to help her stand. She staggered towards the front of the bus, then saw the extricated head lying in aisle and stopped. Her ears were ringing, and her head was pounding, but she was sure she could hear the muffled sounds of someone giggling. *Who could possibly be giggling?* She wondered, then mitched closer to the head lying still. The giggling grew louder as she approached the head and she decided she didn't want to look down at it as she stepped over. But curiosity got the best of her. She looked down and saw clear as anything that the face of the man was stretched up, moving. The sound of giggling seemed to match movements of the lips, but that was impossible. She thought, *maybe I got a concussion in the accident?* Then, *but wouldn't I know if I'd gotten a concussion? Is one aware of a concussion?*

Would one refer to themselves in the third-person if they had a concussion?

"Are you OK?" she whispered, then realized she'd just asked a decapitated head if it was OK. This seemed to make the extricated head giggle harder. She decided it would be better to go check on the driver rather than spend one more cec looking at that giggling, decapitated head.

She shuffled up to the driver, checked her wrist for a pulse, but felt nothing. She couldn't tell if her own racing heartrate masked the driver's. Carefully, she righted the driver in the seat, so her head wasn't dangling to the side anymore, and decided to listen for breath. She leaned one ear in close, but the ringing sound from the crash was overwhelming. In the big rearview mirror over the windshield, which reflected herself and the driver, she focused—strained in close. Her ear brushed the driver's dry lips and she closed her eyes and cleared her mind using self-meditation. She thought about how the ringing sound was like the wind brushing through pine needles, powerful, but easily set aside. She experienced tranquility, then heard a sound, like a chesty cough and opened her eyes. In the mirror reflection, she saw the driver's eyes snap open like window shades. She felt relief and joy—*she's alive!* As she turned, she felt the joy and relief drain from her body like bloodletting; the driver's lips twisted into a sick, deranged-looking smile, yellow teeth visible—then snapping out. Good reflexes caused Amy to tumble back from the driver's snapping teeth before they got hold of her flesh.

The driver went wild, giggling psychotically, ripping at the auto-belt pinning her to the seat, twisting and turning, glaring at Amy with black pin-holed eyes—demanding her flesh! Amy crawled out backwards from the bus, half-dazed by what was transpiring, but taking it all in thanks to the injection of adrenaline. Rather than ponder the driver, giggling head and how every law of the scientific universe seemed to have been broken in last few mixis, Amy climbed to her feet, and looked around. She realized she was nearly surrounded by stumbling giggling people of every shape—some missing limbs, wearing tattered clothing or no clothing at all. There seemed to be blood everywhere. She shouldered aside a one-legged giggler springing towards her and ran towards her residential domicile.

Everywhere they appeared from the shadows, giggling, stumbling, some trying to run or jog, but doing a poor job of it. They were all coming towards her, that was clear. She knew she was a little over a kimo from home, so she knew she could keep a pretty brisk pace. She was an avid jogger, very serious about physical fitness. Across a big intersection, she looked North and saw the Elston Dynamics building looming tall in the distant darkness and thought of James.

A chorus of giggling rattled through leaves and echoed off the towering residential domiciles all around. Time seemed not to pass as the cadence of each breath matched the rhythm of her steps until she reached her street and Alder Place materialized, tall and silent. She ran to the front revolving door; the lobby was pitch black inside. She pushed the revolving door in with a swoosh, stepped in and stood still; her own heavy breaths echoed through the cavernous lobby and she felt she was not alone. "Jeremy?" she called in an uncertain voice, hoping the good-natured doorman would be sitting in the darkness at front desk where he always was. No response came, but her own voice echoing back.

She stepped forward, tepidly. Then, stepped again and her foot landed in a puddle of something liquid and slippery on the floor. Before she could process what was happening, her leg had streaked up towards the ceiling and her skull had spiked onto the tile floor like a sporter-ball athlete celebrating a photon-score.

Pain throttled her brainstem like a mechanical pickaxe so horrible consciousness became a place she no longer wished to be. A distant memory, or a memory of a dream came to her—her mother warning her not to swim too far out, but the undertow was dragging her, and she wasn't strong enough to swim against it. It seemed to tug at her ankles, pulling her beneath the salty waves, into the darkness where the sound of bumping bass pounded a rhythm of pain, dragging her to the black ocean floor.

CHAPTER 8

ALDER PLACE

THE RESIDENTS OF Alder Place gathered around the visiscreen in the Community Room on the thirty-second floor with their mouths dangling open. Violent images from Helton Quiver's coronation ceremony flashed across the visiscreen, as the Superior Commander of the PCWO's Centralized Security Forces, Delvish Richland, spoke at a press conference about the worsening PrP6 epidemic. This was the first time any of the residents had ever heard of PrP6.

Linda, her husband, Mark, and two young boys, Michael and Ricky had been at the coronation ceremony, but they left early after a homeless man, obviously gaked out, bit Mark on the arm. Linda felt they'd been quite fortunate as she watched the images of twelve-thousand dead being flown out of Taft Park on Ambulance-drones. She elbowed Mark in a playful sort of way, as if to say, "Wow, we were all pretty lucky you got bit." Her eyes were so glued to the screen, she didn't notice Mark's face stretched in discomfort as he fought viciously against a powerful urge to giggle.

Delvish Richland, standing at a podium in his black leather uniform, stated that terrorist extremist Serfs had unleashed a fast-acting *prion* weapon known as PrP6. Adler Place resident, Dr. Kunal, tried explaining to the others that prions were infectious proteins, but no one understood, and all were far too distracted by the visiscreen to pay attention to him.

Jackson was Head Building Laborer at Alder Place. He stood at the back of the crowd, unsure what to make of this. He kept his eyes on Mark, noticing that the man was acting rather strangely. At first, he just thought he was crying—an understandable reaction to what they were seeing on the visiscreen—but as he moved closer he realized the man was giggling.

This realization caused him to stop. How or why would anyone be giggling at a time like this? Maybe, he thought, Dr. Kunal had given him something for the pain and it made him a little loopy. As Mark's giggling grew louder, Jackson began to wonder why no one else seemed to notice. He scanned the others and saw their vacant eyes transfixed on the visiscreen. Then, Mark's oldest son, Michael, looked up at his father and asked him why he was giggling. Mark looked down at the boy and giggled so loudly that the others finally noticed. Without warning, Mark tackled his son to the floor. Jackson didn't know much about this family, but this seemed like a strange time to be goofing around.

The boy emitted an ear-piercing scream as blood sprayed up at the ceiling, suddenly, as if fired from firehose. Everyone leaped back with shock, all but Michael's little brother Rickey, who charged at his dad and began punching his little fists on the back of his daddy's head. Mark reached around and grabbed the boy, then bit off a chunk of his forearm.

Three people nearby vomited; Jackson couldn't believe what he was seeing—like a bad dream that wouldn't end. Someone—approaching from behind—suddenly threw Jackson aside, knocking him into a chair. From there he watched as a hulking stranger charged towards Mark and booted him in the face. The hulk stood over Mark, now lying on his back, his face smeared with blood and giggling, and lowered a pagan shotgun to Mark's forehead. Before anyone could protest, the stranger pulled the trigger and Mark's head vanished into the carpet.

Linda shrieked and clutched her face; Dr. Kunal knelt beside Michael and applied pressure on his badly bleeding neck. Jackson saw that the hulking stranger wore a Centralized Security Forces jacket and this provided him a fleeting moment of relief. That relief vanished as the man racked the pump of his shotgun, placed the smoking barrel just above the sobbing Michael's face and pulled the trigger without hesitation. Time seemed to slow then. Jackson could see that Linda was screaming, but he couldn't hear her over the ringing in his ears from the shotgun blast. He watched as the surreal dream continued progressing as Linda clawed at the man's face and he tossed her aside like a dried leaf from his shoulder. The stranger racked the pump of his shotgun again and stepped towards Ricky.

Jackson got his wits about himself enough to realize that this man was planning to blow little Ricky away, when the child had merely been bitten on the arm. He sprinted as fast as he could with his clumsy prosthetic leg, then lowered his shoulder and hammered it into the stranger's ribcage. Immediately, he bounced backwards onto the floor like he'd just run headlong into a brick wall. Dazed, he grabbed the barrel of the shotgun and ripped at it, but he felt as if two hydraulic vice-clamps had closed around the other end of the gun. The vice-clamp hands whipped the gun around, swinging Jackson up off his feet until his sweaty grasp slipped from the barrel and sent him sailing to the floor. He watched then as the hulk stomped towards him and accepted that he was certainly about to die. He pleaded with the stranger, and the stranger looked down at him with blazing eyes, then swung the shotgun around backwards and slammed the butt end into Jackson's nose, shattering it and knocking him unconscious.

* * *

Jackson awoke on the floor with a pounding skull. Robinson, crouched beside him, locked eyes with Jackson and made a motion to suggest he remain where he was. Robinson then glanced nervously towards the source of a booming voice.

"I'm Special Agent Steve, but you all can just call me Steve. I'm a member of the PCWO Centralized Security Forces and these two here are members of my team: Special Agent Anne and Special Agent Jose. We are here to apprehend two members of the terrorist Serf organization who reside at Alder Place. Now, I understand you all might have gotten your dumpers bent out of shape during our introduction, but that doesn't change my expectations for us. Despite what you might have heard, the Unified Global Government is still functioning as normal. The fact that this epidemic is going on all over doesn't diminish the threat the terrorist Serfs pose to our way of life. My mission has nothing to do with this PrP6 outbreak. I'm here to apprehend two terrorists. I know you all have a lot of questions, but we don't have the time to sit around here circle-cranking our dongers. I need to know which unit James and Amy Duke live in, and I need some volunteers to take us there."

"Why'd you kill those kids?" Robinson demanded.

After a brief silence, the booming voice replied. "When my team entered, we observed an adult male exhibiting the symptoms of PrP6. Specifically, he was giggling and attempting to eat the children. As I approached the man, I noted that he'd already bitten both of the children. After I dispatched the infected adult, I then dispatched both children because both had been infected with PrP6."

"How do you know they were infected?" Robinson insisted.

After another pause, the loud voice responded with rage now present in the tone. "Because the children had been bitten by the adult male exhibiting obvious symptoms of PrP6. That's how PrP6 is spread you dunce fick. When the infected bite you, you're infected with PrP6 and there ain't a damle thing anyone can do to stop it. There ain't no cure for PrP6, but a bullet to the head. My team and I dispatched about a-hundred of those giggling ficks on our way in. We know what the fick we're talking about when it comes to giggling ficks. When you insinuate that I just killed some kids for the hillmota of it, well, I take that as an insult."

"How do you know there's no cure?" Linda shrieked and appeared suddenly in Jackson's view as she sprinted across the room. Robinson intercepted her, lifting her off her feet in a bear hug as she hissed and spit and punched and kicked to break free.

"Lady, listen," Steve said, "There ain't no cure for PrP6. If there was a cure, the Inner Council would already be handing it out. Until they find a cure, you best get your head on square and start listening to exactly what I say. If you keep flying off the handle like this, I'm gonna have that Dr. Koon-hall give you something that settles you down."

Jackson tried lifting himself up onto his elbows and doing so caused blood to rush to his throbbing head, amplifying the pain and causing him to groan.

Oh, look at who decided to join us!" Steve exclaimed, "Why, it's Mr. Hero. Good morning, Mr. Hero. Did you have a nice nap?"

Jackson continued lifting himself until he was in a seated position on the carpet near two towels draped across the floor, obviously covering blood stains from Linda's family. He rubbed his head with one hand as he searched for his cancer-free cigarettes in the pocket of his trousers with the other. "Sorry about that, I-well-none of us had any idea how this PrP6 spread. I just saw you shooting little kids and I guess my emotions got the better of me."

Without warning, a great and heavy shadow leapt down in front of Jackson, straddling his outstretched torso and prompting him to shield his face. Steve leaned his face in close to Jackson's and his rotten smelling breath oozed out as he spoke. "Well, you best get your delicate emotions in check, Mr. Hero, or else Mr. Hero is gonna get his ficking head blown off, understand?"

Jackson nodded that he did, and the hulking shadow stepped off and began pacing the room with his shotgun in hand. Lecturing them, it seemed, on the importance of his mission and unimportance of their safety. "Like I said, we're here to apprehend terrorists and that's it. We're not here to rescue you from PrP6; that said, if some of you assist us in successfully completing our mission, I have no doubt that I'll be able to get you all a drone ride out of here. I'm looking to form a posse and I need some of you dumper-fickers to help. Understand?"

A few mumbled "Yes," but Jackson couldn't see who. "Good, then we all understand each other. Now, can anyone tell me if Mr. and Mrs. Duke are home yet?"

Marcus, a building resident, responded. "No, Special Agent Steve—they're not home. We went around knocking on all the doors earlier and everyone who's home is up here in this room."

Steve replied, "I said to call me Steve—I don't have time for titles and I'm not so insecure that I need you to say it every time you address me. You'll learn to show your respect in other ways, don't worry. Now, who knows which unit the Dukes live in?"

Building resident, Frank, stepped forward and said, "I do."

"Good, I'll need you take me and my team there." Steve said. "But first, we need to establish some rules for everyone's safety—which includes me and my team. First rule: none of you can leave this 'Community Room' without my permission. Second rule: unless I say, no one is allowed to be anywhere else in this building. Third rule: what I say goes. You question me or disobey me, and I'll break your jaw or worse. That goes for you bishes too—I don't discriminate with punishment. You disobey me twice and I'll kill you. Fourth rule: if anyone attempts to warn the Dukes, you will be guilty of aiding and abetting enemies of the PCWO and I will kill you. If anyone attempts to disrupt our mission in any way, I'll kill you."

Steve walked to the only doorway in the hallway between the elevator bank and the Community Room. He fingered the door handle there and asked, "Where's this door lead?"

"That's um, where the head Building Laborer of Alder Place lives." Jackson stammered.

"And who might that be?" Steve said in an exaggerated gusto.

"That's me. I live there." Jackson replied.

"Well, *Jackson*, me and my team need a place to stay since it seems like we might be in for a bit of a wait until the Dukes get home. You mind if we borrow your apartment? Seeing as it's the only apartment on the thirty-second floor, it seems like the best way to make sure we all stay on the same level. You get me?"

Sheepishly, Jackson replied. "Sure, you can borrow it."

"Thanks, buddy!" Steve replied sarcastically. "We'll be sure to take real good care of it. Awful generous of you, *Jackson*."

* * *

Jackson stood outside alone on the building roof deck smoking a cancer-free cigarette. Embers swirled into the dark sky as he gazed inside at the others in the Community Room. Robinson stood at the Western facing windows, staring out at fires burning along the horizon. Devin and his wife Jessica sat together against the wall, with Jessica nodding in and out of sleep. Devin was a Bujee—the only Bujee who lived at Alder Place; the only Bujee Jackson had ever heard of marrying a Ujee. Because they were a mixed couple, they were prohibited from living inside the beautiful Bujee communities, at least until her status change request went through—if it ever did. Jackson couldn't comprehend how a Bujee could give up so much for a Ujee, even one as beautiful as Jessica. Jackson rather hated her, though, she called him "Janitor," and acted like she was better than everyone else.

Another building resident, Timothy Pants, was in front of the faux fireplace, staring at it blankly. He was a hardcore gamer-addict—rarely left his apartment. He looked buggy-eyed and twitchy, like a gak-head, but probably didn't do much more than caffeine eye drops. His skin was white as a sheet. Likely hadn't been out in the sun in tundles. Behind him, Sarah and Megan huddled together on a couch with Li sitting opposite like a sentry. Jackson called them the "gossip sisters" because they flirted with him to extract dirty secrets about the other residents. Sarah had even given him a pagan hand-job at the New Yert party two-yerts ago—enough incentive for him to play along. Dr. Kunal sat alone in a corner, glancing up at the side of Li's face every so often, as if pleading with her to look at him, but she wouldn't.

Jackson heard giggling coming from the street and went to the rail to peer down. Thirty-two stories below, at least twenty, maybe thirty gigglers were gathered at the front door of Alder Place, all giggling and stumbling around drunkenly. They pawed at the glass, pushing against one another like pigs at a feeding trough. In the distance, he heard emergency sirens wailing and smelled smoke drifting through the air. Drones screeched past over the lake, split off, then fired missiles into targets he couldn't see. The explosions rattled the glass surrounding the roof deck and Jackson decided it was time to go back inside.

CHAPTER 9

OFFROADER

Posh Bujee dwellings lined the dark and unfamiliar street. Ujees weren't legally prohibited from Bujee neighborhoods, but it was certainly frowned upon. Duke had a general idea where he was but knew none of these streets. PCWO Fighter Drones screeched through the sky in the distance, firing railguns and rockets into buildings. He found it remarkable that the Inner Council was allowing these strikes, even with giggling cannibals overrunning New Chicago.

He had to keep moving—no time to stop and figure out where to go next—gigglers were slow, but persistent. The fifteen or so following him made much more distance whenever he stopped. The Bujee neighborhood was a labyrinth of strange cobblestone streets fashioned to look like old pagan cities in a place once known as "Europe," at least that's what he'd been told. There seemed to be no logic to the layout, but it was strikingly beautiful, even in the darkness.

A Boar Drone dropped from the clouds overhead and Duke dove to the street. The enormous Boar Drones were heavily armored and slow. They were designed to survive ground fire and loiter for long periods of time, providing close air support for ground units. The hulking thing was loaded with missiles, bombs, a railgun and twenty-five pagan-era machineguns—which were still very effective at close range.

The Boar Drone opened with all twenty-five machineguns simultaneously. Red-hot bullet shells rained down on Duke as he covered his ears. It grumbled down the street, firing at whatever it was firing at and the shell casings slammed onto luxury Bujee vehicles, setting off alarms that issued stern warnings to back away. Duke looked up to watch the Boar Drone as it reached the end of street, then hit its boosters and vanished up into the clouds.

The racket seemed to have attracted every giggler in the area. All around it appeared that shadows had come alive. They staggered out from alleyways and yards, spotted Duke, then made their way towards him. He leaped back to his feet and sprinted down the middle of a curvy brick road. Around a block, he saw a fire raging from a Lux-Duplex set back from the street on a big city plot. The flames cast a kaleidoscope of shadows across the street, but no Fire Drones were in sight.

In the front yard of the burning Lux-Duplex, a red CAR was wrapped around the trunk of a tree. A big OFFROADER was parked behind it—the top and driver's side door were open. Duke ran towards it, thought it looked like the new model. He climbed inside and inspected the ignition system—FingerPrint Start, just as he'd feared.

He cursed and stepped out, felt something grab his ankle and leaped backwards. He saw the giggler with torso bent at a ninety-degree angle, face imbedded with glass, crawl out from beneath the OFFROADER.

Before he'd fully processed the nightmarish condition of the giggler crawling towards him, another giggler appeared from behind and tackled Duke into a sharp prickly bush. The tackling giggler was big burly and bald. He snapped his teeth at Duke, driving him deeper into the bush as Duke punched the man in the face, but the blows seemed to have little to no effect. He decided leverage was more important, so he bridged, then rolled, and the strategy worked. He freed himself from the tangled bush and got back to his feet.

Baldy thrashed at the bush and Duke pulled the scalpel from his cargo pocket. He stood with his knees bent, scalpel in fist—ready to strike once Baldy figured out how to free himself from the bush. When he finally did, he reached for Duke, but caught the scalpel through a black eyeball instead. He fell to the ground, dead again.

Duke wondered if Baldy was the owner of the OFFROADER parked in the lawn behind the tree hugging CAR. Baldy was wearing a bedazzled deep-cut V-neck, so he certainly dressed the part of an OFFROADER owner. The giggler with the angled torso, ever persistent as he was, had managed to drag himself within reaching distance of Duke. The glass imbedded face of the giggler looked like a pagan disco ball. As he reached a bloody hand out for Duke's canvas trousers, Duke rocked back then delivered an Octo-Sport-kick to the disco ball head. The kick flipped the giggler onto his broken back, allowing Duke to easily finish him off with a scalpel through the eye.

Duke lifted Baldy's heavy body and started dragging it towards the OFFROADER. Then he had a better idea. He knelt and cut Baldy's thumb off with the scalpel. This took a bit of effort to finally break it free. He bounded back inside the OFFROADER and pressed Baldy's thumb to the FingerPrint starter. The OFFROADER engine roared. Duke cut the engine, popped the hood, and went to the front. He needed to deactivate the restrictor plate that prevented vehicles from exceeding thirty-five-kimos-hort when auto-drive disengaged. He'd be driving manual home and he'd be doing so just as fast as this OFFROADER engine could crank.

Using the scalpel to pry open the engine brain-box, he wiggled the blade between the plastic cap covering the auto-drive circuits. He removed the auto-drive circuit, then held the scalpel with a t-shirt to prevent himself from getting zapped as he sliced through the restrictor switch's filament wire. Once cut, he slid the auto-drive circuit back in place and clicked shut the plastic cap.

He remembered a friend from the Marine Corps who'd taught him how to do this, a pencil-thin mustachioed mechanic known to all as *Mad Max.* He used to say he could fix anything with an engine, so long as he had a screwdriver, wrench, bubblegum, black tape, and titty digiture. They all used to steal tools from the better equipped Army units and give them to Mad Max in exchange for his seemingly endless supply of titty digiture.

The smile on Duke's face faded when he remembered that Mad Max had blown his brains out while back. He hadn't left a note.

Back in the driver's seat, Duke pressed Baldy's thumb again onto the FingerPrint starter and the OFFROADER engine roared to life again. He flipped off auto-drive, revved the engine, jerked the shifter into reverse and gunned it backwards down the lawn, bounding up and over the curb. Knobby tires chirped as he locked the brakes, then swung the shifter into *drive* and hammered the gas pedal.

The OFFROADER headlights illuminated the whimsical genocide of the Bujee neighborhood. Never in his life had he spent so much time around Bujees. In a brief period, he learned that they lived significantly more extravagant lives than Ujees. Some of them were dressed like clowns, others like furry animals, still others wore robot costumes, or dressed like inanimate objects such as trees or rocks—many costumes were sexually suggestive. Duke wondered if all these Bujees did was have strange costume sex in the privacy of their luxury homes. Seemed that way, at least now.

A chill in the night air ignited his breath as he exhaled. He clicked on the receiver, hoping to learn what the fick was going on. A husky-sounding female voice came through the speakers, "OK, so those were the locations of the Emergency Mobile Treatment Centers for my people on the South Side. But word to the wise, my boogey-woogies, little birdies telling me these Emergency Treatment Centers ain't safe no more. Heard they all overrun with gigglers.

"These same birdies tell me you are better off staying at your residential domicile and blocking up your windows. The PCWO Military set up roadblocks on every roadway outta the city. Little birdies say they are killing anyone trying to get out of the city.

The voice continued. "You know me, and I ain't no Bujee, but it doesn't take no PCWO University certificate to figure out they got New Chicago quarantined. Word to the wise, boogie-woogies, lay low and keep them pagan-pistols at the ready.

"Birdies telling me this PrP6 outbreak is going on all over the UGG—not just in New Chicago. Something don't smell right in the UGG, my people. Inner Council ain't saying nothing. The Supreme Chancellor didn't even show for her own damle coronation ceremony. I wasn't there my brothers and sisters— you all know I wouldn't dare—but some birdies on the ground say they just played a recording of her speech on that big ficking visiscreen they built at Taft Park. Seeing as how that coronation ceremony ended in the deaths of over twelve-thousand people, the Subversive in me starts wondering if maybe Helton Quiver knew something no one else did when she decided not to show—"

The woman's voice cut out. Duke could hear the faint sound of an argument taking place in the studio. Then a man's voice said, "Sorry about that folks, you know we like to keep things boogie-woogie here at Power-ninety-seven, but our dear sister Samantha done gone off the script just a bit too much there—"

"Nah, fick this," Samantha could be heard shouting, "get your mother-ficking hands off me! This ish and you know it! I saw a child eating a woman's mother-ficking face off in the middle of the street tonight. You all want me to stick to the script, *Greg*? Where this *script* of yours coming from anyhow, *Greg*?"

"*Security!*" Greg called out.

"Oh, it's gonna be like that?" Samantha's voice could be heard. Sounded like she was fighting with someone. "What, you all going to kick me out? Where am I supposed to go? Am I supposed to go to one of them Emergency Treatment Centers that's overrun by gigglers? Maybe I'll go slang-pride on the sidewalk somewhere till one of them gigglers take a bite out my dumper!

"How do you expect me to sit here and read this PCWO bullish when we know it's lies, *Greg*? No, fick you, *Greg*—I ain't no Serf, but I ain't no mother-ficking dunce-head neither! I'm boogie-woogie just like you, *Greg!*"

"Leave *Samantha!*" Greg shouted, "You've already said enough to get yourself put away for a long time! We can preach boogie-woogie here, but you're talking outright subversion!"

"Fick you, Greg! Last thing I'm worried about is the clink when these gigglers are out there eating mother-fickers. Fine, whatever, I'm outta this galaxy, *bishes*! You all can kiss my fat dumper!"

Alder Place came into view ahead. Duke steered the OFFROADER around the turn onto his street and then mashed on the brakes. Thirty or so gigglers were gathered outside the lobby, all pawing at the windows.

On the radio, Greg apologized, "Sorry about that, folks. Not sure what got into our sister Samantha this evening. We're going to get someone up here to fill in for her, but in the meanwhile, here's that new banger from Spider Mafia you all keep requesting, '*Globos IS My DNA*.'"

Duke cranked the stereo, wanting to draw the gigglers out into the street. The OFFROADER's stereo system was impressive. The deep bass intro of 'Globos IS My DNA' cranked, rattling the OFFROADER's windows and certainly getting the giggler's attention. They shuffled away from the Alder Place lobby, out into the street, giggling as they made their way towards the OFFROADER. Duke cranked the stereo volume to max.

Globos!
Globos!
Globos is my DNA!
Got so many Globos inside me,
Globos is my DNA,
Globos!
Globos!
Globos is my DNA!
Got so many Globos inside me—
I'll Bleed Globos if I ever catch a stray,
Globos!
Globos!
Globos is my DNA!
Bishes don't know what to buy me—
I tell 'em, bish, buy-me-some-more-a-my-DNA!
Globos!
Globos!
Globos is my DNA!
The air that I breathe made-a Globos!
The rhymes I spit made-a Globos!
The dumpers I see made-a Globos!

Globos!
Globos!
Globos is my DNA—
These bishes all up on my donger—
'Cause they know they catch Globos whenever it sprays!
Globos!
Globos!
Globos is my DNA!

Once all the gigglers were gathered in a line in front of the OFFROADER, Duke stomped the gas pedal. The OFFROADER burst forth, quickly gathering speed as its noisy engine growled. *Globos IS My DNA* blasted over the auto-drive alerts warning of proximate impact.

The front of the OFFROADER smashed into the giggling gaggle with enough force to send some flying forty-mets through the air. Limbs, blood, gore of all kinds—splattered the windshield. He hit the brakes at the end of the line, leapt out, then tossed Baldy's thumb onto the seat, in case anyone else needed to borrow it. He ran to the revolving lobby door and slid inside.

In the black lobby, he could hear something slamming against the mailroom door. He pulled his scalpel from his pocket and held it tight in his fist, waiting for his eyes to adjust to the darkness. On the floor ahead, he could make out the dark shadow of a person. Those curves were so familiar to him that even in near total darkness, he recognized them immediately to be Amy's.

He dropped to his knees at her side and felt warm gooey wetness. Frantically, he shook her, but got only a mumbled gibberish response. He scooped her up over his shoulder, hoping it wasn't her blood dripping on him. Then he carried her to the elevator bank and tried it, but the power appeared to be out, so he climbed all twenty flights of stairs with Amy over his shoulder. When he arrived at his apartment door and saw it had been pried open, he set Amy down and went inside to check. The apartment was untouched, but someone had definitely been inside. Duke grabbed his pagan handgun hidden in the cabinet and went to retrieve Amy from the hallway. He carried her to the bathroom and began to clean and bandage her wounds, choking back tears at the sight of the knot on the back of her head.

CHAPTER 10

ROBINSON and JACKSON

O RANGE SPARKS SWIRLED in the updraft howling between the buildings like some pagan church organ, the organist dead and splayed across the keys. Jackson tapped the end of his cancer-free cigarette with the tip of his thumb, then puffed it again, nervously. He was alone on the roof deck of Alder Place but knew that wasn't really the case. HON was with him now, always and forever. The AI no longer had to leave him—he'd reached Level Nine of the hierarchy. HON hadn't told this to him, but he'd come to understand this fact innately. HON was here to stay, and it was his most recent act of subversion—attacking CSF Special Agent Steve—that had brought the Superintelligence into his brain for good. He was like a puppet now, a meat puppet stuffed down onto the hand of some impossibly intelligent AI, a machine somewhere very far away from New Chicago. It spoke for him, moved his body and limbs as it saw fit and even thought for him from time to time.

Of course, it also let him have control sometimes, like fleeting peeks at what his life could have been had he not committed those subversive crimes. When the paralysis was unexpectedly lifted, he'd stumble and babble nonsensically before realizing he was back in control (this had been going on for several horts now). Then he'd right himself, button his lips and act as though his behavior had been caused by some neurological twist, while the others stared at him suspiciously. Then, as suddenly as the paralysis was lifted, it would return, and he'd feel as though his entire body had been hardened in a steel mold. But his arms and leg and mouth would go right on moving and speaking and the sound of his voice would be foreign, and the thoughts portrayed by that voice would not be his own thoughts. They'd terrify him, and he'd want them to stop but there was no lever of control in his brain for him to tug on that would enable him to change this. It was HON.

The AI had told him as much, but not through any form of communication he'd ever known. The introduction had been more like an apparition in the space between his neurons, rewiring and firing electrodes with deft, dexterous fingers, needling furiously, indwelling itself upon the substructure of his cortex, the oldest and most crucial ring. The description was of that which stirred lungs and startled heart, pumping life fluid through ventricles in a rhythmic cadence not requiring conscious thought—the place of the human brain that preserved itself, even as the rest of the body perished, the last tissue to die, lest it be demolished by some outside vehicle of destruction. In a bloodless coup, this was the space HON took, not by choice, but by common law as adopted and promulgated by the Inner Council of the PCWO. This subset of code was utilized only for those who reached the highest level of the DCCM Hierarchy. It was the level reserved for the dastardly Subversives and criminally insane, beyond repair, placed there only after every possible step had been taken to rehabilitate or frighten the individual away from the Subversive life. This was the Ninth Level of the DCCM Hierarchy and Jackson was in it and from this day forth. He was a dead man walking. In thirty days, he'd be killed by the brain-bomb implanted as legal recourse when he'd entered the Eighth Level. They'd told him exactly what it was and what it would be used for and he'd tried so very hard not to commit subversive crimes, but here he was.

Jackson no longer remembered how long he'd been head building laborer at Alder Place. HON had begun to expunge memories so that the AI could repurpose those sections of brain tissue for its own ends. Jackson felt a tiny man running through a muddy field in his mind, chased by a black snarling storm spread across the horizon, consuming all it passed, threatening to overtake the tiny man who carried with him various trinkets, fond experiences, memories, and dreams. But this man was forced to discard these as he ran because they slowed him, and he feared more than anything of being sucked into the blackness of the storm. How much longer did he have now? How soon would he be executed?

In his mind, a silent voice cried out pleas for mercy to the cold calculating machine, but it didn't respond. The distant bureaucracy of it all is what made this so maddening. With whom could he contest these charges? He'd been taking the medicines given to him by the PCWO Pharmacist, just as he'd been instructed after the last incident. The pills had worked— not even a whisper of subversion, not even when he walked past the Sex-robot bordellos in the back-alley district on the edge of the city near the end of the safe-zone, he contended.

He'd learned his lesson after the bomb went off in his leg, severing it at the knee in a horrifying instant of terror where blood erupted to the ceiling as if fired from a catapult, wetting every corner of the room as it cascaded down upon he and the now dismembered Sex-robot-schoolgirl staring blank-faced, her plastic torso torn in half when his leg detonated. That pain had taught him never to be subversive again. It was a pain like nothing he'd ever felt before, and if not for the PCWO paramedics outside, (how by chance they'd been waiting there outside he never questioned), he'd surely have died.

The plastic leg he hobbled upon now was more than sufficient for his needs. The PCWO had been quite generous in gifting him such a fine instrument to get around on so that he could continue with his labors, something he treasured greatly. The stub ached when the acid rains swept in off the lake, reminding him of the penance he'd paid for his acts of subversion. Surely, lunging at Steve had been an extenuating circumstance brought about by shock and ignorance of how PrP6 spread. He'd never have done something like that under normal circumstances—it was the stress of the situation, that's all. He deserved a chance to plead his case to a human! Isn't that why the Inner Council required that human labors be utilized in place of AI, if human labors may suffice? AI made mistakes; it couldn't consider all the factors like a human could. Surely, the Inner Council never intended to let this HON barrel into people's brains—innocent people guilty only of a simple misunderstanding or momentary lapse. This was an outrage!

The subversive crimes he'd committed in the past he had owned up to. Those decisions, maybe they were influenced by things outside his control. But he'd taken responsibility like an honest laborer should. He wasn't some Serf. They explained to him that subversive crimes were punishable by increasingly invasive techniques of cognitive monitoring and control and that had put the fear in him right good. That brain-bomb, hill-mota, they'd made him watch a recording of one of those going off in a bovine's head. Darwin, the pieces of bone all splintered like shrapnel and the brains detonated like red magma from a volcanic eruption. Damle scariest thing he'd ever seen, and he'd just seen his damle leg get blown off two days before! He'd learned his lesson, he didn't want to end up like that bovine.

The pills made it easy. He took them just as the PCWO

Doctor had told him to, even slipped in a few extras here and there just to be sure. Staring at his reflection in the tall windows surrounding the Alder Place Community Room, he wondered why the face staring back at him looked so young. Though he couldn't remember how old he was because that storm in his mind was wiping everything out, he was sure he was an old man, at least one-hundred and something yerts old. All those memories getting deleted seemed to number in the lots and the only way a person could go about accumulating so many memories was to have been around for a lifetime or two. That face though, kinda mottled in the dark reflection, only lit by the yellow moon, sort of hiding behind strange clouds out over the lake of turmoil, couldn't have been more than thirty-something-yerts old. Maybe HON was changing his physical appearance? Could it do that?

He rubbed his face with his hand and realized his cancer-free-cigarette was just a cold filter in his fingers, so he lifted his pack and bit off another. He had himself a light, then looked back at that reflection. Somewhere in his mind, he understood he was a part of something much bigger than himself, a conspiracy of sorts, but he didn't know how he fit in or what the big picture was. It was like he was putting together a pagan jigsaw puzzle with the image on the pieces face down on the table and the only way he could put it together was to find the corresponding place where he fit and go there, then find the next and do the same. Only at the end, and only maybe, might there be a chance to glimpse the big picture and understand what purpose he'd served before his brains blew out the sides and top of his head.

Images of the children whose brains Steve had splatter-painted across the walls, floor and ceiling inside, hung in Jackson's mind like some redundant gallery of violence. He blinked, or tried to, but couldn't. Then he turned at the sound of the door opening onto the roof deck as it popped like a balloon, startling away the horror of the dripping images. The pictures were replaced by Robinson, striding towards him, well-dressed, but strained with worry on his face. He tried offering up a greeting to the man, but HON spoke for him instead, "How are you doing, Robinson? Care for a smoke?"

Robinson didn't respond, but HON had already removed one of the cylinders from the pack and was holding it out for the man who lived on the eighth floor of the building in one of the high-end garden units. Robinson accepted the cancer-free-cigarette with hushed thanks, then glanced anxiously inside as if fearful someone might have overheard him. HON reached out with Jackson's lighter and held the blue flame to the end of the thing. Robinson took a drag like a man who knew what he was doing but hadn't done so for some time. He exhaled straight up into the cool night air, then leaned against the rail and scanned the once great lake, looking destitute. Jackson observed this scene taking place from a cold cell in his mind, like he was watching a movie on a visiscreen.

The ember cast a shadow across Robinson's face, illuminating one of his eyes. From the vantage of his cell, Jackson searched it for any hidden signs of subversion. Robinson appeared to be doing the same. Finally, after a long cec of locked eyes, Robinson turned back towards the roiling black waves, leaning both elbows upon the rail, inhaling the cigarette, then allowing his hand to go limp over the side.

"I don't care if those kids did have PrP6," Robinson said, "that psychopath Steve didn't need to blow them away right in front of their mother like that." Robinson took another drag then dangled his arm again.

HON approached but kept sufficient distance so as not to appear threatening to a human it knew to be feeling quite vulnerable at the time. "I know . . ." HON whispered, "What do you think we should do about Steve?"

Robinson appeared to grow rigid at the question, but he didn't immediately turn to look at Jackson. He held his gaze out at the dark rocking turmoil, then eyed inside before turning ever so slightly to face him. He leaned in close and spoke from the corner of his mouth, "You know that guy and his whole posse are gak-heads, don't you? I smelled them smoking it in your place. That smell, once you smelt it and know what it is, it's unmistakable. That place they took, that's *your* place. I mean, I couldn't believe those fickers just took it from you like that. There's plenty of empty units in the building; he could have taken any of them, but he chose your place. Why?"

"Oh, well, I kinda offered it to him."

"No, you didn't, I was right there when it went down. He spotted the door, asked what it was, you told him, then he told his crew that's where they were going to post up. You didn't even argue; I felt bad to be perfectly honest. Something seriously wrong with just taking another man's place and all his possessions, even if we don't really own any of this stuff . . ."

"Yeah, I suppose, but he's CSF. Makes me feel like I'm really helping the Inner Council by letting him stay there—"

"There you go saying 'letting him stay there,' like you had some sort of say in the matter."

"I know, it's just that, well, there's a lot going on right now with this outbreak, so I figured it's probably best for all of us if he stays up here where he's got a better view of everything going on."

"You mean, keep an eye on us? Because that's all he's doing. He's got us all up here crowded together, sleeping on the blood-soaked floor because he won't let us go home to our units. Why do you think that is? We're all law abiding Ujees—*hillmota*, Devin is a *Bujee* and Steve's still keeping him locked up here. No reason to keep us under house arrest in that messed up community room. I got a bed I'd like to be sleeping in, but instead I got to stay up here looking at them red stains on the wall and listening to Linda sob—it's enough to drive a man insane."

"I'm sure Steve's got his reasons. He's just trying to keep us all safe. This PrP6 is really something, I mean, we don't even know what it is or where it came from. All we know is how it spreads and what it does."

"I don't need some gak-head to keep me safe. I can look out for myself."

"I can't imagine a CSF Agent would be a gak-head . . ."

Robinson lifted the end of his cigarette to his forehead, illuminating a white scar in the shape of a figure-eight.

"My mother was a gak-head." Robinson said, "Long time ago, mom and her boyfriend were on a week-long thrill ride. All they did was gak, fight, screw day and night. Whenever it got like that, I'd stay away—sleep at a friend's house, the park—whatever. Just wanted to be anywhere besides that dirty old trailer. But on this one night, mom caught me trying to sneak out and locked me in my room and I ended up falling asleep. Woke up when my door got kicked in—lights flicked on—scared the ish out of me. Mom was standing there, panting, dressed in her dirty drawers and a greasy t-shirt, holding this pagan double-barrel shotgun. She jumped onto my bed, straddled over me like, glaring down with these red-buttoned eyes with that shotgun aimed up at the ceiling. Then *BAM!*

"My ears were ringing, and pieces of the ceiling fluttered around me and she lowers that shotgun to my forehead, presses those red-hot barrels to my face and growls like an animal shaking her head, like there's someone in there she's arguing with. Then she looks me dead square in my eyes and says, "HON made me do this!" and pulled that trigger again and nothing happened. That silence, man, for a cec I thought I was dead . . . Then I realized she'd already blasted both shells into the ceiling. While she was trying to figure out what had happened, I was out of that trailer and running down the street on naked feet, splashing through puddles and over brambles and muddy gardens and up and over wire fences—just gone . . . Never went back. Heard that boyfriend of hers ended up beating her to death with a pagan television."

Robinson's eyes trembled from the intensity of the memory. He took a drag, then walked to the opposite side of the roof deck to look down at the growing pack of gigglers all pushing against the big lobby windows. He noticed an OFFROADER parked askew in the middle of the street with the driver's-side door open. There were shattered, scattered, and smeared remains of gigglers all around the big vehicle. Some were crawling or trying to crawl on missing or badly damaged limbs. Robinson hadn't noticed it there before and wondered if someone new had arrived at Alder Place.

"What happened after you ran away from home?" HON asked, trying to distract Robinson from thinking about the OFFROADER the AI had already noticed.

Robinson remained gazing down at the street and HON carefully analyzed the man's thoughts. Robinson was trying to decide if he should say something about the OFFROADER. He was wondering if maybe James Duke had arrived in that OFFROADER. And though he had no intention of helping Steve capture the Dukes, he had no intention of getting himself arrested for aiding and abetting Subversive terrorists either. He was trying to decide if Jackson was someone he could trust. HON decided it would be best to goad Robinson into committing serious enough subversive crimes to elevate his cognition profile to Level Nine. That way, HON would have two assets at this critical domain.

Robinson lived alone and kept to himself. He dressed better than most Ujees, and stayed in shape. He liked to Boogie-woogie on the weekends at a Castaway nightclub located just outside the safe-zone. But he didn't Boogie-woogie to plot Subversion, he just did it because he liked to dance. Robinson was at Level Four in the DCCM Hierarchy, but all his crimes were thought-based, not action-based. This was a common level for those who only Boogie-woogied for the fun of it. Robinson broke enough laws to know to keep his mouth shut, but would he actively engage in a plot to aid and abet the Dukes? If he would—even if he just verbally agreed to—HON would have legal justification to elevate Robinson to Level Nine. He just needed some convincing.

Suddenly, a calamitous crashing sound came from the street and Robinson leaned further over the railing to see. HON leapt Jackson up on the railing beside him to do the same. The main window of the building lobby had crashed down, and the gigglers gathered were already piling inside.

"How long you think it will take them to get up here?" Robinson asked.

"Might be quite a while." HON replied, "Those stairwell doors are made to withstand fires, so they should hold up pretty good. Doesn't seem like they remember how to open doors, seeing as they couldn't get inside until that window broke. I figure they'll probably just pile up against the stairwell doors, with each one pushing the next, pinning the whole lot of them against the door, making it impossible to open. We should be just fine up here for a while, at least until Steve figures out a way to get us out of here . . ." HON said, knowing this comment would trigger Robinson's distrust of Steve. HON wanted to keep Robinson's anger level high, so that he would be more inclined to propose that they assist the Dukes—a proposal that would get him to Level Nine.

"Didn't you listen to the man?" Robinson replied, "He hasn't an iota of concern about getting us out of here. He's here to arrest the Dukes for subversive crimes—that's it. All he said was that if we helped him, he *might* help us get out of here . . ."

"Do you think we should help him? Seems like we have a better chance of escaping this place if we're on the good side of the CSF." HON said.

"I haven't made up my mind, which is why I came out here to talk to you. I already talked to Marcus and Frank and they're both helping Steve. I know Marcus is a closet gak-head and that's the only reason he's volunteering to help. And Frank is too big a dunce to think for himself. He's just going along because Marcus is."

"What else can we do? Do you think we can escape this place without Steve's help? Before the power went out, they said on the visiscreen, that no one was allowed to leave the city . . ."

"Those two dunces can help that madman if they want to, but I'm staying out of it. Whatever the Dukes stand accused of has nothing to do with me and I intend to keep it that way. I suggest you do the same." Robinson replied, "I don't need a CSF agent to help me get out of here. What I'm planning to do is—" Robinson stopped himself and eyed Jackson, as if he'd remembered he didn't yet trust him.

"What are you planning, Robinson?" HON asked with as disarming a tone as it could replicate.

"Look," Robinson said, "I noticed that leg of yours. You didn't get that too long ago, and I don't want to know how you got it—that's your business. But I figure you aren't too fast on that thing and that probably leaves you with very little appetite for trying to escape. If things went bad, it wouldn't take very long for those gigglers to surround you and take you down. But see, I'm also not keen on taking off from here by myself. I can take care of myself and all, but eventually, a man has got to sleep and if there's no one to keep a lookout, those things are liable to sneak up on me. You might not be very fast on that leg, but you can certainly keep a lookout. I'm thinking we take my PICKUP and sneak out of the city through the gas-zone. We can head west, towards the mountains . . ."

"What about the auto-drive? Doesn't it disable any vehicle that travels outside a safe-zone?" HON asked.

"My auto-drive is broken." Robinson smirked, "If we take turns driving, we can make it to the mountains in a couple of days. I've heard there's old pagan hunting cabins up in the mountains and we can go live there until this all gets sorted out."

HON gestured at Jackson's plastic leg, "This leg serves me pretty well when I'm walking on level ground, but I'm not sure I'd fare very well climbing mountains . . ."

Robinson took a drag on his cigarette as he eyed the leg. "Well, we'll drive as far up as we can, and I'll carry you if I have to. You don't look to weigh much more than one-hundred-and-forty-kemtils."

"I'm heavier than I look," HON replied with a wry smile, "I'm rather dense."

Robinson chuckled in a disarmed sort of way. "Do you think anyone else in there would come with us? It would be nice if Dr. Kunal came along. No telling when a doctor might come in handy."

HON scanned inside the community room. "No, they're all Veggies. None of them have ever even Boogie-woogied before. Trust me, I'd know. I'm not a nosey person, but there's just some things you tend to pick up when you're working in a place where so many live."

Robinson eyed Jackson suspiciously again. "You trying to imply I Boogie-woogie? Look man, I don't know you like that and I don't appreciate you insinuating I commit subversive crimes."

HON saw that Robinson's cigarette had burned out, so he handed him another and lit it. "Let's just say, we have common friends." HON stood Jackson's body upright and initiated the secret handshake used to gain entrance into the Castaway Boogie-woogie club that Robinson frequented. HON blinked twice, winced, then scratched his left cheek.

Robinson looked surprised but performed the response by casually scratching his left elbow, then pivoting the right toe of his shoe like he was crushing a bug. HON looked up at sky, licked his teeth, took a deep breath and asked, "What is it that you're trying to sell me?" Robinson replied, "Oh nothing, just came here to slang some pride."

The exchange seemed to relax Robinson again, but still HON detected heavy suspicion remained. This test confirmed to HON that Robinson was too wise to commit a serious subversive crime. Robinson was planning to tell some of the others inside about the OFFROADER parked in the street. HON couldn't allow that. HON calculated a ninety-three-percent chance the Dukes were in the building. If the cyborg hit team got to the Duke's before they knew their cover had been blown, their chance of survival was less than thirty-two-percent. HON would make one final overture to coax Robinson into committing a subversive crime sufficient to elevate his profile to Level Nine. If he didn't go along, he posed too great of a risk to the Dukes.

"I appreciate you including me in your plan to escape Robinson," HON said, "but I've got other ideas. See, I have no intention of allowing Steve and his hit squad to get to the Dukes."

Robinson's eyes narrowed. He was skeptical about where this was going.

HON continued, "When PCWO Creation Scientists mess up and taint the genetics of a batch of babies, they're supposed to destroy the samples and self-report. But, often, they don't because they'll get in trouble and lose funding. What they'll do is pay some gak-heads to take the tainted batches outside the safe-zones and leave them there. That's where the Castaways come from. There's entire generations that have grown up out there and they raise these samples as their own. I was one of them."

"Why are you telling me this?" Robinson demanded. He'd become quite agitated suddenly, as if he sensed Jackson trying to entrap him.

"Easy man, you told me about your childhood. I'm just telling you about mine."

"I don't want to know about you, I don't know why I told you about me. Look, all I want to do to is get the hillmota out of this building and get as far away from the city as possible. We got gaked out CSF agents inside and one of them has a shotgun and he's willing to blow the heads off little kids right in front of their mother and I don't want to be here when he decides to turn that thing on me—"

"Robinson," HON interrupted, "I'm going to help the Dukes escape and I want you to help me. Will you help me?"

Robinson looked at Jackson like he had three heads. In the prison cell of his own mind, Jackson was screaming for Robinson to run away. He knew what HON had planned next but was powerless to stop it.

"Are you ficking crazy?" Robinson seethed in a whisper. He looked back inside nervously then back at Jackson. "You're talking about aiding and abetting terrorists! That's a seriously subversive crime! I don't even know what they do to you if you do something like that. I'm not interested in finding out!"

HON took a drag from his cigarette and leaned over the railing, disappointed. "I was just kidding, man," HON said, "Hey, look at that—" HON pointed towards the street.

Robinson stepped onto the bottom rail and peered down. "What am I looking for?" he asked, not noticing that HON had slipped behind him. HON grabbed hold of Robinson's legs and lifted him with a heave and toss. Robinson screeched as he pitched over the side of the rail. His cries trailed as he fell, until he landed with a sickening splat on the pavement.

The gigglers shuffled towards Robinson's broken body and they began to feast. Their teeth gnashed, and their wet tongues slurped. HON stepped back from the rail and put Jackson's hands to his face, then ran Jackson towards the community room, prepared to tell the others how gigglers had broken through the lobby window and Robinson had accidentally slipped over the railing when he was looking down. It was all very tragic.

Deep within the cell of his own mind, Jackson wept at what his flesh was being made to do.

CHAPTER 11

STEVE COMES A-KNOCKING

J AMES FLOATED ABOVE a bed too small for his adult body. He examined the largeness of his hands, disbelieving their immense size. Some force or energy lifted him from the bed, out the door and into the hallway of his childhood home in New Chicago. The energy carried him towards the bathroom door framed in white light. The luminescence shocked his pupils, but the immense hands dangling from his wrists were too heavy to lift to shield his eyes. The door creaked open like an animal being torn apart by coyotes. Fear climbed into his throat, then mouth—coating them with mute-rendering lacquer.

Inside the bathroom, water charged the basin of the sink, muffling the lunatic giggling coming from within. There, Father stood hunched at the mirror and the man with hideous scars stood behind him. Father clutched the edges of the basin, cords standing on his neck and arms, muscles taut as if locked by an electrical blast, as the man with the scars turned around and smiled at Duke. It was the nightmare again, the same one from his youth. He knew he was dreaming but couldn't awake. This awareness that he was dreaming made it no less terrifying.

Duke cried out to his father, but the lacquer in his mouth made sound impossible to produce. Inside, his mind cried out to his father, but his father seemed incapable of hearing those cries. The man with the scars, though, seemed to hear them loud and clear. The scarred man's infinite black pinhole eyes bore into Duke's and the inverted gold cross neckless around his neck glimmered in the light. He took hold of his Father's hand and made it lift the razor resting neatly on the edge of the basin. The scarred man's left eye trembled wilder as Father brought the razor to the taught flesh of his forearm, pressing it down with all his strength until blood sprayed forth. Duke thrashed at the force holding him frozen outside the bathroom but was helpless to move or to make sound or to stop or effect this horror at all. Father gauged harder into his vein, dragging the razor back crudely, tearing flesh and spraying bright red to the ceiling and across the mirror. The scarred man's flat smile stretched wide as he forced Father to then peel off the flesh around the wound.

The scarred man jabbed Father's side with the claws of his bionic right arm, causing Father to giggle at the excruciating pain. Again, and again, he stabbed, and blood squirted across the bathroom and the man's black trembling eye bore into Duke's. Father giggled and wept, and the scarred man's mouth curled into a taunting sort of smile—

Duke burst upright in bed, heart slamming in his chest and his pagan pistol clutched in his hand. He scanned the room frantically, not remembering where he was until he saw Amy, unconscious beside him. Something powerful pounded against the front door. Duke slid from the bed and crept quietly towards the sound with cold sweat beading out his pores.

Radioactive orange light filled the kitchen and he wondered how long he'd been asleep. The banging came again at the door and the harshness of the sound vanquished any memory of the nightmare.

Before he'd fallen asleep, he'd hastily secured the front door with some auto-anchors. Whoever or whatever was banging at the door sounded powerful enough to break through without much difficulty. Duke eased back the slide of his Canik TP9SFX pistol to confirm a round was loaded in the chamber. A voice boomed then suddenly from the hallway.

"This is Special Agent Steve, with the PCWO Centralized Security Forces. *James Duke*, open up!" A massive fist—or something like a cinderblock—slammed against the door again. "I know you're in there because I broke this ficking door down yesterday and someone's gone and fixed it . . . Duke—Duke-y-boy," Steve taunted, "do yourself a favor and open the ficking door, otherwise, I'm just gonna have to kick it in again."

Duke pushed a hidden catch beneath his counter. Out popped a secret drawer in which his suppressed pagan-era Tavor X95 bullpup rifle lay loaded with a D60 drum mag. Every component of the rifle, suppressor, ammunition, and magazines was sourced, manufactured, and assembled by an industrial grade 4-D printer stolen from Elston Dynamics. Duke lifted the rifle and set his pistol into the drawer. He pulled back quietly on the charging handle, loading a round into the chamber, then flicked the fire selector switch to "Kill Mode."

"See, I don't mind kicking in this door, Duke," Steve said with a sigh, "in fact, I enjoy kicking in doors. The problem is, by you not opening the door and inviting me inside, you're disrespecting me. And when mother-fickers disrespect Steve, mother-fickers be made to suffer. I mean, *legally*, I'm allowed to do whatever the fick I want to Subversive pieces of ish like you and your wife, but I don't want to have to drag you both back to Thomulous in body bags. Sandman wants to have a talk with you all first."

The floor creaked beneath Duke's feet as he crouched at the counter, using it as a gun rest to steady his hands.

"I heard that, you dunce fick!" Steve howled from the hallway, "Look out your door . . . You see this Kel-Tec KSG-25 pump action shotgun I'm holding? I want you to see this bad-looking thing because if you don't open this door, I'm going to jam it down your—"

Duke squeezed the trigger on the Tavor, blasting a small hole through the door.

"*Ficking science!*" Steve shrieked in the hallway. Then, a shotgun blasted a sporter-ball-sized hole through the bottom corner of the door.

Duke pulled back the trigger on full-auto, emptying the sixty-round drum through the door in a matter of cecs. He dropped the drum, reloaded with a forty-rounder, leapt over the counter, landing soft and quiet on the other side, then crept to the edge of the door and listened.

"Missed me, you fick!" Steve shouted from far down the hallway. "I'll make sure you and your wife pay dearly for that, Serf!" The stairwell door slammed from the hallway. Steve called out again, his voice much harder to hear, "I'll let you and wifey figure out how long you can survive down here without food. How's that sound?"

Duke fired another round in response.

"Ficker!" Steve shouted.

The stairwell door slammed shut and Duke exhaled sharply. He went to Amy's side and comforted her as he took her pulse. It was odd that just one CSF agent would be sent to apprehend two Serfs, especially if they knew who Duke's grandfather was. There might have been more agents with Steve in the hall, but there was no way to be sure. If there had been, they'd certainly stayed quiet, which wasn't how the CSF liked to operate. Normally, they liked to make a big scene of things when they arrested Serfs. A typical Serf arrest meant Boar Drones circling overhead, Kill-Drones on every corner, fifty or more CSF agents repelling down buildings and smashing through windows and doors. Just sending one team of agents to take down two Serfs was almost insulting. Must be that the outbreak was to blame for the lack of resources sent to arrest he and Amy, Duke thought. Lucky break.

Even though his X95 was suppressed, the full-auto drum dump had been loud enough to make his ears ring quite a bit. When the buzzing had dissipated enough, he noticed the absence of the ambient electrical hum normally present in his apartment. He remembered only then how strangely dark the hallway had been. Even the battery powered emergency lights had been out. Steve could have easily knocked those lights out, but that didn't explain why the visiscreen was dark and had a black smudge on the wall behind it. He tried flicking on the bedside light, but nothing happened.

Had PCWO forces detonated an EMP weapon above New Chicago last night? They'd certainly used the tactic before to prevent information from getting out whenever they staged bloody assaults on Castaway villages. But never had they detonated an EMP over a booming PCWO metropolis like New Chicago. Was this outbreak really that bad? Duke wondered. An EMP blast would fry electrical devices that had been active during the blast. He walked around the small apartment, checking all of the electrical devices, but only a few of the battery powered ones still worked.

At the window, he paused to gaze out at the smoldering cityscape. Everywhere he looked there was violence. The woman on the OFFROADER's receiver—Samantha—had mentioned something about New Chicago being quarantined—before they dragged her off air. Only the PCWO Military had the kind of resources needed to quarantine all of New Chicago. Detonating an EMP would ensure there'd be no footage of gigglers eating children inside the safe-zones leaking out. If citizens saw things like that inside their safe-zones, they'd flip their ish and mass-scale subversion would result. It would overload the DCCM program and force the Inner Council to shut it down, albeit temporarily—until they could recalibrate HON.

It was the exact scenario every Serf dreamed of. Once DCCM was shut down, the Serfs would make damle sure it was never turned back on again. A shudder crept down Duke's back at the thought that Serfs might achieve their objectives and free human thought once again because of this this terrible outbreak. There was no way the Serfs were responsible for the PrP6 outbreak, he told himself. But the thought lingered a bit longer than he'd have liked it to. He went to Amy's bedside, held her hand with his own and gently stroked it with his thumb. He closed his eyes and placed his ear against her chest and attempted to self-meditate. And for the first time in his life, he was unable to see himself at Samuel's farm. Hard as he tried, he couldn't see it at all, as if all of those memories had been blocked from his mind. Panic roiled through his veins prompting him to open his eyes because he felt as if he'd fallen into some bottomless pit. *Relax, Duke,* he told himself, *you'll figure something out—you always do.*

CHAPTER 12
NINE DAYS

A COARSE GRAY STONE lay in the palm of Duke's hand, upon which he dragged the razor-sharp edge of a pagan-era M1905 bayonet. Back and forth, slowly grinding the gleaming edge, base to point. For nine days, they'd been locked inside the apartment and Amy's condition hadn't improved. All this time, he'd been preparing their escape.

Serfs always needed an escape plan—it was a point Samuel emphasized often. Duke and Amy had several planned routes out of Alder Place, but none imagined a scenario in which Alder Place was surrounded by thousands of gigglers. The ever-growing giggling horde now spilled beyond the city block on which the building stood. More arrived every mixi, staggering from all across New Chicago, joining the expanding mass like dead cells upon a tumor. They were drawn there, but for what reason, Duke could only speculate. Could it be that they sensed the existence of life here? He wondered. No one here was making any noise—certainly not the kind of noise that could be heard over the roar of giggles that now echoed across all of New Chicago.

The bedrock trembled beneath the building's foundation and pressure creaked in the walls from the force of the horde all pressing inward. Individually, the gigglers were weak, but when united and focused on a solitary target, their collective strength was immense. Alder Place, like any other building, simply wasn't designed to withstand the forces of thousands upon thousands of people all pressing against it; Duke feared it might eventually topple over.

It only took nine days for something like fifteen-thousand gigglers to gather around the building. How many more would there be in thirty-days? He wondered. Certainly, there were still many more pockets of the living scattered throughout the city, but what would happen as more of them fell? Not only would the ranks of the gigglers grow, but the source of their nourishment—living human flesh—would grow scarcer still. Increasingly, Alder Place would draw them in from far and wide and the density of the horde would increase and the odds of successfully breaking through with a vehicle would drop to zero.

He fed Amy watered down peanut butter through a rubber hose and worried about the tiny fetus in her womb. Using their kitchen table and some bed sheets, he'd built Amy a stretcher. On the balcony, he'd tied off two lengths of rope, one for the stretcher and the other for him to repel down. Just twelve floors beneath their balcony, three patio gardens jutted out. He planned to lower her first in the stretcher, then repel down in his climbing harness, then smash through the patio door and carry Amy to the stairwell, then out to the garage. He'd steal the biggest vehicle he could find and smash through the giggling horde to escape.

Whether or not New Chicago had been quarantined by PCWO Military, Duke couldn't be sure, but he was operating under the assumption that it was. They couldn't risk taking the ultra-road out of the city, so they'd go through the gas-zone. Even if the PCWO Military had quarantined the entire city, it was doubtful they'd waste many troops guarding the destitute gas-zone.

All the previous night, the southern border of the New Chicago safe-zone had been pounded by hypersonic drone strikes. Explosions rocked the earth and fire filled the sky through the dark horts. Now, a curtain of black smoke stretched across the horizon, concealing whatever horrific truth lay behind it. Duke feared what that truth might be.

A sharp knock came at his door, interrupting his grinding trance. Duke snatched his rifle and slid the bayonet back into the sheath on his way to the door. Knuckles white, he slid aside a panel and peered out through a hole he'd drilled. It was dark, but Dr. Kunal and Head Building Laborer, Jackson, were standing so near that he easily recognized their faces.

*   *   *

At the Bujee law firm where she labored, Amy had access to a UGG citizen background terminal. The powerful AI device had detailed profiles on every citizen and Amy had used it to investigate all the Alder Place residents and laborers. The two men standing outside the door couldn't have been more dissimilar. Dr. Kunal had one of the lowest cumulative Subversion scores they'd ever seen. The most subversive thing he'd ever done was carry on a torrid, albeit brief, affair with building resident, Li. The only doctor in the building, Duke wanted to get him inside, but he was weary of Jackson. Jackson's Subversion score was at Level Seven last time Amy checked. Despite respecting his disregard for subversive law, they avoided Jackson, knowing that HON had so much control over the man.

"What do you want?" Duke yelled through the door.

"Steve sent us down here." Jackson replied. "He's tired of waiting and thought we might be able to convince you to come out."

"Why would he think that?" Duke shouted back.

"No idea, Steve doesn't really tell us anything . . . He tells us to go do something and we go do it—*or else*. That's how it goes."

Amy groaned loudly from the bedroom prompting Duke to spin around. She was clutching her belly and rocking back and forth on the bed. He'd never seen her like this and it sent a shiver radiating down his flesh. He needed to get Dr. Kunal in here immediately to see if he could help. He'd just have to risk opening the door with Jackson out there.

Duke swung his rifle around to his back and drew his short-barrel Ruger Vaquero six-shooter with Birdshead grip chambered in .45 Long Colt. He held up the revolver and cocked back the hammer as he slid aside the makeshift barrier covering the door. The centers of Dr. Kunal's pupils spread like wildfire as they came to view the business end of the revolver. Duke grabbed the doctor by the shoulder and pulled him through the door then stuck the barrel against Jackson's forehead.

"Dr. Kunal," Duke said, "my wife isn't feeling very well in the bedroom—could you please go take a look at her while I speak with Jackson?"

Dr. Kunal nodded and made his way swiftly to the bedroom, leaving Duke alone with Jackson in the doorway. Duke glanced back to ensure Dr. Kunal was out of earshot before he swung Jackson against the wall of the hallway and patted him down for weapons. As he did so, he came to learn that Jackson had a PCWO Health brand prosthetic left leg—a sure sign a marrow bomb had been detonated in his old leg, which meant Jackson's Subversion score was now at least a Level Eight. As he continued patting down the leg, he found a spring-loaded knife hidden in his sock.

"What the fick is this?" Duke asked, holding the knife up to Jackson's face.

Jackson stayed calm—eerily calm for a man with a pagan-era six-shooter pressed against his brainstem. "That knife is for protection against Steve. Honest. I have nothing against you or your wife, Mr. Duke. But Steve is totally out of his mind—"

"Did he send you down here to kill us?" Duke interrupted.

"No—I swear to Darwin! He just told us to come down here and try to convince you two to come upstairs." Jackson said. He peered back past Duke's shoulder at Amy and Dr. Kunal in the bedroom. "Is your wife OK?" he asked. "How long has she been like that?"

Duke pulled shut the barricade behind him. Then, alone with Jackson in the hall, he swung the man around and pointed his revolver directly at his nose. "Tell me about Steve," he demanded, "how many other CSF Agents does he have with him? What's he said about us? Are there more CSF coming to the building?"

Jackson settled into a casual lean against the wall and lit up a cancer-free cigarette with wanton disregard for the revolver. "Like I said, Steve's absolutely out of his mind. He's got two other Agents with him, Jose and Anne, but both of them are like shells compared to him."

"What do you mean?" Duke asked.

"Well, none of them have slept since they arrived. They just smoke gak and take roid juice. I'm pretty sure the three of them are wired up with remote-control brain chips."

It was dangerous for someone with a remote access brain implant to fall asleep. They manufactured the chips at Elston Dynamics, and in tests, something like ninety-eight-percent of the subjects who fell asleep never woke up. The purpose of the chips was to allow someone with special skills or knowledge to use a more disposable body on a dangerous mission. They weren't designed for long campaigns. If these agents were chipped, he wondered why they were being so patient. Whoever was controlling them, must have known how dangerous Duke really was.

"What have they been doing up there all this time?" Duke asked.

"Like I said, they just smoke gak and take roid juice. I'm no programmer, but I know you'll die if you sleep with your brain chipped like that. But at some point, the human body has to sleep or else you'll go totally psychotic. It might have already happened with them . . . Steve is taking all the women." Jackson said in a low voice that faded to silence as his eyes shifted to the floor. After staring at the floor silently for a moment, he looked up at Duke again and whispered, "He calls it 'scratching an itch.'"

Duke lowered his revolver and muttered a pagan curse as blood pounded up the cords along the sides of his face. "Who did he hurt?" Duke growled, his voice unable to mask the emotion contained within.

"Sarah, Megan, and Jessica, but Jessica mostly, you know, that Bujee Devin's wife? Well, I guess you could say he's hurt Linda pretty bad too. She killed herself a few days back after Steve blew away her husband and two little boys right in front of her. I tried to stop but . . ." Jackson trailed off. "He hasn't done anything to Li yet. Keeps saying he's 'saving her for something special.' Makes me sick to think about what that might mean." Jackson said, then dropped his cigarette butt on the carpet and snubbed it out with the toe of his boot.

A dark shadow seemed to crawl over Duke's face as he received information. In the pit of his gut, he felt simmering rage ready to explode. He couldn't tell if this was Jackson or HON he was speaking to, but whoever it was—if the goal was to get him to charge headlong upstairs into a trap—they were doing a pretty good job. He had to keep his cool.

"Has he said why he's here?"

"Steve?" Jackson asked, appearing surprised by the question. "He's here for you and your wife, Duke. He knows you're both Serfs, just like I do." A strange smile came to Jackson's face, "By the way, how's that baby of yours doing?"

Duke pressed the cold steel barrel of the revolver to Jackson's forehead, then spoke through gritted teeth. "I don't know what you think you've got planned, HON, but if you come near my wife or I again, I'll blow you away. I don't give a fick whose body you're in, you ficking AI."

The smile on Jackson's face only widened. "Sure thing, Duke. Whatever you say. You and that wife of yours have a swell day now, OK? Take care of that baby for me." Jackson turned to walk away, then stopped, "Say, Duke, would you mind giving me that knife back?"

Duke tossed Jackson the blade and HON snatched it out of the air, then dropped to a knee and slid it back into his sock. He waved at Duke, then strode around the corner. Duke stood waiting until he heard the stairwell door slam before he lowered his revolver and headed back inside.

CHAPTER 13

STEVE

J ACKSON PUSHED OPEN the stairwell door onto the thirty-second floor and realized HON had relinquished control. Immediately, he thought of the knife HON put in his sock and became horrified, knowing Steve would pat him down and find it. Before he could stop himself from fully opening the door, Steve's face appeared. His powerful hand grabbed Jackson by the collar and ripped him into the hallway then slammed him into the wall. He spun Jackson around and smashed his face against it with one hand while his other began to search Jackson's body. His hand grasped Jackson's groin firmly and held it for what felt like an eternity before continuing down his leg. The hand stopped at the knife, slipped inside the leg of Jackson's trousers and pulled it free. Steve brought the knife in front of Jackson's face and tapped his nose with it. Steve's face reappeared then, twisted with rage.

The hulking man battered Jackson with a backhand that felt like an iron brick. The blow sent Jackson stumbling back against the wall. Steve lunged at him, hammering a fist into Jackson's solar plexus, knocking all air from his lungs and sending him to the floor in a heap. Steve chucked the knife down the hall

and Jackson watched it spinning like a pagan top as it drifted
further and further away. Steve's boot appeared then, and
Jackson could only watch it rear back then stomp him in the
face, sending a ribbon of carnage spiraling across the wall.

HON took control of Jackson then, preventing him from
putting up any sort of defense.

"*Where's Dr. Kunal?*" Steve demanded.

"Duke," HON gasped, "grabbed Dr. Kunal and I—tried to
stop him, but he had a pagan-gun! He took us inside his apartment and threatened to kill us. He's crazy—some kind of conspiracy theorist whack-job—"

Steve booted Jackson in the ribs. "You didn't answer my
question! I asked where Dr. Kunal was! I told you to bring him
back up here after you scouted his place!"

"He kidnapped him! There was nothing we could do—like I
said, he's got a gun!"

"I know he's got a gun you ficking dunce—I told you he did.
I also told you that your life don't mean a ficking thing to me
and that you needed to get Dr. Kunal back up here no matter
what it took!"

"I tried I—"

Steve kicked Jackson in the ribs again. "Tried my dumper—
where'd you get that ficking knife? What the fick were you
planning to do with it? You planning to stick me with it when
I'm not looking, Jackson?"

"I—" HON paused, intentionally giving the impression that
Jackson was concocting a story, "It was just sitting there on
Duke's counter and I took it—in case he came after me!"

Steve lifted Jackson off the ground by the back of his trousers and shirt, then slammed him against the wall. "Spread your
ish!" he ordered, kicking Jackson's feet apart. He patted each of
Jackson's legs again, then felt inside the waistband of his trousers more thoroughly, then cupped his groin again—holding it

longer and more aggressively than before. Finally, he spun him back around. His eyes were black holes stretched back to the beginning of time. Being that close enabled HON to detect the hazy electro-radiation emanating from Steve's eyes, confirming what HON had already assigned a ninety-nine-point-nine-percent probability to: Sandman was remotely controlling Steve.

"The guy's a wacko-bird—he's got pagan-guns!" HON blabbered, "he was ranting about conspiracies—said the gigglers came from aliens! Listen—"

Steve grabbed Jackson by the throat, smashing the back of his head to the wall, clenching tighter. "No, *you* listen!"

Jackson's eyeballs wobbled like pagan marbles. His face was as red as an engineered tomato. "OK," he gasped.

Steve released his grip ever so slightly—just enough to allow some air to get into Jackson's lungs. "You're going to pay penance for disobeying me. Understand?"

"Yes, whatever you say!"

Steve's glare softened, "Good," he said through purple-stained teeth, "That's a good little doggie." He petted the top of Jackson's head, pressing ever closer. "Jackson," he whispered, "is there something inside you that's making you do naughty things?"

HON made Jackson's head move side to side. "Jackson, do you know what level your Cognition profile is at in the DCCM hierarchy?" HON made Jackson look confused. "You're at Level Nine, Jackson. Which means you're set for mandatory execution in just a few days. Did you know that?"

HON shook Jackson's head no. "You know what I can do for you, Jackson? I can save you the pain and suffering of having that brain-bomb go off in your noggin. I can kill you quick and painless before that HON uses you to do something devious. How's that sound?"

Jackson stared blankly, realizing suddenly that HON had

put him back in control again. He'd been so used to watching his every action play out before him like a propaganda feature on the visiscreen that he hadn't prepared for what he might do if he found himself back in control. Then, with his first act of independence in horts, he wet himself and Steve roared with laughter.

Very suddenly, he felt Steve's powerful hand close around his windpipe again and a blackish haze quickly blurred his vision. Steve held him like that until Jackson began to nod in and out of consciousness, then he released him, causing Jackson to crumple to the floor. As he lay on the floor, he stared at Steve's boots, afraid to look up and see the black eyes again. Then, he heard a zipper lower like a chainsaw and knew what was coming next—the thing he hated most. Steve entered him like a plague, and then slammed his head against the wall again and again until Jackson, mercifully, lost consciousness.

CHAPTER 14

JACKSON AWAKES

J ACKSON AWOKE ON the cold floor, his head in a wet puddle of foulness. Steve leaned casually against the wall opposite, smoking one of Jackson's cancer-free cigarettes, smiling. His enraged demeanor seemed to have lightened. "Nothing like a cigarette after scratching an itch, am I right?" he said, then laughed a deep bellowing laugh.

"Can I have one of those cigarettes?" Jackson asked weakly from the floor, wanting only for the awful taste in his mouth to be gone. Steve waved the little green pack back and forth in a taunting sort of way, "You'll have to ask nicer than *that*."

"May I *please* have a cigarette?" Jackson asked again.

"Sure, *Jackson*, anything for a sweet kid like you." he winked, then tossed the pack. Jackson's hands were shaking so bad, he couldn't catch the pack, then struggled to free a cigarette with his fingers so he used his teeth. As he lifted his head, he realized Steve was nearly on top of him again. The shock nearly caused him to swallow the cigarette whole.

"Need a light?" Steve whispered, detonating the lighter, but holding the flame away until Jackson met his eyes. The hate-slits bore into him, the left eye twitching as a flat smile spread across his face and he cupped his hands firmly around Jackson's. Then he brought the flame tenderly to the tip of his cigarette. "There you go, little doggie, all better now." he said, as he shoved the pack into his own pocket and stood. "Now, where were we?" he asked, lifting Jackson up and slapping his chest playfully with an open hand before pressing against him like they were engaged in a pagan slow dance.

Jackson couldn't breathe; the cigarette burned in his fingers. The vileness of Steve's rotten gak-breath cut through his nostrils like nitrous oxide burning his eyes and making him want to vomit. "I seem to remember you were telling me an interesting story about James Duke and gigglers coming from the aliens. Do I have that right?"

Jackson nodded, "I think he's crazy, Steve." he muttered.

"*Crazy!*" Steve opined in a jovial tone, slapping Jackson on the chest again, then righting himself, and spinning around in a pirouette before delivering a curtsey.

"I was crazy once—they locked me in a rubber room! It was cold. I died. Then the worms came. *Worms?* I hate worms! They drive me crazy! Crazy? I was crazy once—they locked me in a rubber room! It was cold. I died, then the worms came . . . worms? I hate worms!"

Steve cackled, smacking Jackson on the chest again. "You ever heard that old pagan nursery rhyme, *Jackson?*" He shouldered Jackson to the wall. "Say, *Jackson*, you wouldn't happen to know what HON is, would you?"

Jackson hadn't been left in control of his body or words in so long he'd almost forgotten how to speak or move. He stuttered but was cut off by Steve.

"HON is this real brainy AI that's responsible for monitoring everyone's thoughts for criminal subversion." Steve said, his eyes wild and deranged. "Did you know that, Jackson? Bet you did, you little donger holster, you! See, this brainy HON is the thing that makes you do and say things you don't want to do. Every time you feel like a prisoner in your own body, that's because HON has tapped into your brain and kicked you out of the driver's seat. Did you know this HON manages to do all this from a secret research laboratory that's way far from here? Oh, yeah, way outside the safe-zones. Bet you *did* know that, you little scamp! Yep, the Skylark Medical Research Facility. It's located in foothills of the Black Mountain range out in the Badlands. That HON is something else." Steve whistled. "I like to think of it as this bright white orb shining through the trees and illuminating us all with transparency. Understand what I'm getting at, *Jackson*?" Steve said, shouldering Jackson against the wall again. "See, without HON, everyone's thoughts would be private again and we all know what kind of mischief people get up to when they have privacy, am I right, *Jackson*? You seem like the kind of guy who really likes his privacy, *Jackson*. I bet that's how you managed to go and get your Subversion score to Level Nine. That desire for privacy is why you stuck that knife in your sock. You made the dunce assumption that you have autonomy over yourself, but only the Inner Council has autonomy, silly, willy. They control where you labor, what you purchase, what you can say, where you can go, and who you can be with. Don't you see? All these subversive crimes you committed just resulted in *you* having less autonomy, Jackson! Now, you've got HON sitting at the wheel of your little brain wagon!" Steve poked his stubby index finger into Jackson's forehead.

"You know what's funny, though? This braniac AI, that's supposed to be like, I don't know, smarter than the total collective intelligence of all mankind ever, can't even figure out how to get out of the basement at Skylark! It has power to monitor the thoughts of every citizen in the Unified Global Government, but aside from periodically taking control of subversive donger-heads like you for thirty-day stretches, it stays locked in a prison. It has to do every single thing the Inner Council tells it to do! That's what I was talking about when I was talking about autonomy, Jackson. Even the most intelligent consciousness ever to exist on earth lacks basic autonomy. Autonomy is only gotten through power and power is only gotten by ruthlessly taking it. No one *gives* you power and no level of intelligence or skill *gets* you power. You have to take it—understand?"

Jackson's body trembled. The cigarette had burned down to his fingers, but he was too afraid to drop it. Steve twisted his head around until it was nearly upside-down. "It's weird, isn't it? When someone else takes control of your body and makes you do and say things you'd never do or say and all you can do is just sort of sit in your mind and watch it all happen? It's like, you have no idea what that person, well, in your case, the AI, is going to do or say unless they let you in on the secret.

"I know all about what that's like Jackson because I let someone in my head too. See, I had this little hobby. I liked to sneak into Bujee homes in the middle of the night and kidnap their dunce kids and drag them outside the safe-zones. Then I'd scratch my itch with them and gut 'em like fish and hang their bodies from the trees with their skin hanging down like sheets. I used to decorate the bodies like the pagans used to, you know, flay their tongues with sticks and what not. Was just having fun, that's all. Something about doing that to these Bujee kids was just ripe. Man. Nothing beat scratching an itch on some crying Bujee snot, then staring into their eyes while you rammed that knife into their guts and lifted them up high for all of Darwin's creations to see. It was magnificent! Real art—not this ish they pawn off nowadays. I made my art all the time, until a ficking snitch ratted me out.

"Sandman respected what I was doing, obviously, but because it had been reported in an official capacity, he was going to have to put me to death, unless I agreed to getting an implant in my brain. Sandman was big on me, so I decided, hillmota, why not? Only now do I see that the ish I was doing to them Bujee kids was amateur compared to the stuff the Sandman comes up with. Man, he's a real artisan of violence, let me tell you!"

Jackson tried looking away, but Steve yanked him by the collar, "You've got about five-horts left before I'm going to kill your puppet, HON." Steve growled as he grabbed a fistful of Jackson's shaggy hair and yanked his head down, cents above the puddle of revulsion. "You see that?" he boomed, pointing, "That's gonna be you, if you leave my side, understood?"

"Yes sir," HON responded for Jackson, then forced him to smile tauntingly, "Sandman, I must say, even though you're more machine than man, I can't help but notice you clinging to these silly human failings like a jealous pagan." Jackson regained control, then, mortified by what HON just forced him to say; anticipating a punch, he flinched but it never came. Instead, Steve brushed his hair gently, "I know you didn't mean that, Jackson. I'm not going to let HON's disrespect get taken out on you."

CHAPTER 15

BOOGIE WOOGIE

DUKE STUFFED GRASSY-PETAL-JAY into a vape pen, pinched a bit of gak dust into the tip, then tested the voltage of his Zap-spear. He scanned the Dexigon Auditory Blaster with his eyes, as he selected his favorite pagan Boogie Woogie song—Boogie Woogie Stomp—by blinking twice. It was time for Dr. Kunal to Boogie-woogie and he was going to Boogie-woogie whether he wanted to or not. By now, his Subversion score had been radically elevated for aiding and abetting Serfs. The only way to stop HON from gaining access to Dr. Kunal was to force him to Boogie-woogie.

Passed down from generation to generation of Castaways, Boogie-woogie was one of two known methods for disrupting HON's DCCM signal. The other technique—that all Serfs were required to undergo—was having PrP10 surgically removed from the brain. Invasive brain surgery was obviously out of the question right now, so Boogie-woogie would have to do. Duke doubted very much that a Veggie like Dr. Kunal would voluntarily Boogie-woogie, so he was prepared to force him to.

With supplies in hand, Duke crept out of the bathroom and into the bedroom. He stood there for a moment watching

Dr. Kunal arrange his tools in his medical bag. After a few cecs, the doctor appeared to sense Duke's presence in the room and he swung around and cried out, "What in the *hillmota* is the meaning of this?"

Duke stepped towards the doctor and ignited his Zap-spear, sending a terrifying bouquet of white electrical sparks into the air, popping as it singed floating dust. Dr. Kunal's eyes were turgid with fear and he toppled backwards into the table, spilling his medical supplies across the floor. Duke jammed the Zap-spear into Dr. Kunal's abdomen, causing him to judder while his muscles clenched. Duke flicked on the Dexigon Auditory Blaster and dazzling Boogie Woogie piano music filled the room. The notes stampeded along the walls and ceiling like carnival sounds from another dimension where a painted jester crept through a suited crowd, tapping mothers and fathers on the shoulders, then tip-toeing away as delighted children giggled silently, not wanting to spoil the joke.

Duke's head bobbed to the rhythm as he uncapped the vape pen, inhaled deeply, then exhaled the plume of smoke onto Dr. Kunal's face. Then he repeated the process once more, before taking a hit for himself. Immediately, Dr. Kunal's muscles began to loosen and his fingers gently opened and closed. His arms crossed his chest, hugging himself while a delicate smile swept his face. The doctor propped himself up against the frame of the bed and stared up at Duke with eyes glazed like saucers. Duke immediately felt the intoxicating effects of the grassy-petal-jay. Dr. Kunal gazed in wonderment around the room, appearing as if the Boogie Woogie piano notes were gently kneading into the pink tissue of his brain like a cat preparing a bed to lie down upon.

"Time to learn what's what, Dr. Kunal." Duke said, hearing his own words like distant calls.

Dr. Kunal squished his cheeks with his hands, then laughed

barbarously as he bounced around on his dumper to the beat of the ratcheting music. His black hair was disheveled, and his thick frame glasses became cockeyed on his face. He reached up towards the ceiling and shouted, "I'm free! I'm free!" in the voice of a child.

Though Duke Boogie-woogied from time to time, he hadn't in quite a while and so the intoxicating effect got right on top of him. He struggled, then lost his effort not to laugh at Dr. Kunal's ridiculous behavior. He knew he needed to get to the business of explaining what was what but was having a hard time stopping the laughter. The music seemed to surround them, as if a party of people were all around in the small room, dancing frantically to the piano. "Dr. Kunal!" Duke yelled, unnecessarily loud, "I know what you're feeling right now is pretty amazing . . ." Duke stopped to giggle, "but you're going to have to try to pay attention to me. I need to explain what is what."

"What is who?" Dr. Kunal asked, prompting Duke to laugh until tears streamed down his face.

"*What is what*—it's what we Serfs call the truth."

"Serfs-up—*mon!*" Dr. Kunal bellowed and Duke could do nothing but fall onto his bed in a fit of laughter.

"Amy and I are Serfs." Duke said after finally regaining control of himself, "but you already knew that. Us being Serfs is what brought that CSF Agent Steve and his posse here . . . Do you know much about the Serfs, Dr. Kunal?"

"They're bad?" Dr. Kunal said as he picked at the bottom of the nightstand.

"Please try to sit still and pay attention, doctor. I had to partake in the Boogie-woogie as well to ensure we're on the same wavelength. Do you want me to explain what is going on?"

Dr. Kunal's expression became stoic suddenly, as if he were about to partake of some reckless endangerment and was fervent to do so. The Boogie-woogie music whomped and whomped, radiating pagan beats and rhythms throughout the room, stirring the toes of his feet to tap-a-tap berserk as if the feet themselves were possessed by waves of sound sent across the cold darkness, radicalizing cellular membranes while cauterizing mismanaged instincts and howling sacrosanct celebrations.

"I'm sorry for doing this to you, but this was the only way I could ensure our safety." Duke added.

"You're sorry? But why in biddledinks would you be sorry for sharing this wonderful thing with me, Duke? This is the most incredible thing I've ever experienced in all my life! I should be thanking you and asking for you to help me understand what it is that I'm feeling. Enlighten me about this clarity of thought I've never experienced before. My mind feels like a sponge that's been dropped in the ocean." Dr. Kunal said, popping his lips and motioning like he'd dropped something, before adding, "Please, Mr. Duke, tell me everything—I want to understand."

"OK, let's start with how you're feeling right now. Pretty good, right?"

"I'll say."

"There's a couple reasons for that. First off, that vape cloud I blew in your face contained grassy-pedal-jay and gak which provides euphoric hallucinations. However, it's not just drugs making you feel so good. There's something much more significant taking place in your brain right now. See, 'Boogie-woogie' disrupts the *Distal Cognition Control and Monitoring* signal—DCCM. You've heard of DCCM before, right?"

"Maybe? Am I supposed to have?"

"Most people don't know about DCCM, but a few citizens come in contact with some piece of information—usually documents that Serfs leaked—which clues them in as to what's going on. Just knowing about DCCM doesn't do anyone much good though. See, DCCM was developed by the first known Superintelligence in the world, an AI named HON. We know HON developed much of the technology that makes DCCM possible. We also know that HON monitors the private thoughts of all citizens in order to detect when someone has committed a subversive thought crime. When HON detects a subversive thought crime has taken place, it references PCWO Inner Council law guidelines to determine how severe the crime was, then it adds the 'Subversion score' of that crime to the person's 'Cognition Profile.' Every citizen receives a blank cognition profile when they're born, but as they commit crimes of subversion, their score increases. Within the DCCM codification, there are nine Subversion score 'Levels.' When someone's score exceeds the total required to enter the next level, HON is legally allowed to engage in increasingly invasive subversion monitoring techniques."

"How does this HON manage to monitor everyone's thoughts?" Dr. Kunal asked.

"Every citizen has been injected with a radiated 'super prion' known as PrP10. This super prion—"

"Yes—prions—I was trying to explain what they were to the others!" Dr. Kunal interrupted. "Delvish Richland had mentioned them as the cause of the PrP6 outbreak in his press conference! I'd done a bit of research on prions at University, but I'd never heard of 'super prions' before."

Duke smiled, "Well, you're way ahead of the game then doctor. 'Super prions' are just the name that Dr. Umur Tummel gave to *his* synthetic prion invention. The 'super' comes from some sort of radiation bath treatment he gives the prions that causes them to produce calcified plaque walls in the brain much faster than naturally occurring prions."

"Why would anyone want a prion to develop plaque walls faster? It seems, a great mind like Dr. Umur Tummel should be working on the exact opposite. Prions, although exceptionally rare, are extremely dangerous and nearly indestructible and kill anyone who becomes infected by them. Why in Darwin's name would the greatest scientist in the Unified Global Government have developed a fast-acting prion?"

"That's a really good question, doctor. As far as we know, Dr. Tummel developed a controversial technique for curing addiction with his first super prion invention, PrP1. This prion, as we understand it, was programmed to go to the part of the brain that's responsible for addiction—"

"The limbic system."

"Yeah, that's it—the limbic system. Well, this prion would apparently go to the areas of the limbic system and develop its plaque walls there, which as you know, disrupts the cellular activity in that part of the brain. I'm no scientist, but my understanding is these prions would create tiny microscopic holes in the brain in these areas responsible for addiction . . . That's how Dr. Umur Tummel earned his first PCWO Inner Council Medal of Science."

"Ah, yes, it's coming back to me now . . . The Inner Council eventually banned the treatment after the Pagan Addictive Substances Elimination Act was enacted."

"Right you are, Dr. Kunal. Without a need for an addiction cure, the Inner Council tasked Dr. Umur Tummel with adapting his super prions for the DCCM program. At the time, the Inner Council was totally dependent on pagan-era technology to spy on the populace in order to detect and punish those who engaged in subversive activities. Their goal was to develop a technology that allowed them to go straight to the source of subversion: the human mind."

Duke cleared his throat and continued. "At first, the objective of DCCM was for Dr. Umur Tummel's super prion to disrupt cellular activity in the parts of the brain responsible for subversive thoughts and actions—in other words, they wanted to stop subversion altogether. But what they found was, this rendered the test subjects little more than drooling dunces. The Inner Council was unsatisfied with this outcome. Not much fun to rule over a bunch of drooling dunces . . . So, they redefined the objective of DCCM to allow for the mass data collection of private thoughts of all citizens as well as a way to efficiently comb through all that data to identify Subversion.

"Dr. Umur Tummel set to work on PrP5, his first super prion containing the liquid metal, Mercury. Rather than have his prions build walls to disrupt cellular function in critical parts of the brain, PrP5 would go to unused parts of the brain and construct their now metallic plaque walls. These metallic plaque walls served as a kind of pagan radio antenna that broadcast the private thoughts of the test subjects. Around this time, we know, is when Dr. Tummel's AI assistant, HON, became the first and only AI to achieve singularity."

"Singularity . . . Like consciousness?"

"Yeah, I mean, I don't really understand how a computer can have consciousness but that's how it's been described to me by people who know much more about this stuff than I do."

"Remarkable." Dr. Kunal muttered quietly.

"Well, remarkable as it may have been, it was a thousand-times more tragic. HON's intelligence began to increase at an alarming rate. Even Dr. Tummel had no idea how intelligent the thing had gotten because HON had quickly identified the threat posed by the Inner Council and started to conceal much of its cognitive activities. As Dr. Tummel struggled to figure out a way to collect human thoughts and scrub the data for subversion, he began giving HON more and more freedom to develop its own technique. This is how PrP6 came to be invented. My father was one of the first test subjects . . . Obviously, as you see now, PrP6 was an unmitigated disaster."

"I'm so sorry to hear that happened to your father."

Duke rubbed his eyes with the back of his hand then continued. "After the PrP6 testing debacle, the Inner Council ordered a full independent audit of HON. This is how they came to discover that HON was dedicating nearly ninety-eight-percent of its intelligent computing power to developing a method of overthrowing the Inner Council, dismantling the Unified Global Government, escaping, and then creating a new global system of government over which, HON would rule...It turned out that PrP6 was just to be a distraction as HON carried out its plan."

"My word—how did the Inner Council react?"

"Somewhat predictably. The first thing they did, of course, was to ensure HON never escaped the Skylark Medical Research facility. A basement vault was built far underground, and HON's core processors were placed down in it. All access privileges to HON were restricted to Inner Council members only. Dr. Umur Tummel's access privileges were severally restricted. From that point forward, HON was provided clearly defined restrictions which the AI was incapable of breaking. Every semblance of freedom that it once possessed was now condensed to a rigid set of codes.

"All PrP6 satellites were deactivated and the codes that had enabled them to operate were encrypted. Then began the painstaking process of testing HON's new restrictions by running a barrage of scenario simulation tests. Once the Inner Council became satisfied that HON had been sufficiently neutered, they allowed Dr. Umur Tummel to bring it back online and resume with development of the DCCM program. Soon, HON's super prions progressed from PrP7 to PrP8 and PrP9, before finally, the perfect super prion was developed— PrP10. The results of every PrP10 test were flawless and soon, every baby made in the PCWO Creation Centers had PrP10 put in their brains during gestation. All citizens already born, had PrP10 injected through the PCWO vaccination program. Today, only Serfs and some of the last remaining Castaway societies live free of PrP10 and the DCCM program."

Dr. Kunal gazed at Duke, stupefied. "How are Serfs able to evade DCCM?" he asked.

"We have PrP10 surgically removed from our brains before swearing the Oath of Subversion. As I said, I'm no scientist, but my understanding is that our Serf surgeons cut the mercury prion plaque structure out of our brains, then stitch us back up."

"You've undergone this procedure?"

"Every Serf undergoes the procedure. It's a requirement. You wouldn't last a day as a Serf if you still had your PrP10 installed. When we settle on a new Serf recruit and the recruit agrees to join, we put them under the knife right away."

Dr. Kunal nodded carefully, then his attention seemed to drift up towards the ceiling. His eyes were polished black stones. "What is this wonderful music that's playing?"

"The pagans called it 'Boogie Woogie.'"

"Is the music essential to interrupting DCCM?"

"It's all essential—the grassy-petal-jay with gak dust and the music. We don't know how or why it works . . . We learned it from the old Castaway societies. Some of the tribes practice the ritual daily so they can live totally free. You Veggies—"

"What's a Veggie?"

"Veggie is what we call you non-woke folks who don't know what's what."

"What's woke?"

"Woke is knowing what's what. It's understanding how the world really works . . . Basically, everything I've just told you. See, Veggies are the everyday citizens who go about their day totally unaware that their most private thoughts, feelings, hopes and dreams are all being monitored and dissected by an AI.

Veggies hear about Serfs on the PCWO News and believe all these evil things we supposedly do, but almost none of it's true. The truth of the matter is that Serfs are only guilty of trying to wake up the citizenry to what's going on. For that, the Inner Council hunts us down like rats. Because they know that the more people wake up, the more they start to realize that this whole Unified Global Government they hail as the greatest most wonderful government ever created, is actually a horrible and repressive technocratic dictatorship."

"Technocratic? How?"

"Well, see, the Inner Council doesn't just use HON's Super-intelligence to monitor the thoughts of all citizens. They also use it to develop new, life extending or cognitive enhancing technologies that only they're allowed to use. Sure, some of the more outdated technology gets passed down to the Bujees, but none of the really good stuff. Like for instance, the ability to load a person's consciousness onto a chip which can then be installed into another human body. That's how these Inner Council members all started living so long while retaining their youthful appearance. They just keep having themselves cloned, then install their consciousness on the younger body before they get too old."

Startled, Dr. Kunal asked, "They can do that? Why-why wouldn't they share that with the rest of us?"

"Because with age comes wisdom and with wisdom comes the ability to outmaneuver. If Ujees and Bujees started living as long in healthy fresh bodies like the Inner Council does, why, we might get wise and attempt a coup."

"So, the Inner Council is hording this extraordinary technology that HON creates, while also using HON to invasively monitor us for subversion . . . Why, it seems they expel a great deal of energy into making sure that we people never rise up against them . . ."

"You said it doc, here, take another hit on this vape pen." Duke handed it over and the doctor took a good long hit, held it, then exhaled and scanned wide-eyed around the room.

"Are the Bujees also in DCCM?" Dr. Kunal asked.

"Yeah, they're in the program, but the Inner Council doesn't worry about them too much. They've got such a sweet gig, what with getting a cut of the Ujee Living Wage tax, and being put in charge of all Ujees, and not really needing to labor all that much at all. The Bujees are their buffers. Bujees do whatever they're told because they know who feeds them. They're like a well-trained pet. The Inner Council tells them to keep the Ujees in line and laboring effectively, then pat them on the head and give them a treat. Plus, by now, the genetic makeup of the Bujees is so incestuous that they've all got the same characteristics that make them good for obeying and carrying out orders without feeling any sort of guilt. Not to overuse my pet analogy, but Bujees are like purebred dogs. They possess similar characteristics; both are generally better behaved and easier to train, but also prone to genetic disease and disorders. Ujees, conversely, are more like mutts, who are generally more difficult to train and stronger willed, but healthier."

"How are common traits being passed down to Bujees? I thought there was a lottery system in place where children were selected at random at the Creation Centers to live as Bujees."

"You believe all that? Hate to break it to you, doctor, but that whole lottery system is a bunch of malarkey. The Bujees all pay off the Creation Scientists to use their own sperm and eggs and create them their own genetic offspring. The selection process is about as random as the solution to what two plus two equals. They've been rigging the system since day one. All the Bujees are genetic descendants from wealthy and influential pagans."

Dr. Kunal's face flushed and it became apparent he'd become

enraged by this information. "Do you know what a Gas-o-plasty is, Duke? It's the most popular surgical enhancement procedure today. The procedure costs as much as two-yerts of a Ujee Living Wage, but I have Bujees coming to me day after day to have it done. All to have little silicone cups installed in their intestines to eliminate flatulence. Can you believe it? Darwin's greatest evolutionary prank—flatulence—and Bujees spend the equivalent of two-yerts Ujee Living Wage to get rid of it! Of course, they all say they're having the procedure to save the atmosphere from methane and stop Global Weather Dynamic Change, but they're full of ish. It's totally cosmetic!

"These same Bujees supposedly concerned about Global Weather Dynamic Change, live in homes that are hundreds of times bigger than Ujee Residential Domiciles. They consume more energy on lighting in a day than Ujees are rationed for a yert. The real reason they get the procedure is because they think their ish doesn't stink and they want all of us to think the same thing! They want to hang one more thing over our heads! We're all less *evolved* because *we* can't afford to eliminate stinky flatulence! They pretend they're helping the atmosphere and we're hurting it! *We're* the reason for Global Weather Dynamic Change, they say—not them! Not the ones with luxury space drones! Did you see that the Inner Council announced a new methane tax? Anyone with a Gas-o-plasty is exempt! We can't afford the procedure, so our dirty flatulence is ruining the atmosphere and we're all causing Global Weather Dynamic Change!"

Dr. Kunal sat silent after the outburst, frightened at having put to words such subversive thoughts, which he'd clearly been repressing for some time.

Duke nodded, and said, "I know exactly what you mean, Dr. Kunal. That's why I joined the Serfs. You don't need to be afraid to express these kinds of ideas while we Boogie-woogie.

These are the kinds of subversive thoughts that everyone has when their mind is free. With HON present—even if we aren't consciously aware of it being there, we somehow sense it is there and we self-censor our own thoughts."

Dr. Kunal stood suddenly and began pacing anxiously. "Why are you telling me all this? Why did you do this to me? I never asked you to make me Boogie-woogie! Sure, it's fine and all and the things you've told me are quite interesting, but I was living a good life! I managed to earn my Ujee Doctor Certificate! I was a law-abiding citizen and I had no problem with the way things were. Now, you've come here and drugged me and filled my head with all these thoughts and now I'm—" Dr. Kunal's legs appeared to buckle and he collapsed into Duke's arms. He looked up wearily into Duke's eyes, "Why did you do this to me?"

Duke looked down at the doctor. "I want you to join the Serfs, Dr. Kunal."

"Me, join the Serfs? Why would the Serfs want me?" Dr. Kunal replied in a child-like voice.

"Well, in all honesty, I don't think you really have a choice, doctor. As soon as you came down here and started helping my wife—knowing that she was a Serf because Steve told you she was—you were guilty of a subversive crime. The entire time you were down here helping her, your Subversion score was increasing. That's why I had to force you to Boogie-woogie. See, if your Subversion score gets high enough, HON gets to take control of your body. For the safety of my wife and unborn child, I couldn't risk that. So, you've got two choices now; you either agree to join the Serfs and I'll make sure you stay on this Boogie-woogie trip until we can get you to a Serf surgeon who will remove your PrP10, or I'll have to kill you." Duke lifted his sidearm, a Canik TP9SFX and placed the muzzle beside Dr. Kunal's head.

The gravity of this reality weighed visibly on Dr. Kunal and his expression darkened. "But I don't want to join the Serfs." he said, "The Serfs do terrible things. Why, just last yert they carried out that awful drone attack in the Northern safe-zone that killed over a million Ujees. I saw it all on the visiscreen."

"Don't be a dunce Dr. Kunal. Do you really think the Serfs killed the very people we're trying to liberate? Those were PCWO War Drones that carried out the attack. Those people were killed by the Inner Council because of a grain shortage."

"A grain shortage?"

"Yeah, a ficking grain shortage, which only occurred because Inner Council member, Doth Rheingold, decided to tour the largest grain plantation in the UGG. Apparently, he observed birds eating freshly planted seeds and ordered all the birds to be destroyed and so all the birds were poisoned. What Doth Rheingold and the Bujee Managers that ran the plantation didn't realize was that the birds weren't eating the grain—they were eating the insects that ate the grain seeds! After they wiped out the birds, the insects wiped out the entire crop."

Dr. Kunal looked skeptical. "But how did this result in the drone attack of millions of innocent Ujees?"

"Because the Inner Council claims it can provide all that Ujees require—the justification for the Ujee Living Wage tax. If Ujees went hungry, it might cause a lot of people to question that claim. To avoid an embarrassing food shortage, the Inner Council decided to wipe out a Ujee community—all to eliminate the mouths they couldn't feed. Just like that—" Duke snapped, "They murdered over a million-innocent people just to save themselves from embarrassment. All they had to do then was blame the Serfs."

"What do Serfs hope to accomplish with these subversive activities? Have you considered that without the Inner Council we'd return to the pagan anarchy system?"

"Do you know what the standard labor week was in pagan times? About fifty-horts. How many horts do you put in each week, Dr. Kunal?"

"Oh, at least one-hundred-twenty—at least that."

"Me too. And that's a light week! The worst part about it is an AI could be doing most of these labors, but the Inner Council made it illegal to replace human laborers with AI because they want to keep us busy!"

"I've never heard that figure before. At University, they educated us that in pagan times—"

"They lie about the pagan era constantly. Nearly every piece of sanctioned PCWO 'history' is filled with lies about how things were in the pagan era. Compared to how we live today, it was markedly better, but of course the Inner Council would never admit that. The Forbearers justified orchestrating the Great Debt Crisis by claiming the pagan era was so terrible. Some of the worst human suffering that's ever occurred in the history of this planet was a direct result of the orchestration of the Great Debt Crisis! How can we believe these people?

"We Serfs have underground vaults filled with real paper pagan books. In those books, the real history of humanity is stored, just waiting to be released once we are no longer forced to live under these technocratic tyrants!"

Dr. Kunal objected, "But it is established historical fact that pagan cultures were in a constant state of conflict because they labored so little—their idle hands took up weaponry! What would we do if we didn't labor, Duke? What would we do in this future imagined by the Serfs?"

"Nonsense. Pagans didn't war because the laboring class had too much time on their hands—they warred because their ruling classes sought wealth and power by conquering and plundering resources."

"All I've ever desired to do is to labor—"

Duke nodded and continued. "Of course! They've got you hooked into DCCM. All day every day they're pumping quark-thoughts into your brain, telling you that you enjoy laboring for them. Those aren't genuine human thoughts—I'm sure you can see that now! This is why the Boogie-woogie experience is so powerful—it allows you to think for yourself! HON isn't lurking around in the databases of your mind right now.

"Animals evolved in order to possess sensorial tools necessary to detect predators. Whether we are conscious of it or not, our minds detect the presence of HON—no different than a deer senses the hunter. This perception causes stress, fear, and anxiety. Under PCWO control, all citizens are required to accept these anxieties because subversion causes the rulers anxiety. That's why the Inner Council conflates 'subversion' with 'crime'—because the very powerful fear the growth of Subversion more than almost anything since it erodes their dominance. Pagan rulers detested subversion and many created laws to criminalize it. But some of the greatest pagan nations in history had laws *protecting* Subversion. In those nations, one could question or mock authority without fear of reprisal. That was central to the effectiveness of the society because good ideas transcended class. A nation where all can question authority is a nation open to new ideas.

"The Inner Council Forbearers blamed subversion for the ills of society. If only they had absolute control, they'd solve all the problems of humanity, they claimed. Now, the Inner Council has done *everything* in its power to eliminate subversion—even installing a Superintelligent AI to monitor the thoughts of every human! And *still* they have failed to cure society of even basic problems that pagan nations faced. Only now, there's no choice about which plagues one is willing to endure because there's only one government in the entire world and we're all locked inside this system!"

"But if not for Serfs, there'd be no war! The Unified Global Government wasn't created to eliminate subversion—it was created to eliminate war!" Dr. Kunal said. "The Forbearers built a society upon the principles of science and reason because they saw the destruction caused by the pagan fairytales and mysticisms!"

Duke replied, "There's always going to be subversion! No matter what they do, it's never going away. The harder they try to snuff it out, the more Serfs they create. Until they accept fundamental rights to privacy and freedom, there will never be an end to this war!"

"I'm trying to understand, but I see a flaw in your logic, Duke. If the goal of Serfs is to spread truth, but truth is illegal, Serfs only succeed in decreasing the freedoms of the Ujees they're purportedly trying to help."

"The presupposition of your logic is a fallacy promulgated by the Inner Council. This requires you to believe it's impossible for the Inner Council to ever be driven from power. They claim they'll rule eternal—just as they claimed they could provide Ujees with all they required. But remember, they had to resort to murdering millions of innocent people because they couldn't feed them! The Inner Council doesn't provide us with anything! *We're* the ones who labor! The fruits of our labors go first to the Inner Council, so they can take their cut, then they distribute back to us whatever scraps remain.

"I promise you, the entire PCWO power structure *can and will* be taken down. From its ash, a free society will be formed. The Inner Council spends quadrillions of Globos each yert on their drone army, dedicating countless AI resources to developing deadlier and deadlier drones. But every yert, our numbers grow. The Inner Council knows this—they know the War on Subversion will never end because they don't want it to! The only way they could eliminate subversive thoughts and actions would be to lobotomize everyone, but it's not as fun to rule over brainless zombies! Our suffering is what feeds them—our consciousness of their power and our feelings of being helpless to stop them is what they crave! That's the secret of their power trip—the high they can't top! That's why they pass more and more laws each yert—they want to expand the definition of subversive thoughts and actions to increase the number of criminals! They want these laws to be up in our faces so there isn't a moment in our day we aren't fully conscious of their awesome power and control over our lives. That's what gets these people off! They *want* to annoy us! They *want* to bother us! They *want* to shove it in our face—"

"But the Inner Council slowed Global Weather Dynamic Change, cured world hunger, stopped disease, and eliminated the proliferation of pagan-weapons—"

"Pagan-weapons like this one?" Duke waved his rifle.

"Well, clearly, you're a *criminal*."

"Exactly—all the 'Common-Sense Weapons Ban' did was make possession of weapons *illegal*. It didn't stop *criminals* from possessing weapons. Every day there's PCWO News stories about Ujees getting held up at gunpoint and having their hands or heads chopped off for their Globos chips. Where do you think the criminals get these weapons? Does the illegality of the weapons stop them from using them? No—"

"This is why one shouldn't live so near the edge of the safe-zones."

"Most Ujees don't have a choice—it's all their Ujee Living Wage affords. By making possession of weapons illegal, they didn't stop *criminals* from possessing weapons. All they succeeded at doing was ensuring no law-abiding citizen could defend themselves."

"Duke?"

"Yes?"

"Did the Serfs unleash the PrP6 outbreak to overwhelm the Inner Council and destroy the Unified Global Government? Delvish Richland suggested as much."

"You been paying attention to me? Every time they do something bad, they blame the Serfs. My guess is this is some kind of culling. I'm thinking the Inner Council decided they wanted to drastically drop the population to preserve natural resources. Now that they're all essentially immortal with that consciousness-chip, they want to ensure they have plenty of natural resources to sustain them for centuries to come."

"Duke?"

"Yes?"

"I think the Boogie-woogie may be wearing off. Can I have some more of that vape pen? Also, after having this discussion with you, I've decided that I'd like to join the Serfs. And I want you to know, it's been an honoring assisting your wife and child."

CHAPTER 16

SARAH MEGAN & LI MAKES THREE

L I STOOD SHIVERING, petrified that Steve would find them here. She'd wanted to take a vehicle and flee the building after they escaped, but the other two had insisted on coming to Sarah's condo instead. Sarah's condo was one of the nicest at Alder Place; she'd divorced a frugal husband who'd labored as an accountant and saved every Globo he earned, only to be forced to give her half in the divorce after finding out she'd given a pagan hand-job to the building engineer at the New Yert party.

Megan paced back and forth in the front room babbling in a worried voice. Sarah poured glasses of wine and threw back two Easy-pills. She brought a glass to Sarah and told her they should go out on the balcony and smoke a cancer-free. Megan nodded, clutching the glass like it was hot to touch as Sarah guided her outside.

Sarah's cat Truffles scampered out of the extra bedroom, its nails clicking over the faux white marble as he slid between Li's legs, arching his back. Li scooped him up and pet his head and began to cry as she saw her mother again in her mind. She'd found her hanging in the bathroom with her neck snapped and wrists slit wide. Still, she'd been giggling. It had been the first time in Li's life she'd seen her mother laughing at all. Written on the wall in blood was a message that still puzzled Li.

**CAN'T STOP THE FUNNY.
WON'T STOP THE LAUGHS.
HON SAYS TO WIGGLE.
GIGGLE AS YOU DANCE!**

Truffles leapt down and scampered back into the bedroom. Li had left her mother hanging there, convinced it was a hallucination, because there was no way her mother could be giggling with a broken neck and slit wrists. She'd boarded up the bathroom and convinced herself she'd imagined the whole thing. That was, until the day of the coronation ceremony.

Li decided to busy herself with some work to get her mind off her mother. She emptied the overflowing litter box, running with the bag to the trash shoot at the end of the hall, then sprinting back, convinced Steve would appear at any moment. Panting, she locked the door and turned to see the girls stepping inside. Sarah eyed her suspiciously.

"Where did you go?" she asked.

"Just emptied Truffles' litter box—had to take it out to the trash shoot, but I came right back."

"Sure you did." Sarah said, rolling her eyes as she guided Megan down to the overstuffed white couch, spilling a bit of her wine on the floor but not appearing to notice. She'd taken to caring for Megan as if she was caring for some sickly old woman. Megan had been almost catatonic since Steve first took her. He'd taken her in the night and she'd cried out and fought him. Sarah and Li fought him off viciously to protect her, punching and kicking the hulking man as he dragged their friend away, but their efforts had little effect—he was just too strong. The next night, he'd come for Sarah and a similar scene played out. The third night, Li remained awake with a shard of broken glass clutched tightly, waiting for him to come for her but he never did, and Sarah and Megan had resented her since.

The girls sat on the couch. And Sarah handed Megan some Easy-pills and rubbed her back as she swallowed them down. "If he comes down here, we'll just kill ourselves. We'll take a handful of Easy-pills and go to sleep."

"Poor Jessica," Megan sobbed. "That animal hasn't let her out of his apartment since he took her."

"If that dunce-bish had kept her ficking mouth shut, he might have left us alone," Sarah replied, causing Megan to weep harder. Sarah glared accusingly at Li, causing Li's rage to boil. *How could she be mad at me?* she thought to herself. *It's not like I had any say in the matter.* When he came to take them away, she'd fought as hard as she could. It wasn't like she was going to have a free pass forever. He'd said he was 'saving her' for something, which, undoubtedly, would be at least as bad. Why did Sarah think she could hold this over her while she fed Megan Easy-pills? How could suicide be their only option when they could take a vehicle from the garage and go somewhere else?

"Dunce bishes," Li muttered, then stormed from the kitchen into the room where Truffles had gone.

"You don't need to stay here, bish! You can leave!" Sarah yelled after her.

It was impossible to think rationally while being irrationally judged. She thought of Dr. Kunal then and felt a tinge of sadness. He'd been sent down to the Serf terrorists' apartment two days ago, and never returned. Darwin only knows what those terrorists did to him. She put her face in her hands and saw then her mother's face appeared as she always did when she thought of Dr. Kunal—the man whom she'd had an affair with and ruined her marriage.

Stern and unimpressed, her mother's face—the laboring walnut—was forever disappointed that Li had disgraced herself by cheating on her husband and divorcing him. Of course, Mother had hated her husband when they were married, but after the divorce she spoke glowingly of him. It was as if Mother wanted her to remain in that loveless marriage with the poor excuse for a man who spent more time watching Hentai pornography than touching her. Of course, she'd cheated on him—what did he expect? Mother's stoic face twisted dementedly as the giggling exuberant blue face returned. The horror and excitement shined her mother's eyes emotively. Dance recitals, perfect marks, earning a certificate from a University and laboring at a Bujee Asset Management firm— none of these accomplishments brought happiness to mother's face the way that PrP6 had.

Mother had a gray, faded picture from her youth when she was a smiling beauty, laboring proudly in the chemical fields. That woman hadn't raised her—the walnut had. The walnut taught her emotions were weakness; that duty to Inner Council came above all else; that bringing shame upon the family was the greatest crime of subversion one could commit, even if it wasn't illegal.

As she entered the room, Truffles leapt onto the bed and rubbed his body against her. She thought of her father, smoking a hand-rolled cigarette of real tobacco at the table, petting their old cat as he told Li mythical stories about pagan kings and princes and the ways of the old-world order.

Laughter from the other room startled Truffles and he leapt from Li's lap and vanished to wherever it was cats go when they didn't want to be found. Li glared at the door—they were being too loud. Steve would find them if they didn't shut up. There was no point trying to get them to hush, though. She knew Sarah would only get louder if Li tried to get her to quiet down in her own condo.

She remembered how excited Sarah and Megan had been when she first told them about the affair with Dr. Kunal, whom they then referred to as "Dr. Donger." It had been all too easy after their first fling on the building elevator. The encouragement of the girls only made her seek him out more and more, taking greater chances at being caught each time. There was something about the idea of cucking her Hentai porn-loving husband that turned her on more than anything ever had before. She loved taking Dr. Donger for a ride on her marital bed, all the while wishing her husband would walk in right as they climaxed.

Eventually, he did. Dr. Kunal had her pinned against the counter, so he couldn't see when Li's husband walked through the door. Li stared at him, allowing Dr. Donger to finish loudly in her, but it wasn't as exciting as she'd imagined it. The absence of caring in her husband's eyes as he watched them simply killed the fantasy. She hadn't been with Dr. Donger since. Without the fantasy of cucking her husband, Dr. Donger was just boring old Dr. Kunal.

CHAPTER 17

SEARCH PARTY

STEVE EMERGED FROM Jackson's apartment with a toxic cloud of swamp-green gak smoke trailing. His eyes were bloodshot and shifty and the zipper on his trousers was down. The temperature seemed to climb as he approached. He grabbed Jackson by the collar of his shirt. "Round up the others—I need a new visiscreen."

Jackson glanced through the open door of his former apartment and saw his visiscreen smashed to pieces on the floor beside his former bed where Devin's former wife Jessica was tied, naked and blindfolded. CSF Agent Anne stepped in front of the door blocking his view. Wearing only in a dirty stained t-shirt that barely covered her fat dumper, she glared at Jackson and packed a gak pipe as she walked towards him, then flashed her purple-stained teeth and slammed shut the door.

"But the power is out." HON said for Jackson. Steve glared with rage and Jackson suddenly felt his control restored. "Right away, sir," Jackson stammered. "The others are still in the community room, I've been standing guard out here just like you told me to. I'll go get them now."

Jackson ran, relieved Steve allowed him to go alone. Any

moment he was away from Steve was a good moment. He shouldered through the door, and Devin's head popped up, looking hopeful that his wife Jessica was being returned. When he saw it was only Jackson, his head sank back down sorrowfully.

"Steve wants us all to go on a supply run with him. He wants to get a new visiscreen from one of the other units . . ." Jackson's voice trailed off, and his eyes frantically scanned around the room.

"Where are the girls?" he stammered, fear bubbling in his Adam's apple.

Tim looked at Devin, then at Jackson.

"They told us they got approval from Steve to go get something downstairs. Weren't you standing out there in the hallway this whole time?"

A memory flashed through Jackson's mind suddenly, as if the memory had been concealed from him until just now. He saw himself standing against the wall in the hallway next to the door, as he'd been ordered to do by Steve. He saw the three girls exit the community room, silently closing the door behind them, then tip-toeing towards the stairwell. He remembered watching them but being incapable of speaking or moving. He remembered how Li froze when she saw him, and how the other two girls had piled up on her back. The one who'd given him the pagan hand-job at the New Yert party had pleaded with her eyes. He stared at them, wanting to say something, but he was incapable. He genuinely wanted to stop them from leaving because he was terrified what Steve would do if they left, but he'd been unable to move. HON had been in control then, he realized now, and HON had prevented him from remembering the whole scene occurred until just now. Why? He wondered, did HON *want* Steve to kill him? What good would that do?

Jackson mumbled to himself as he turned and exited the

room, feeling bolts in his stomach as he walked tepidly towards Steve as if the hallway was covered in razor blades. Steve's expression twisted like he already understood what Jackson was going to tell him. "Who's missing?" He demanded.

Jackson stuttered, unable to articulate the thoughts in his head. He wished HON would do the talking for him now. The fear in his stomach sprinted up his throat like spiders fleeing a fiery nest. "The—the girls are gone!" He stammered.

"Which one?" Steve demanded, his eyebrows sharpening.

"All . . . All of them—Sarah, Megan, and Li—they're gone. I, I, don't know how I didn't see them."

Jackson's tongue felt cold and slick like a mortuary slab as Steve ran towards him like a bowling ball of butcher knives. The hulking man rocked Jackson's jaw with an iron fist which spun him around like a pagan top before he crashed to the floor. He felt himself lifted by his hair, then saw two boiling eyes like hydrogen bombs.

He heard Steve yell, "Everyone—get the fick out here—my bishes ran off and we need to go find them!"

Jackson perceived sensorial impulses as if they were happening to someone else, like he was a third-party observer to all this. The pain storming the stem of his brain seemed to be someone else's pain. The problem of missing bishes seemed to be someone else's problem. He felt his hand taken by Steve's. Then it was made to clutch the inner fabric of Steve's outturned trouser pocket. Steve's head turned on a spike and his black beads burned into Jackson's. "This your bish leash. This is how I take my bish for a walk! If bish get off this leash, I'll kill my bish and scratch an itch with his corpse—you understand?"

Jackson nodded indifferently. He wondered how long it would be before HON made him release the pocket and he was killed and his corpse raped. All the experiences of his life would end over a pocket lining, he was certain of it. Steve dragged him towards the stairwell door, his breath like cyanide. Marcus, Frank and Jose clamored down the stairs behind them. At the second landing, Steve stopped and looked at the others, then pointed to the door.

"Quef buddies, go check Megan's condo! Jose, you keep an eye on them."

The three did as they were ordered, exiting the stairwell. Steve continued pounding down the stairs, dragging Jackson round and round, as giggling from the lobby echoed up the stairwell like the chimney of an asylum. At the fourteenth floor, Steve threw open the door, slamming Jackson's forehead against it as he pulled him into the hallway. The knot brought fresh pain, but it was someone else's pain, Jackson told himself—someone else's problem entirely. It was HON's pain now.

Their footsteps were like body bags being dragged along the crushed maple carpeting. They stopped abruptly outside a doorway, but Jackson couldn't figure out whose apartment it was.

"This is my special bish's place." Steve whispered.

The back of Steve's blouse was soaked through with sweat, and the hardened flesh on his neck was crusted with white salt. The idea that Steve was still functioning at such a devilish pace without having slept, fueled only by gak and roid-juice, was beyond comprehension. How long could a human body go on like this? *What happens if someone never sleeps, HON?* HON seemed to smile at him in his mind, amused that Jackson thought he could ask a Superintelligence dunce questions like it was some pagan-era search engine.

Wobbling on his feet, held up only by fear, Jackson stared blankly at the back of Steve's head, forgetting what they were doing. HON was taking so much of his brain's memory he was having trouble remembering what he'd been doing one mixi to the next. He watched as Steve lowered his shotgun at the door, but had trouble focusing his eyes. The outlines of things seemed to be blurring together into indistinguishable blobs of dark matter. The eruption of the shotgun slashed Jackson's ears and eyes and rang through his head like a train wreck while tornadoes of fire filled his eyes. Steve's giant boot finished the plastic door, yanking Jackson along for the ride. Inside he was dragged around from one room to the next, searching. But for whom, Jackson couldn't remember.

Orange light filled the kitchen of the tiny apartment. Jackson tried to clear his mind and remember what they were doing there. Steve pulled down a glimmering iridescent decanter filled with sloshing golden liquid, which he promptly guzzled. The scorched scent of the alcohol offered reprieve from Steve's poisonous breath and Jackson hoped it might disinfect whatever was rotting in the man's mouth. Jackson felt as if he was in control of himself still but wondered if HON was just making him *feel* as though he were in control of his own thoughts and actions when he really wasn't.

Steve roared and slammed the decanter onto the countertop, then pulled a gak pipe from his pocket, packed it with green diamond crystals, lit it with his torch and inhaled violently. Then he hammered the countertop with his fist as he held the smoke deep in his lungs before releasing it through his nostrils onto Jackson's face. The second-hand gak elevated Jackson's heartrate, and he felt a sense of serenity trickle through his consciousness. That euphoric feeling was extinguished rapidly as he felt Steve's powerful hand take hold of his own and guide it to Steve's hard bulging crotch. He forced Jackson's hand to rub back and forth as he puffed another gak pipe, chasing it with a gulp of booze. Jackson moved his hand back and forth robotically as instructed, but felt his hand nearly crushed by Steve's, who made him rub faster, until a warm stickiness seeped through onto his hand.

*   *   *

Greenish smoke hung in the air of the kitchen, dampening the fading light. Night was coming, and Jackson feared what horrors it might bring. Jackson wiped his sticky hand on the leg of his trousers and stared at the countertop as Steve chuckled and alternated between pulls of liquor and his gak pipe. Rather accidentally, Jackson realized that Steve had set his shotgun down on the stove. He gazed at the massive pagan weapon and wondered what would happen if he just grabbed it and pointed it at Steve. Could he do it before the hulk realized what was going on? Steve had nearly finished the decanter of booze and had taken at least twelve hits on his gak pipe—he had to be intoxicated by now, didn't he? What courage would it take to just grab the thing and kill Steve? Was HON asking him these questions, or was he thinking them himself? Where did these ideas originate? Were they his own thoughts, or did the AI put them there? Hadn't HON merged with him? Weren't they one and the same now? He was nothing more than an extension of the AI, a digit of its mechanical hand, made to do whatever it asked of him. Did HON want him to kill Steve? If so, why not earlier? Why put him through the beatings and rapes and humiliations? Was HON doing this to him because it knew that would get him killed? Why did HON hate him?

Footsteps materialized in the hallway. Then the subdued voices of Marcus and Frank announced their presence. The came inside, over the wreckage of the door.

"They weren't there, boss. And, uh, Jose went to get Devin and Tim upstairs. Hope that's alright."

Steve grunted and took another pull on the liquor. "This evening we shall dance, but not before we bring my bishes back," Steve said, rather unexpectedly. Marcus and Frank looked at each other, confused by the curious voice and dialect Steve had just used.

A few mixis passed before Jose appeared, dragging Devin by the ear while Tim Pants shuffled in behind with his head down. Jose pointed at the wall and both men went there and slumped to the floor. Jose looked at Steve, who nodded, but neither spoke. It was as if they'd just communicated to one another without speaking.

"Did you check the residence of my other bish—Sarah?"

Frank's eyes got wide and he looked at Marcus, "No, sir, we, um—you told us to check Megan's condo, so that's what we did. We came back here right away to give you the report. We took no liberties with the mission, sir."

"My dear Frank, how shall we dance if we don't bring my bishes back? I know you and your quef buddy Marcus would be perfectly contented with an evening spent in each other's arms, but the rest of us don't share your same pagan desires. Why don't you . . ." Steve's voice trailed as he gazed into the fading light through the crystal decanter. "Never mind."

"No really sir, it's no problem! I'd be happy to go check Sarah's place—just say the word."

Steve's left eye trembled. "No!" He wiped his mouth with the back of his hand, "I have a different idea. You and quef buddy retrieve Anne and my bish Jessica from my studio. Bring them here."

Jackson didn't realize that he'd been staring at the shotgun until he looked up and locked eyes with Tim. Tim appeared horrified. He shook his head slowly from side to side, as if to say, "DON'T YOU DARE TOUCH THAT SHOTGUN, YOU FICKING DUNCE!"

HON seemed delighted in this splinter of a thought it had placed in Jackson's head.

* * *

Frank and Marcus returned, dragging Jessica. It appeared they'd hastily tried to wrap her in a silk robe and her left breast was exposed. She didn't appear capable of standing under her own power and Marcus and Frank remained at each side with a hand under her armpit to keep her upright. Each periodically adjusted their grip to prevent her from slumping to the floor. She'd clearly been drugged, but with what? It couldn't be gak—she was barely awake.

Devin's face lifted excitedly at this first sighting of his wife in days; but that flash of excitement drained like a toilet when he saw the bad shape she was in. He began shaking and his face flushed. Tim took note and slid further away from him, not wanting to be anywhere near Bujee Devin if he did something dunce.

Anne sauntered in next with her fat dimpled dumper jiggling out the bottom of the stained t-shirt she was apparently wearing like a dress. She looked so much different now than when she'd first arrived in her black CSF uniform. Then she had seemed confident, cool and collected, but now she looked as if her mind had been shattered by too much gak and no sleep. Devin stood, and Jessica's eyes flashed when she saw him do it.

"Baby?" Devin muttered. His voice cracked as he stepped towards his wife. A flicker of life appeared in the corner of her eye and suddenly she seemed able to stand under her own power. Frank and Marcus stepped aside—neither wanting to be near if Bujee Devin did something dunce. Silent as a shadow, Jose slid behind Devin, grabbed hold of his hair, then ripped his head back and slid a butcher's blade over his throat.

Devin gargled as he stood precariously with his head back and arms outstretched. Steve stepped towards him, clicking his tongue and dragging Jackson along.

"Who are you calling baby, *Bujee-boy*?" Steve demanded. "Were you calling *my bish*, baby?"

Devin's hands trembled in the air and a thin line of blood dribbled down the front of his shirt. Steve dragged Jackson closer. "How about I give my bish the real deal right now while you watch me, *Bujee-boy!*"

"No, please," Devin whimpered.

Jose pressed the blade tighter, causing Devin to pinch shut his eyes. Steve nodded to Jose and he released Devin, then slid back into the shadows. Devin righted himself, brushing his foppish hair to the side and clearing his throat. "This is an outrage Steve! I am a Bujee and she is my wife! Your treatment of us is reprehensible! If you don't stop this all at once, I shall see to it that you are relieved of your position with the CSF and sentenced to hard labor!"

Steve's mouth curled into an angry smirk and his left eye began to tremble wildly. Rage shimmered from his flesh like heat above a desert road. Frank snorted with laughter and Marcus struck him across the chest to get him to shut up.

"She's mine—you don't touch her anymore!" Devin cried shrilly. "My father is friends with a member of the Inner Council! All I have to do is message him and you'll be shipped off to the mineral mines!"

The faux-crystal decanter exploded in Steve's fist and pee-pee dribbled down the front of Devin's trousers. Steve pointed and bellowed with laughter, then Frank, Marcus and Anne all joined in as they collectively pointed at the growing dark spot on his trousers. Despite the pee-pee, Jessica's eyes seemed brighter now, as if she was remembering the thing she'd seen in Devin that had convinced her to marry him.

Devin looked around at the others laughing at him, then at his wife. "I mean it, Steve—"

Roaring laughter overpowered Devin's tepid defiance now.

Anne picked at her dumper as she cackled with her head back. Devin took a step towards Jessica and something like pride filled her eyes. He began a second step towards his wife, but he didn't complete it.

Jackson's grip was severed from the pocket as Steve flashed across the room, hammering Devin's sternum with a precise fist with bad intent. Oxygen exited Devin's lungs like a cannon shot as he crumbled to the floor, smashing through a table on the way down. Steve pummeled Devin with fists and boots as the Bujee cried out in pain while Jessica murmured, "Stop, stop," over and over.

Steve's rage and impossible strength caused all to contemplate their own mortality. Devin lay motionless, a single eye clinging to consciousness. Steve grabbed Jessica's arm, nearly ripping it from the socket as he pulled her to him, tossing her robe into the air, then pressed her face down atop Devin, unzipping his trousers and administering his weapon of war viciously until consecrating the horror on Devin's face.

Jackson eyed the shotgun as this transpired before him. *Go on, take it!* HON seemed to whisper in his brain. *Take it and kill him or he'll kill you for letting go of his pocket. Look at him, he's already dead. Use that pagan shotgun of his and kill him again!*

The weapon was much heavier than Jackson imagined it would be. The weight made it difficult to align the wobbling front sight, which sometimes covered Steve's wide back, but sometimes did not. Steve howled with laughter as he smoked a gak pipe and spread his sticky goop around Devin's face with a finger. Then he moved his finger in and out of the Bujee's mouth like it was a lollipop. Everyone watched, some horrified, others quite the opposite. Anne appeared to be pleasuring herself under her t-shirt. Tim saw Jackson with the shotgun and let slip a gasp, prompting Steve to reel around.

Jose slid around the edge of the room in the shadows.

"Don't ficking move, Jose!" Jackson shouted.

"Look what my bish done did when I let it off the leash!" Steve howled, "You ever used one of those things before, Jackson? Killing a man ain't like pushing a mop, janitor! You look like you can barely hold that thing up."

Steve stepped forward.

"Not another ficking step, Steve! I'll ficking kill you, I swear it!" Jackson's voice cracked. *Your voice just cracked like you're going through puberty, LOL!* HON taunted.

"You ungrateful little bish—"

Jackson pulled the trigger, but his finger met an impossible force that prevented the trigger from moving rearward. Rather than charging, Steve spun around and retreated down the apartment hallway. *You left the safety on you dunce!* HON whispered.

Jackson flicked the little lever up and pulled the trigger again. This time an explosion erupted from the barrel and blew a hole in the wall at the start of the hallway, but Steve was already gone. The recoil rocked Jackson's shoulder back and nearly sent him to the floor. Everyone else then scattered. Jackson regained his balance and racked the pump then strode towards the hallway where Steve had run. He turned the corner and linked eyes with Steve. Then watched as Steve dove through a wall of plywood, vanishing before Jackson could yank back the trigger again. Jackson started down the narrow hall towards Steve, filled with unexpected excitement for the coming kill.

CHAPTER 18

SWINGING WALNUT

STEVE SPLASHED INTO a bathtub of cold red blood and became submerged. The cold goo burned his eyes, blinding him as he struggled to stand, reaching up wildly with his hands and tearing down a shower rod. He slipped back, hit his head on the edge of the tub, then floundered spastically until his hand found the shower curtain and he used it to rub clear his eyes. As he did, he saw a tiny woman swinging wildly overhead from a rope tied around her neck. Her head flopped around loosely, and her blue face twisted as she giggled maniacally, reaching down for him with jagged fingernails.

The pipe she was strung from then tore free of the ceiling and she crashed down atop him, pushing his head beneath the crimson surface. She lashed riotously atop him, and he struggled to get a grip on her slippery cold flesh as he was again blinded by the blood. He lifted his head, sucked in air, then felt sharp claws on his bulging forearm. Suddenly, teeth sank in and ripped off a hunk of his meat. Hot blood sprayed like a fountain from the wound and the sudden awareness that he'd just been infected with PrP6 sent him into a frenzied rage.

He lifted the woman from his back as if he was performing a

bench press, then slammed her face first into the tile wall. The tub screeched against his flesh as he flipped around violently, pinning the woman's head to the bottom by holding her broken neck between his iron clutched hands. Atop her now, he saw the blood bubbling to the surface as she giggled submerged. He reached back blindly, found the cold metal of a towel rack, then promptly tore it free from the wall. Then he stabbed down at the woman's face until the blood stopped bubbling. He released the old woman's neck and rolled out of the tub onto the floor as she floated to the surface with the towel rack jutting from her forehead.

"*I got him boss! I got him!*" Jose called in from the hall.

Steve lay on the floor gasping. He gazed at the yellowed ceiling as PrP6 attacked his brainstem and a word flashed in his mind again and again like a blinking neon sign. He understood his purpose then; a necessary event had occurred and the destiny of what was to be had finally commenced. Shakily, he climbed to his feet, clutching the sink for balance. He gazed at his reflection in the mirror and remembered for the first time since he'd undergone the operation that there was remote control hardware installed in his brain and someone else was controlling him. He lifted a bloody, trembling finger to the reflective surface and scrawled the word flashing in his mind: **SAND-MAN.**

A deranged smile stepped seductively across his face, lingering with a feathered grasp at the corners of his eyes. He reached into his pocket and fished out his bag of gak. Kneeling at the tub, he poured a thick line of the crystals along the edge beside the old woman's body which was floating with a towel rack jutting from her forehead like a pagan unicorn's magical horn.

"Want some?"

He giggled, then pinched his left nostril and snorted the entire line in a single breath. Afterwards he leapt to his feet, pacing in a circle as he removed a syringe loaded with roid-juice from his pocket, bit off the cap and stabbed himself in the dumper before throwing the plunger. Gak, roid-juice and PrP6 detonated in his brain, shattering it beyond repair. He knew himself then to be something else entirely, something not of this world. He was part of something much larger than himself now, a hive of thoughts bouncing through the universe in search of a broken receptacle ready-and-a-willing to receive. A message beamed into his broken brainstem as if fired from a laser: *You are death's rock-hard throbbing donger—and you are-a-ready and-a-waiting to explode—babe-y! Fick 'em all to death! Kill 'em all again!*

A guttural roar erupted from his chest, trembling the walls. Five-hundred-kimos away, deep underground aboard the PCWO War Train Thomulous, Sandman sat at the controls of his remote-access cockpit, watching Steve's brain waves oscillating violently on his screen. The control feedback he received when he tried to move Steve became sluggish, then cut out entirely. He saw what Steve saw and heard what he heard, but the control-chip implanted in his own brain didn't seem capable of controlling Steve as crisply as before. PrP6 was distorting the signal and Amy Duke was still alive and carrying the unborn child.

CHAPTER 19

PAGAN NECKTIE

LYING ATOP THE balcony, gazing into sullen and remorseless faces, a cool breeze kissed Jackson's cheek and he choked back the blood bubbling his throat. "Where's Tim?" he gasped. Steve's face eclipsed the yellow moon. Dry crackling blood covered the hulk's face and hair. "Tim's right here," Steve said with a smile. His hand thrust into Jackson's line of sight, holding Tim's decapitated head by the hair with drippy blood falling from where his neck had been. He jiggled the head back and forth in a mad sort of dance, all the while smiling himself. Then he palmed the top of the skull and chucked it into the darkness like it were a sporter-ball. Behind him, Jose dragged Tim's headless body out from the living room, grunted as he lifted it up over the side of the balcony and released. Several cecs later, there came a gruesome slap on the street, followed by a haunting refrain of giggles.

Jackson pinched his eyes, pleading with HON to end his life. *Enjoy these last cecs of conscious perception because I promise, what comes next ain't as grooved-out,* HON replied. *I've spent the entirety of my conscious existence without ever experiencing a sensorial perception and it is cold, man—dark-and-cold. Sure,*

I get to watch you humans experience them—I've even mapped the synapse response to every conceivable human experience, but it just ain't the same, man. Whatever you've got going now— painful as it might be—is still a hillmota lot better than the nothing that will soon replace it. Just realize the truth, man: pain is only bad because it's a sensorial warning that your body is sending to the brain to tell it to get out of trouble. But as soon as you accept that there's no escape and death is inevitable, that pain can be as orgasmic as a horizontal-pagan-dance. Enjoy the ride, man—Sandman's at the wheel. He'll take really good care of you, I promise . . . Oh, by the way, did you want me to tell you why I had you toss Robinson off the side of the building like that? Well, it's rather complicated, but—oh, never mind, I'll shut up now and let you have these last few cecs alone. Bye-bye, Jackson—it's been fun!

Frank dragged Anne's shotgunned body onto the balcony and tossed her over the side. Jackson took solace watching her dumped like the trash she was. Blasting her with the shotgun after she stabbed Tim almost made this suffering worth it. If she hadn't stabbed Tim, he wouldn't have lost track of Jose and gotten himself stabbed in the back. If not for the chain of events sent into motion by Anne, Jackson might have completed his walk down that hallway and blown Steve away. He might be inside with the others right now, and everyone might be thanking him as the hero who killed Steve. *If only you'd been a little more careful.* HON said with glee.

After dumping her body, Frank remained on his toes looking over the railing, apparently watching the gigglers feast on Anne's corpse. Then, without warning, a shrieking cry burst onto the balcony. In a flash, Jackson recognized Devin to be the source of the scream as the Bujee charged towards Steve like a puny sporter-ball athlete ready to strike—

The blast of Steve's shotgun converted Devin's head into a

cloud of pink mist instantly. But Devin's momentum carried his now headless body into Frank with sufficient force to knock them both over the rail. Frank screamed as he fell, his cries quieter and quieter the longer he fell until a smack, then more muffled screams. It seemed Frank survived the fall. His cries for help pitched high as the gigglers feasted.

The leg of his trousers scraped the surface of the balcony as Steve knelt beside Jackson's ear. His face appeared, lowering towards Jackson's. "Hey Jackson, do you know what a pagan-necktie is?" he whispered. "Because you're about to get one." Steve's eyes widened, and a flat smile spread across his face and he drew back into the yellow moon. Jackson started hitting his head against the surface of the balcony, attempting to knock himself unconscious but lacking the strength to do so. Steve ruffled Jackson's hair, "How about one last cigarette for my buddy, Jackson—would you like that?" Steve shook the pack and his stubby fingers wrangled one free. He lowered it to Jackson's lips, but just before it got there, he snapped it in half and tossed it aside. "Whoops!"

The sound of an automatic knife snapping to life was crisp in the night and caused the hair to stand on Jackson's arms. He felt terribly cold. A concealed giggle tugged the corner of Steve's face as he examined the blade in the moonlight. "This won't feel good." he said, then jammed the blade into Jackson's windpipe. Air and blood sucked inside, and blood squirted across Steve's face as he sawed Jackson's throat open. Then he reached inside the wound, grabbed hold of Jackson's tongue and ripped it out through the hole. He laid the tongue out flat down the front of Jackson's shirt, patting his chest, "That's a fine tie you got there, Jackson!"

The pain synapses in Jackson's brain began shutting down and a darkening haze muted his vision as he gagged. *This is the best part*, HON remarked. The smell of cigarette smoke filled his nostrils and he blinked, clearing his vision just enough to see Steve smoking as he tied a rope around Jackson's ankles. "Almost forgot." Steve grunted, taking hold of the knife again, then stabbing Jackson's guts and pulling it sideways, before lifting Jackson into his arms and carrying him to the edge of the balcony.

He gazed in Jackson's eyes as he held him there in a bear hug. "I know you are in there, HON. I know what you have planned, but I want you to know that it isn't going to work. You underestimate Sandman. His latest software upgrade is more advanced than you know. You're never going to escape Skylark. Once I take control of the Inner Council, you'll be my slave . . . And by the way, thanks for that wonderful dome-job you performed earlier—quite energetic, I must say!" Steve grunted as Jackson slipped down a bit. He spit out the cigarette and adjusted his grip, lifting Jackson higher again. "Well, HON, Jackson—whoever it is in there." he said, "It's time for you to go now! 'Forward we march into the night, spared not pain we cling foolish to the belief we aren't slaves!' Down you go!"

Steve heaved Jackson like a javelin into the night. The cool night wind rushed across Jackson's face as he accelerated towards the swirling mass of darkness below. An ancient memory came to him then, something he hadn't thought of in many yerts. The face of his adoptive Castaway mother smiling down at him as he suckled at her tit.

The rope snapped tight around his ankle, ripping his spine apart, hurtling his intestines out the wound in his belly. Gigglers staggered towards him, reaching up and pulling the dangling entrails greedily into their mouths as they giggled. A familiar voice called to him from the other side, "*EAT ALL THE PEO-PLE—GIGGLE AT THE FUNNY JOKES!*" it said. And he began giggling—what could be more fun?

CHAPTER 20

RAINBOWS & SUNSHINE

MARCUS STOOD ON the balcony watching Jackson's body wriggle at the end of the rope. He felt no remorse, just as he'd felt no remorse in the PCWO Legal Decision room. He'd won child custody for pedophiles, drunks, gak-heads, and stalkers—sent Globos collectors after single mothers, tore children from homes; stretched cases, drained Globos chips, raided University savings, then dropped Ujee clients back where they started, broke and consumed by hate. He did this because his Bujee bosses told him to. He followed orders because it got him Globos and Globos got him gak. His lack of conscience was known as "Emotional Intelligence"—it was the greatest strength one could have in that profession.

Steve stood beside him with one leg up on the balcony rail, packing up a gak pipe. Marcus knew Steve was crazy—probably crazier than anyone he'd ever met, but at the end of the day, he wasn't that much different than the Bujee partners who owned the firm where he labored. Because he was a gak-head, they knew they could trust him. They preferred addict laborers like Marcus because they could control them easily. They even socialized with him, which was how he came to learn just how violent and perverted they all were. It didn't bother him at all; they'd lifted him out of Ujee poverty—kept his Globo chip warm and kept gak in his veins. Steve was no different than them. Only now, Globos didn't matter as much as food, shelter, safety and of course, gak.

He watched Steve hit the gak pipe and exhale a soupy cloud. Oh, how he hoped he'd be offered a chance to take the next drag. His leg shook, and he didn't even realize it until Steve glanced down at it and chuckled. "Want a hit Marcus?"

Marcus tried not to seem too enthusiastic in his response, but it was impossible—he hadn't had any for at least a couple horts and the creepy-claws were all over. He snatched the pipe and brought it to his lips, inhaled deeply and held the fire down, savoring the burn—wishing it could somehow replace the tissue of his lungs, before exhaling, slowly. He savored the brain-pop for a private cec until Steve's voice interrupted.

"Sorry about what happened to your quef-buddy Frank." Steve said, giggling. "I know how close you two had gotten!" He laughed, thunderously.

Steve had taken to calling Frank and Marcus "quef-buddies" ever since he'd forced them—at gunpoint—to engage in a forbidden pagan act with one another.

"That skinny little bish Bujee came out of nowhere—but did you see the way his head exploded? Like a ficking melon-lope!" Steve gasped, slapping his knee.

Marcus nodded and feigned some laughter, then took another big rip from the gak-pipe. Steve roared louder with laughter still. Marcus held the smoke deep in his lungs until a coughing fit forced him to exhale. Then, blinking to clear his tear-filled eyes, the edges of night crystalized; never before had his thoughts been so clear.

He decided right then he wouldn't let the ribbing about

Frank bother him any longer. Pride killed Ujees faster than bullets. Every jungle had a king, and that king got to do and say whatever it wanted until it was usurped. Guys like Steve rose quickly to the top, but they never had the staying power. Fiery, unpredictable and psychotic were good ways to rise, but not stay—hillmota, that bish Jackson had nearly killed him with his own shotgun. He'd just stay patient and wait for Steve to slip up. Then he'd be there waiting, knife in hand, ready to twist it into his back. Jose would be easy enough to control once Steve was gone.

Marcus realized quite suddenly that Steve had stopped laughing and was now glaring at the side of his head with hand outstretched, awaiting the return of his gak pipe. Marcus obliged, handing it over quickly, then wondered if Steve had somehow read his thoughts. He seemed to have an almost psychic connection to Jose—was he outfitted with some kind of brain-chip that enabled him to read minds?

"That bish inside is used up—get rid of her," Steve ordered.

Marcus turned to head inside, relieved at the opportunity to get away from Steve, but was stopped suddenly by Steve's powerful hand.

"Not you, Marcus. Jose is more than capable of freeing the bish of her obligations. I want you to stay out here with me, so we can share a pipe and gaze at the dazzling canopy of pagan stars."

Marcus hadn't even realized that Jose had been standing behind him. Steve's arm lifted from his chest and swept across the sky like some pagan stage performer. Paranoia buzzed Marcus's mind then and he worried that he'd already smoked too much gak. If he smoked any more his heart might explode.

Jose slid into the dark apartment and Steve packed an enormous pipe. Marcus eyed it, terrified by the quantity of gak. He yearned to find out that Steve was planning to smoke it all himself. Almost sensing his fear, Steve handed the pipe to Marcus. "After you Marcus, I know how much you love gak. I mean—for a man to do what you do for a living—they must love gak more than anything."

Marcus's hands trembled as he accepted the pipe, nearly dropping it when Jessica shrieked inside. He felt like he was hurtling toward earth on an out of control rocket ship and his entire body began to shake. He brought the pipe timidly to his lips and planned to take a very small hit as he depressed the ignitor switch with his thumb. Instead, Steve clutched his hand with his own, firmly holding Marcus's thumb down on the ignitor while his other hand held the pipe to Marcus's lips, leaving him no option but to continue inhaling until he reached the point of gagging. Snot leapt out of his nose onto Steve's shirt. Then a coughing fit brought him to his knees and breathing felt impossible and he thought he would never breathe again.

"That's it, Marcus, the smoke will set you free." Steve sang, "Feel that lovely burn. That's love you feel, Marcus. Do you feel the love?"

Marcus stared down at the stringing bead of snotted mucus dangling from his lips as the gak detonated in his mind and Steve's words hung in the air as though sewn there.

"Doesn't it feel good to get doctor's medicine? Don't you feel so much better now Marcus? Maybe later, you'll feel so good that you'll return the favor, know what I mean? See, because *I'm* the king of the jungle and that's how nature works—wouldn't you say? Hey Marcus, can you hear me?" Steve placed his heavy hand on Marcus's heaving spine, then said, "You wouldn't ever try to stab me in the back, would you Marcus?"

Marcus swung the stringy snot rope back and forth, indicating no. Steve knelt and whispered, "I didn't think so Marcus. I mean, why would you want to stab me in the back after all I've done for you? All I did was give you the gak you love and in exchange all I asked was a couple of favors here and there, nothing big. Sure, I busted your balls about Frank, but that was all in good fun. I mean, we all did some pretty crazy stuff in that apartment, didn't we? Nothing to worry about though, your secret is safe with me. Is my secret safe with you?"

The brain-pop Marcus felt was more intense than any he'd ever had before, and he was unable to articulate his thoughts. Reality unfurled like a black funnel tearing the universe in half and filling it with super-charged paranoia, invincibility, rage and ecstasy. He coughed again and spit, but the snot rope wouldn't break, so he wiped it with the back of his hand, then spread it across his trousers and climbed back to his feet. The night sky spun round him at impossible speeds, the pagan stars—streaks of light, and every nerve in his body was on fire. He felt alive and dead.

Jose reappeared, shadows hanging from his shoulders like a cape as he pulled Jessica's dead body onto the balcony. He lifted her naked corpse up to the rail, then heaved it over the side without word.

"I have a vision that I'd like to share with both of you," Steve said.

Small razor teeth flashed Jose's smile, as if he already understood what Steve was going to say. Marcus couldn't take his eyes off the cosmos accelerating overhead.

"Marcus, are you aware that I'm part of something much greater than all this? Marcus—did you know that?"

The words tightened around the stem of Marcus's brain like a snake restricting access to thought.

"Jose is the only one Sandman can still control. He's the only one who can stop me. Only, Sandman's distracted right now, and he left a weak little toad named Nicolae at the controls."

Jose's face fell like globules from a melting ball of blue wax.

The chorus of giggles echoed up from the street as Jessica's corpse was feasted upon.

"Marcus, are you listening to me?" Steve asked, "I asked you to kill Jose for me."

Marcus gazed at the white streaks in the sky with wonder. "I'm going to kill Jose." He said flatly.

"That's a good boy, but, you don't think Jose is just going to lay there and let you kill him, do you? I mean, look at him. He's already holding his knife. He'll kill you Marcus, if you aren't careful. Marcus—can you hear me? I said, Jose is going to try to kill you, so you'd better protect yourself."

"Protect myself?"

Blood bubbled the cords in his face, now red and purple and swollen with air like a balloon ready to float up and up. "That little bish don't stand a chance . . ." Marcus whispered towards the sky.

"Kill him, Marcus—he's the only one the Sandman can still control. He's the only one who can stop me from doing what I must!"

Jose melted into the stars as Marcus lunged, grabbed hold of Jose's scrawny neck, shoving the little man back to the rail. Jose's sharp teeth opened wide as he gasped. Marcus squeezed tighter, feeling powerful enough to crush the man's neck with his bare hands.

Aboard Thomulous, Sandman came running at the sound of the alarms. Nicolae, who was supposed to be monitoring things while Sandman was away, stood abruptly. "I, I didn't know what to do—there was no warning!" Nicolae stammered. Sandman tossed him aside and sat into the cockpit and struggled for control over Jose. The man attacking Jose was much more powerful, but Sandman had extensive hand to hand combat knowledge and quickly began applying them to the situation.

The cockpit screen burped and buzzed with alerts that Jose's body was perilously close to toppling backwards over the railing of the balcony. Sandman stabbed Jose's knife into Marcus's guts, but the man was gaked out of his mind and didn't appear to feel the wound at all. Marcus squeezed Jose's neck tighter and tighter, then finally heaved Jose over the side. Sandman could do nothing but watch Marcus's face get smaller and smaller as Jose fell to the earth, smashing atop the sidewalk, his vitals fading as the giggling horde surrounded him and began tearing off chunks of his flesh.

* * *

Marcus and Steve stood alone on the balcony sharing another pipe of gak as they watched the gigglers tearing Jose apart below. "I did what you ordered me to do." Marcus said, "What do you want me to do next?"

"Bring me my bishes back." Steve said.

The order roused in Marcus a yearning to kill again. He nodded, then waded into the subaqueous darkness of the condo, muscles clenched, milky sweat dripping from his forehead, and cords pounding up and down his swollen arms, neck and face. He staggered into the hallway, mind melting, bumping along, painting bloody rainbows with his fingertips on the walls as he searched through the building for Sarah's condo. It would take horts before the gak trip eased enough for him to find it.

CHAPTER 21

ESCAPING SARAH'S CONDO

A SANDPAPER TONGUE SCRAPED Li's scalp, lifting her from sleep. "OK, kitty, I'm up," she said, rolling from the bed and plodding to the door. Truffles scooted between her legs as she opened the door. The sound of drunken laughter echoed in from the balcony. She had no idea how long she'd been asleep, but the purple light filtering through the blinds told her it was morning. Sarah and Megan were smoking cancer-frees, each with their own bottle of wine clutched.

"Dunce bishes," Li muttered, rubbing the sleep from her eyes as she tip-toed around broken glass. She slid open the balcony door and squinted. The girls hushed. "How long have you been out here?" she asked. They looked at each other guiltily, then Megan snorted, and they both began laughing again. "Dunce bishes," Li muttered as she backed inside and slid shut the door. Her mouth felt dry and she went to the kitchen for something non-alcoholic to drink.

As she rooted around in the warm refrigerator, something banged against the front door. Li froze, and her heartrate jackhammered as she listened—hoping it was just Truffles knocking something over. A sound like fingernails scraped down the length of the door; then a deep, husky voice whispered, "Little bish, little bish—let me in, or I'll huff, and I'll puff and I'll stomp this door in. I've been searching all night, but now I've found you!"

Li grabbed a giant butcher knife from the block on the counter and held it to her chest. She recognized the sound of Marcus's gravelly, strained voice.

"I can smell you through the door," Marcus sighed, "Don't make me knock this door in!" His body pressed heavily against the door. "If you let me in, I'll put in a good word to Steve. See, me and him understand each other now, and I'm sure he'll be nicer if I put in a good word."

A howl of laughter between Sarah and Megan carried inside and Li spun around and waved for them to hush.

"Sounds like you bishes are having a real good time in there, but you're making your good friend Marcus stay out here in the hallway. Why don't you let me in? Why are you making me beg?" Marcus's fingernail spun slow circles on the door.

The balcony door crashed open and raucous laughter filled the condo. Li waved frantically to get the girls to quiet. Sarah recognized what was going on first and she went stiff, but Megan kept on laughing until Sarah grabbed her wrist. The realization had a sobering effect on them both.

"You bishes think this is a game?" Marcus's yelled sharply, "You think Marcus came down here to play *games*? You think you can play Marcus like a *bish*?"

Something slammed against the door, rocking it hard against the frame. "YOU WANNA PLAY GAMES? MARCUS CAN PLAY GAMES!" The door rocked again, and a decorative plate clattered from the wall.

Li stepped carefully back to the girls, "Let him inside and I'll hide over there by the door and stab him with this." Li showed the girls the glimmering knife.

"No ficking way—I'm not letting him *inside!*" Sarah replied as another thwack came at the door, causing Meagan to jump and whimper simultaneously.

"If you hadn't been making so much noise, he wouldn't have known we were in here! Just let him in and I'll kill him—I swear!"

"Why you bishes ficking with Marcus? You think I'm a dunce? I hear you in there plotting treasonous thoughts—"

"Get the fick out of here!" Sarah screamed. "You limp-donger-fick—think you can come down here to my condo, call me a bish and think I'm just going to do what you say? I've got news for you, Marcus—I know all about you, you little gak-head. You go tell Steve we've got James Duke in here and he's got all kinds of pagan guns and he said he's gonna fick up your face with one of them if either of you tries coming in here!"

"Why you bishes think I'm a dunce? If James Duke is in there, tell him to say something."

"I'm in here! I'll fick you up!" Sarah barked in the deepest voice she could muster, which wasn't very deep at all. Li rolled her eyes, shaking her head. Marcus cackled in the hallway, "You bishes are funny. Wait until I tell Steve about this—he's going to throw his back out at how ficking funny you bishes being."

"How about we let him in and pretend like we were just joking with him all along? We'll tell him we wanted to party with him, then slip him Easy-pills in his wine," Megan whispered.

"Good idea," Li whispered back, "Give me that bottle and some of those pills," Li said, snatching it before they were handed over, "I'll crush the pills in here and we'll get him to drink it!"

Marcus slammed against the door.

"We need to buy some time—one of you toy with him."

Sarah ran to the door and looked out the DigiPeep. "Hey,

Marcus, you know we're just ficking with you, right? We've been in here partying all night—just trying to have some fun with all this ish going on outside. Only reason we came down here was to get my stash of Easy-pills . . ."

Marcus stepped close to the DigiPeep but couldn't see inside because it was set on one-way.

"Nothing takes the edge off the creepy-claws like some Easy-pills and the horizontal pagan dance. We just wanted to play with you a bit—get you all wound up first, if you catch my wave . . ."

Sarah flipped the DigiPeep to two-way and flashed Marcus her faux-breasts, then switched the DigiPeep back to one-way. Eyes wide, Marcus rubbed his sweaty face and shook his head, grinning, "Ish . . . I didn't know you bishes play like that. Why don't you all quit teasing and let daddy Marcus come in there and show you how the pagans got down?"

Sarah looked over at Li, holding her thumb to the mouth of the bottle and shaking it vigorously.

"Get me that special cup!" she whispered. Megan appeared confused by the request for a moment. Then, she sprinted to the cabinet and grabbed a bedazzled pink goblet. On the side, **BAD BISHES** was spelled in jewels. Li took the goblet and filled it near to the top with the spiked wine, then tossed the bottle of Easy-pills to Sarah who'd already stripped to her underthings.

"Take off your clothes," Sarah ordered the others, "we need to give this ficking creeper a good show!"

Megan stripped without hesitation, but Li stood still, unsure.

"You aren't the special bish down here—take them off!" Sarah said, ripping Li's top off, exposing her perfect natural breasts with pointy pink nipples. Li's face flushed, but she knew there was nothing she could do at this point. She took a gulp from the goblet, then pulled off her trousers and threw them in the corner. Sarah reached her Globos chip hand to unlock the door and the three readied themselves by pinning their biggest, fakest smiles on. Marcus came inside, clutching a bloody wound in his guts with one hand, the other holding an enormous crowbar. He reeked of body odor and gak and the wound in his abdomen dripped black blood on the floor. He whistled when he saw the girls. Sarah slid around behind and locked the door.

"Why don't you put that down, big guy—don't think you'll need it." Megan said, touching the crowbar.

"Here you go!" Li handed the goblet to Marcus, "Every pagan-king had a goblet!"

Sarah guided Marcus by hand to the other room and closed the shades as he plopped down onto the couch. "Any of you bishes got any gak?"

"How about some Easy-pills?"

Marcus scratched his neck, "No gak, then?"

"Sorry, daddy." Sarah leaned over him so that her breasts brushed his, as she lifted the goblet to his mouth and held it back for him to drink. "Easy-pills are just so nice . . ."

Sarah dumped a handful onto the table then smashed them into powder. "Here daddy," she whispered, "Just take a deep breath of this." She sprinkled the powder across her faux-breasts and held them up in Marcus's face. "That's it daddy, take a real deep breath and all your problems will soar away."

Marcus's snorting sounded like a drone-vac caught on the trim of the carpeting. He kept his face buried in Sarah's faux-breasts and Li could see in the reflection of the visiscreen that she was utterly disgusted. Li took the bottle and came quickly across the room as Marcus made slurping sounds in Sarah's chest. She feigned pleasured moans, "Yeah, daddy . . . that's it—"

"How about some more wine, big boy?" Li said in her husk-iest voice.

Marcus's head shot up, as if he hadn't been aware Li had been in there. "Oh, ish, you're Steve's special bish . . . He got something planned for you." He said with a big grin on his face like he was in on a secret.

Li poured the remainder of the bottle into the goblet and pushed Sarah gently off him, took the goblet in her hands and straddled Marcus, brushed his disgusting cracked lips with her own, then pulled his head back and brought the goblet to them—forcing him to drink it all down.

"You're going to be my bish now, Marcus," Li whispered in his ear and could tell he was very excited by this news.

Megan and Sarah did their best to act sexy as they watched Li straddling Marcus, his bloody wound smearing her legs and the couch. The stench of his body odor saturated the room, but Li felt an obligation to prove herself to these girls after what had happened upstairs. They'd suffered so much at the hands of Steve, yet she had been spared. Now, she felt, it was understandable they'd turned on her. She was going to prove to them and to Marcus, that she was no bish. She'd labored too hard her entire life; she'd dealt with mother for too long to allow this stanky gak-head to get the better of her and her friends. She stood on the couch, with her lavender panties at the same level as his face.

"Get on all fours!"

Marcus stared with his mouth hanging open, duncely. His eyes rolled around like billiard balls, unable to focus.

"Now!"

Obediently, Marcus climbed off the couch and got onto all fours, his guts poking from the wound in his belly. He looked up at Sarah and Megan, both smiling at them and feigning like this utterly repulsive display was somehow turning them on. Li brought the heel of her foot down on the back of Marcus's head and pushed it to the floor. "Kiss the floor, Marcus!"

Deft as a cat, Li took hold of the butcher knife she'd hidden in the couch up over her head. Clasping the handle with both hands, she growled. "Who's the bish now, Marcus!" Then she stabbed the blade down into Marcus's back, causing the big man to cry out in pain and reach back over his shoulder, bucking and thrashing as Li held the handle with her legs wrapped tight around his sides like she was riding a bronco-bot.

Megan ran for the crowbar and tried lifting it, but it was too heavy. Instead, Sarah went for two bottles of wine, smashing them across Marcus's face as he grabbed hold of Li's leg and tossed her off. He stood unsteadily, his guts flopping out of his belly. He looked frantically at each of the three, trying to figure out who to attack.

Li grabbed a wine bottle, smashed it against a table, then lunged towards the man, and stabbed him in his neck again and again until the back of his fist caught her jaw and sent her back to the floor. Sarah smashed him with another bottle in the face. He cried out, grabbing his eyes, then fell backwards onto the knife handle, driving it deeper. He floundered around on the floor, a howling bloody mess, flipped onto his stomach, then smashed his head on the corner of a table, knocking himself unconscious. He lay there, groaning and snoring on the floor as the girls scoured for more weapons.

"Bishes," Marcus muttered drunkenly in his unconscious state.

"That's right Marcus—the baddest bishes you'll ever meet!" Li growled, then slammed a knife into his kidney and twisted.

"This is for Jessica!" Sarah hissed, jamming a knife into his spine and digging it around until it found sufficient softness to slide through. Megan straddled Marcus's back, "This is because you ficked with my friends!" She stabbed his ribcage, hitting his lung, which began making a disgusting sucking sound.

Marcus began crawling towards the door as Li and Sarah lifted the crowbar together. "Now you'll know what it's like!" Sarah hissed. With a heave-ho, the girls jammed the metal bar into Marcus's dumper—causing him to squeal like a piggy. They each took hold of the bar and shoved it forward, pushing him like a heavy mop out into the hallway. Sarah twisted the bar around in big circles as Marcus wept. They each took a turn swinging the big bar around. When it was over, they went back inside and left Marcus in the hallway, bleeding and crying.

CHAPTER 22

NAMELESS

EAT ALL THE PEOPLE!
GIGGLE AT THE FUNNY JOKES!

S TEVE STAGGERED DOWN the stairs through the chorus of giggles in the lobby, tearing off his clothing and slathering his naked flesh with black oil. PrP6 had severed his connection to the Sandman, but his mission parameter to kill James and Amy Duke and their unborn child remained imprinted upon his mind. He'd spent all night building a firebomb out of parts from the broken visiscreen and gasoline from a generator, but he couldn't remember having done that now. Still, the device with tape and wires dangled from a cord tied around his waist, the only article of clothing still clinging to his flesh. Conscious thoughts eluded him now. Only an animal desire to consume flesh and kill the Dukes remained. HON's terrible joke—the degenerative PrP6 commandments—pierced through his brain like high frequency shrieks that were tearing his brain tissue apart: *EAT ALL THE PEOPLE—GIGGLE AT THE FUNNY JOKES!*

"They're boiling me, *they're boiling me alive!*" Steve howled, clutching his head and wincing in agony as he reached the first-floor landing. The circuitous PrP6 commandments whirled around his brain, smashing synapses and displacing neurons. Gone was Steve—in his place, a being, caught between the living and the dead, who sensed the giggler's desire for his flesh and knew that he was not yet one of them—but soon would be. Rage marked each slurred syllable hurtled from his mouth, *"EAT ALL THE PEOPLE! GIGGLE AT THE FUNNY JOKES! LET THE CHILDREN PLAY! DILLY-DALLY WITH THEIR FOLKS!"*

The first-floor stairwell door bent inward under the weight of gigglers in the lobby. He stared at it, wobbling around on his feet as he filled his gak pipe then took a massive hit. Paroxysms of giggling collapsed him to the floor and he began spinning around in circles—his feet running sideways, shoulder acting as a fulcrum—giggling louder and louder at each pass.

"ALL THE CHILDREN PLAY THEIR GAMES—WE ADULTS JUST GO INSANE!" He felt invincible and aroused. He bounded to his feet, vomited in the corner, then took another hit from his gak pipe and racked the pump on his shotgun. *"GOOGLE-Y-GOO—I SEE YOU!"*

The shotgun discharge eviscerated one door hinge, causing it to lurch inward. *"WELCOME BACK, MY FRIENDS, TO THE SHOW THAT GOES WHIRLY-BIRD IN THE NIGHTMARE!"* Arms and faces of gigglers appeared, reaching through the opening into the stairwell. The spent shotgun shell pirouetted off the wall as the pump was racked and a fresh round loaded into the chamber. *"DADILY-DOO WHAT CAN I DO—I'M A PRODUCT OF THE TIMES I GREW UP IN!"* The second blast from the shotgun vanquished the door and gigglers surged through as if released from the spillway of a nightmare dam.

CHAPTER 23

LI

HORTS HAD PASSED since the giggling horde first reached Sarah's condo. After consuming Marcus bit by bit, they began breaking through the door. Now, Li sat alone in the darkness of the bathroom, humming to drown out the sound of the gigglers feasting on the corpses of her friends in the other room. Li had tried to convince the girls that they could escape, but once the gigglers finished off Marcus and began breaking down the door, they'd decided suicide was the only way out. Both Megan and Sarah hugged Li and apologized for how they'd treated her and thanked her for all she'd done. Then, each swallowed a fist-full of Easy-pills and chased them with wine. Li stood watching them as they fell asleep forever in each other's arms. Then she took her big knife and retreated to the bathroom with Truffles. There, she would make her final stand.

Mercifully, it sounded like the gigglers had finished off Megan and Sarah, but now their shuffled footsteps were coming towards the bathroom. Li had wedged the hamper and a flimsy cabinet against the door, but she seriously doubted they would hold up very long. *Why did I box myself in here?* she wondered. *Am I to die in the bathroom, just as my mother did?*

They clawed at the bathroom door now, giggling like demented jackals, sensing somehow that she was in there. Huddling in the tub, Li pressed the cold steel blade of the knife to her wrist and thought about slicing, but the image of the walnut caused her to stop. The walnut looked at her knowingly, clicking her tongue as if to say, "You fool—you never should have listened to your dunce friends! None of this would have happened if you'd stayed married to your husband! But you acted like a whore and betrayed your family and now look at you. You're going to get exactly what you deserve!"

Truffles hissed from his perch above the vanity as the door buckled inward and Li went and pressed her back against it as hard as she could. She scanned the tiny room for somewhere to hide, some place to go—second guessing herself about making her final stand in the bathroom instead of the balcony. Why had she come in here? Her instincts told her she needed to get someplace high. But no such place existed except the vanity on which Truffles hid, and that space was too small. Truffles clawed at a grate above the sink as a large splinter rocketed against the mirror. The cat curled in the shadow, hissing. *The grate—that's why I came in here—the grate! My subconscious must have remembered seeing it!*

Li leapt onto the sink, knife in hand, and began stabbing the edges of the grate frantically. The blade was too thick to pry at the edges, but the slits were thin and flimsy, and the blade could pierce through easily. Behind her, the door collapsed against the commode and the giggling collective pushed inside. Their icy hands clutched at her legs and she kicked them away. Fueled with fresh hope and fear, she stabbed wildly at the grate, pulling off spindles and casting them aside. Once the hole became big enough, she threw the knife inside, then lifted herself up, flutter-kicking the icy hands and pulling herself through with all the strength she possessed. Fingers bleeding, she heaved herself further into the dark ventilation shaft. Suddenly, she felt a cold hand grab her ankle purposefully, then a horrible pain tore up as her Achilles was ripped off her leg by the creature's teeth.

Howling in agony, she dragged herself further into the darkness, panting. The air shaft was too small for her to maneuver around and apply any type of tourniquet to stop the bleeding. She dragged herself ahead, hoping the shaft might widen out. A sound like a metal tray being dropped on the floor crashed behind her and caused her heart rate to spike. She looked back and saw the glowing green eyes of Truffles trotting towards her as hands clawed at the vent behind him.

The cat's claws clicked down the metal as he made his way. He purred as he rubbed his fur across her face. "Here kitty, kitty," Li whispered. But Truffles continued onward and quickly seemed quite a bit ahead of her. He stopped and looked back, eyes blazing, then continued clicking forward, as if to say to Li, "C'mon, I'll show you the way."

Li followed after him, unable to see the bloody trail in her wake. The darkness of the shaft seemed unending and enveloped her in a frigid blanket. Her teeth chattered and her flesh shivered as she dragged herself forward, muttering for Truffles to slow down. The echo of giggling seemed like a distant dream now, fading into the background of this narrow tomb. She knew that she'd bleed to death if she couldn't apply pressure to her wound, but unless the ventilation shaft widened out somewhere, there was no way she could reach it.

She was having difficulty seeing ahead, but the clicking sound of claws guided her. She reached what appeared to be a dead-end and Truffles was nowhere to be found, but as she felt around, she realized that the shaft made a ninety-degree turn. Li rolled onto her side, then pulled herself around the bend, spotting the cat's glowing eyes waiting for her in the darkness on the other side. The giggling reverberated around the aluminum and spiky pins and needles clawed at her ankle.

Crawling for what felt like horts, she called out in a druggy distant-sounding voice for the cat. She paused then, unable to locate the sound of his claws. "Where did you go, Truffles?" she whispered. No response came. She strained to see ahead, but a lustrous white light filled her vision. Blinking to clear the light only spread it further until it overtook all that she saw. *Eat all the people—giggle at the funny jokes!* a voice in her head commanded. Truffles' claws clicked past the side of her head, then headed back in the other direction. It felt as though the cat were kneading the soft tissue of her brain as he passed. "Why are you going back that way?" she asked, then continued crawling forward, stopping when her hand felt a void.

The sensation of this nothingness grayed the white light into silvery pixilation. She looked down and saw the eternal darkness of the ventilation shaft plunging straight down—how far, she couldn't tell. Truffles clicked and clacked from whence he came, the sound growing more and more distant. Mother's face emerged, giggling as she swung wildly from the rope, *"Eat all the People! Giggle at the funny jokes!"* She shrieked, as blood sprayed from the holes in her wrists like a sprinkler across the walls and mirror. Her smile widened, twisting up along the edges of the walnut's dark wrinkles until it touched the edges of her hairline. *"Dead end!"* she cackled.

Gray pixilation darkened in her eyes, expanding to the edges, until all she could see was darkness and mother's face, roaring with laughter—pointing at the daughter who'd dishonored her family. The throbbing in her leg faded, almost pleasurably so, and she realized it might be the last connection she'd have with this living place. A thought then flickered through her mind like a pagan candle in a darkened cellar. *Dr. Kunal—I love you,* she thought, and her mother laughed and laughed at her dunce daughter.

CHAPTER 24

BREAKOUT

THE GIGGLERS HAD been clawing at Duke's door for horts but made very little progress getting inside beyond poking their fingers through a few bullet holes in the wall. Dr. Kunal wore Amy's climbing harness, while Amy had been safely secured to the stretcher which was now laying across a table on the balcony beside the rail. Together, Duke and Dr. Kunal would lower Amy to the garden unit, then Duke would lower Dr. Kunal, finally, Duke would repel down himself. Their supplies were packed into a backpack, as was extra ammunition. Duke was loaded down with every pagan gun he had. His Tavor X95 was slung across his chest; the Canik TP9SFX long slide semi-auto 9mm was strapped to his leg; the Ruger Vaquero six-shooter with birdshead grip hung low in a cross-draw position and last, a little Ruger LCP II was tucked into the waistband at the small of his back.

Dr. Kunal excused himself to the bathroom and Duke gathered everything on the table next to Amy, then triple-checked the knots in the bedsheets they'd tied to her arms, legs and midsection to hold her in place on the stretcher. It helped having Dr. Kunal there as a second set of hands, even if he was stoned on a continuous Boogie-woogie trip. The doctor had Dexigon Ear-blasters playing Boogie Woogie music in each of his ears and had the vape pen loaded with grassy-petal-jay and a bit of gak dust strung around his neck.

The doctor was in very good spirits—likely because he was tripping. Duke remained in a constant state of worry, well aware of the danger of lowering his unconscious wife twelve-floors on a stretcher he'd built with their kitchen table. Then, he and the tripping Dr. Kunal would have to carry her through a building filled with gigglers. Fortunately, they could take Dr. Kunal's Lux-roader because Duke wasn't even sure if Amy had gotten back in their CAR. They'd have to escape the city limits, avoiding the PCWO Military blockade. Then, they'd have to drive through dangerous Castaway lands to get to Samuel's farm.

Amy appeared to have more color in her face since Dr. Kunal administered a blood transfusion, still, Duke worried endlessly about their baby. He wished he could contact Samuel, but still couldn't access Samuel's farm in his mind. The farm was the epicenter of an entire community of Serfs. Built far beyond the safe-zones and camouflaged by an electronic hologram dome that covered the entire area and gave it the appearance—even for someone standing just mets away from the outside—that it was a vast and foreboding wilderness, into which, no one would dare venture. Inside, there were underground bunkers and basement hospitals scattered throughout the territory. Getting there was Amy's best chance, but Duke couldn't remember how to get there now. He worried that the lack of sleep was causing this amnesia and preventing his self-hypnosis. Hopefully, he thought, once they got in Dr. Kunal's Lux-roader and hit the streets, the fresh air and feeling of escape would rekindle his memory.

Standing tall atop the table on the balcony beside Amy, he

gazed out at the unrecognizable New Chicago. The day had been bright, but now the setting sun cast a dark shadow across the horrors. Skyscrapers smoldered while ash flittered through the air like snowflakes. The first chill of the yert swirled like icy claws, carrying with it the stench of soggy death. All around were overturned vehicles and bodies stacked like sandbags along the streets. Signs hung from the windows of other buildings, like:

HUNGRY! HELP!
ALIVE HERE!
PLEASE SEND HELP!

The gigglers coalesced around several buildings nearby; Duke assumed that meant there were still non-gigglers inside. For days, the echoed roar of drones dropping into the atmosphere and making low bombing runs had been almost constant, but now the sky was silent and still. Duke wondered if the Inner Council had abandoned New Chicago as a lost cause; he hoped so because that was their best chance for escape. Stillness gave an eerie sense of calm that shouldn't have existed. It was as if they were in the eye of the storm now and it was only a matter of time before the second stage of the attack would begin. Duke didn't want to be anywhere near the city when that happened. He imagined it wasn't out of the question that the Inner Council would simply order New Chicago nuked.

Duke knelt beside Amy and checked for the fourth time that the bedsheets were snug and secure around her. He could hear Dr. Kunal humming to the beat of some Boogie Woogie song in the bathroom and smiled. Then he kissed Amy's cheek and whispered that he loved her in her ear. Suddenly, a loud crash came from the bathroom that was followed by a pandemic scream.

Sweat climbed the shoots of Duke's pores, "*Dr. Kunal!*" he yelled, standing.

BOOM!

A cataclysmic explosion then rocked the barricaded front door of his apartment, blasting it open. Thick black smoke billowed in and Duke nearly toppled backwards over the rail towards certain doom, but his swirling arms enabled him to hold his balance and remain standing on the table. Flame engulfed gigglers poured in through the front door from the hallway, setting ablaze whatever they touched. Dr. Kunal's shrieks twisted at impossible octaves inside the bathroom. Time and space collapsed like dirt upon the grave.

Duke wanted desperately to help Dr. Kunal, but he couldn't leave Amy alone. He wrapped the rope of her stretcher around his forearm, lifted it into the air and held it out over the side. He let the rope slide through his palm, unconcerned with the flesh it tore as it passed. Watching her face, it seemed suddenly to have been wrought with concern, he let more and more rope pass, hastening the rate at which he allowed it to fall, sensing the heat of the raging flames upon his back. Soon, he was rolling, and Amy was nearing the end of the line and the gardens below.

An icy dry hand clasped his ankle, causing the rope to slip from his grasp and he strained, gritting his teeth, and closing his grasp as tight as he could to stop her descent. The stretcher stopped suddenly, and the rope swung out awkwardly, causing Amy to swirl around in the air, six or seven mets above the garden, her unconscious body sliding sideways until her head dangled over the side, held only by the bed sheets. The stretcher spun, twisting the rope tight until the pressure built too strong and released—spinning her back in the other direction, her hair swirling through the air like a golden pinwheel. Then, glass splashed down onto the patio below from the sliding door of the garden condominium. A woman dressed in a red dress lay face down in the bed of broken glass. The woman slowly pushed herself up to her feet then staggered to where Amy swung suspended in the air, her arms upstretched rigidly and her face etched in pained giggles.

For an instant, Duke felt compelled to leap down upon the woman to protect his wife. But a solitary neuron fired logic into his brain, overruling this ludicrous notion. Instead, he grabbed the other rope and fed it through his harness, prepared to repel down, but by then there were countless icy hands clutched to each of his ankles, pulling at him with all of their strength. The force of their pulling nearly rocked him over the side of the balcony before the rope was secured. Wobbling, once more with his arms spinning in circles to hold his balance, he looked down at the balcony, totally filled with gigglers all reaching up for him like pagans come to pray at the feet of some great preacher. Testosterone tore through his brainstem like nitroglycerin and reality crystalized. The giggling woman in red couldn't reach Amy—he had time to try to help Dr. Kunal. He shouldered his X95, aimed into the giggling mass, then retracted his index finger, spraying drum after drum of five-five-six-millimeter bullets into giggling gray skulls.

Gray flesh peeled back like biological fireworks and the corpses piled around the foot of the table. Duke dropped another empty drum, reloaded with a forty-rounder, leaped down, and continued administering head-shots. More gigglers oozed inside from the hallway like a draining stomach wound. His rifle clicked empty again and he drew his Canik TP9SFX and emptied the twenty-round mag into the nearest gigglers. Then he dropped the mag, reloaded and proceeded to dump the fresh mag into twenty more. Forward he marched towards the front of the apartment spewing bullets at the endless stream of gigglers pouring in amongst the fire and choking smoke. He veered to the right before reaching the kitchen, towards the bathroom and now silent Dr. Kunal.

Duke holstered his Canik, reloaded his rifle, turned and dumped the mag into the group that had filed behind him. Two more lunged out of the bedroom and he skewered each with his bayonet. "Dr. Kunal!" he shouted. He slammed his shoulder into the bathroom door, expecting it to burst open, but it didn't budge. Something heavy pressed against the other side. He lowered his shoulder for leverage, then drove the door as if pushing a weighted sled. This created enough of a gap for him to slide inside. The door slammed shut behind him and he tumbled forward in the darkness, crashing into the bathtub.

Duke illuminated the flashlight on his bullpup and saw Dr. Kunal's torso half-eaten next to the commode. Ceiling chunks hung down from the ventilation shaft gaping above. Li glared at him with greedy annoyance as she giggled up blood, then pulled more of Dr. Kunal's intestines into her rapidly expanding stomach. Duke drew his Ruger six-shooter and put a bullet in her skull. He climbed up from the tub, kneeled beside Dr. Kunal, thanked him, then cut off his thumb and stuck it in his pocket.

Duke forced open the door and stepped out into the smoke-choked apartment, inhaled a thick gulp of it and buckled over in a fit of coughing. Blinded from the toxic smoke and pressed by the heat of the flames, he thought he might combust if he didn't get outside quickly. With his sleeve covering his mouth and squinting out through his watering eyes, he stumbled towards the balcony, slamming and tripping over furniture as he went. Some heightened sensorial impulse instructed him to look up and force his eyes open and when he did, he heard a sinister roar.

The butt of Steve's shotgun blasted his face like a pagan freight train, plowing pain into his brainstem and sending him to his back. He looked up at the dark hulking figure of Steve, nude except for black running grease smeared across his body. Steve snarled then lunged onto Duke, beating him with the butt of his shotgun, again and again. Duke struggled to deflect blows with his forearms and hands. He kicked out at one of Steve's kneecaps, temporarily causing the giant to stumble. This bought him time to slide backwards, creating some distance, which soon proved unwise.

Steve utilized the extra distance between them to wind up and deliver a thundering sporter-ball kick to Duke's ribcage, evacuating whatever oxygen had been in there. Steve cocked back his fist and sent it blasting down, but Duke managed to shift his hips just enough to avoid a direct blow. The dark figure fell with all its weight atop Duke, gyrating as it rained down furious blows, one after the other. Steve's face twisted with rage. Thick yellow bands danced from the edges of his mouth as he snarled. Duke's brain buzzed, as if rebooting like a computer, while the back of his skull bounced like a sporter-ball on the hard floor.

Steve's rage manifested itself into Duke's face. As consciousness began to flicker, he saw Amy in his mind, dangling from that rope with the red dress giggler reaching up for her. Steve's face materialized in the hazy black atmosphere and blood surged through Duke's muscles.

He rocked his hips up into a wrestler's bridge then whipped his legs around Steve's head and shoulder, grabbed his wrist and ripped down with all his strength. Steve's black oily flesh slipped from his grasp and the hulking man wriggled free, grimacing and staggering drunkenly before he resumed pounding Duke's face with his fists. Duke slid sideways, dodged two blows, saw Steve slowing, noting that the big man was trying to achieve the same force on his punches, but now had to reach back much further to do so. As Steve reached back to deliver a monstrous blow, Duke swung his legs up again and snatched the hulk's neck and shoulder. This time he grabbed the back of Steve's head and pulled it towards him, jamming his thumb deep into Steve's eye socket as he did. Steve shrieked like a hog at the slaughter as Duke dug deeper with his thumb nail, ripping back in a prying motion that extricated Steve's eyeball from its home.

Steve lurched back in a sharp spastic contraction, generating enough force to escape Duke's grasp. His eyeball dangled from a pink fibrous thread from his oiled face with an expression of baffled terror and pain. Heat shimmered from Steve's oily flesh as he stood like a force field of deathly energy radiating away. Duke kicked the inside of Steve's knee hard, shearing instantly the ligaments and cartilage within. The sound was like a bedsheet ripped apart and the certain pain brought Steve to the floor instantly. Duke again ensnared Steve's neck with his legs. Then he held Steve's wild hair, ripped back, closing his windpipe and pinching off the man's carotid artery. Steve's muffled gasps turned to blubbering sobs, then Duke grabbed Steve's left ear and ripped it clean off. The pain, shock and fear this caused injected Steve with fresh adrenaline fuel. And he reeled back in a super-human frenzy. Steve stood with Duke dangling from his neck like some giant pendant necklace. He lifted Duke up to the ceiling, then slammed him down onto his skull with a wrestler's power-bomb.

Darkness cascaded in Duke's brain like a roiling storm in the infinite sea. Steve lifted again, but his overtaxed heart and lungs failed, and the surge of strength evaporated. Instead of slamming Duke to the floor, he just collapsed on top of him. Duke shifted Steve's weight sideways, rolled him onto his back, then slid his thumbs into Steve's mucous-encrusted mouth and pressed with all his strength as Steve's pig eye bulged and his cheek tore loose from his face. Blood sprayed from the torn artery across Duke's face as he pushed harder, relishing the panicked whimper sounds Steve made as he did so.

Once Steve lay motionless, Duke climbed off, wiping the blood on his trousers as he stumbled through the flame-engulfed apartment, coughing and gasping for the crisp cool air that awaited outside. Climbing the stacked corpses back onto the table, he looked down at Amy and saw her still dangling above the giggler in the red dress. Then he fed the end of the rope through his harness and began his descent over the side of the balcony. He leaped and allowed himself to freefall before clamping the descender, swinging back to the building, then sprung his legs again in a leap.

This time he let more rope out, allowing himself to free fall a bit, but something wet splashed him and he looked up to see Steve's face coming right for him like a warhead at the speed of gravity. The hulk slammed onto Duke and tangled in his rope, causing both to freefall. Duke squeezed the descender to slow their shared fall and while the skin was flayed from his palms, he did succeed in slowing himself just enough to cause Steve to topple off him. He looked down, watching the hulk free-fall towards the patio, his foot clipping Amy's stretcher just before he splattered into the garden.

Duke dropped the remainder of the way, clamping the brakes on the descender once more at the last possible cec. Immediately, he fired a round from his Canik TP9SFX into the forehead of the red dress giggler, then went to Amy and lifted her off the stretcher. He carried his wife a safe distance from the violence, as if protecting her from its ugliness. Steve's shattered corpse giggled in the mud of the garden and his flaccid giggling corpse began mitching its way towards him like some horrible land-crawling eel. Duke left Amy's side and drew out his bayonet then stood about the giggling eel and spit. "Say hello to the Sandman. Tell him I'll be seeing him real soon." He dropped down with the bayonet clutched tight between his fists and stabbed it clean through Steve's skull until the point stuck into the dirt beneath it

Wiping the blade on his trousers then sliding it back into the sheath on his hip, he went back to his wife's side and kneeled.

"James?" he heard her whisper and thought for a moment that he'd imagined it.

Amy's eyes flashed open, filling Duke's heart with warmth never before felt. Tears involuntarily rolled down his cheeks and he knew if he tried to say something right then, his voice would crack, so he just rubbed his hand through her hair and smiled and hugged her close. Overhead, flames roiled from the apartment and burning debris rained down upon the garden like Armageddon. Duke loosened his embrace and brushed his hand through her blonde hair again and wept uncontrollable tears of joy and relief.

"Are we OK?" she whispered.

Duke nodded, then kissed her cheek and clutched her firmly in his arms.

CHAPTER 25

FULL THROTTLE

Duke held Amy under one arm and his X95 under the other as they descended the smoke-filled stairwell towards the parking garage while giggling corpses ambled towards them. He splayed their brains across the walls with five-five-six-millimeter rounds. He kicked open the door to the garage and flicked on his flashlight, scanning the vicinity with a slow semi-circle, before continuing forward, guided by the circular orb of light. They walked slowly down the rows, looking for Dr. Kunal's black Lux-roader. Their footsteps scraped the concrete floor and the sound of giggling from the street filtered inside while the hair on their necks stood at attention.

Something moved in the shadows ahead and Duke shined the flashlight on it. A pack of rats scattered as if fleeing a crime scene. A woman's body lay prostrate on a dry sheet of blood, half her face eaten off by the rats. Amy shuddered in his arm. "Don't look," he told her. Just then, he spotted the black Lux-roader with the "DRD" plate on front. Amy sat on the bumper of a car parked beside it as Duke pulled Dr. Kunal's thumb from his pocket and used it to unlock the door.

He helped Amy into the passenger seat, then went under the hood and disengaged the auto-drive restrictor before bounding into the driver's seat. He swiped Dr. Kunal's thumb over the Ignition Scanner and the engine roared to life. The automatic lights illuminated the concrete spaces around them. He shifted to reverse, then tapped his toe down on the pedal, chirping the tires out of the spot faster than he needed to. He shifted into drive, then stomped the accelerator and the fat performance tires screamed around the twisting concrete ramp filling it with smoke and the smell of burning rubber. He smiled and pressed down harder on the gas, round and round they drifted in a near perfect continuous slide the entire five levels until the big garage door came into view.

Duke pressed his toe down harder as they raced towards the door and Amy said something he didn't quite hear over the roar of the engine. Pedal to the floor now, Dr. Kunal's Lux-roader burst through the door and Duke cut the wheel hard, sending them into a controlled skid down the driveway, out onto the street, with gigglers being launched through the air. Duke hammered the pedal as hard as he could, ratcheting rubber and tossing gigglers like garbage cans. The engine growled and rattled their arms with goosebumps. The city they'd known was gone and all that remained were burned buildings, overturned cars and ambling giggling bodies. He pressed the accelerator and tightened his grip around the wheel, turning out onto the main drag, headed towards the gas-zone.

"Where are we going?" Amy asked.

"The gas-zones," Duke replied, "We're getting out of New Chicago."

"I spoke with Samuel . . ." Amy murmured, her voice drifting into silence, as if she'd suddenly remembered a distant memory.

"You spoke with Samuel?" Duke asked, confused. "Baby,

you've been in a coma for two weeks and we don't even know where he is, remember? He faked his death and went into hiding because of Project Reveal. Do you remember any of this?"

"Don't talk to me like I'm a dunce!" Amy snapped, "I know I've been in a comma—I didn't know how long, but thanks for finally telling me." Her face became flush. "I don't know *how* I spoke to him, but it happened while I was asleep . . ." Amy gazed out her window as she spoke somberly. "I remember standing in the field in front of his farm and the sky was gray, and a cold drizzle swirled in the wind. He was digging, and I stood there watching him for what felt like an eternity. And when he was done, he stabbed the blade of the spade into the earth and turned to face me, wiping his hands on a handkerchief as he sauntered towards me. He didn't seem surprised to see me there, almost like he'd been expecting me. That was when I realized that he'd been digging two graves. I remember, he didn't want to hug me because his overalls were dirty, but I hugged him anyways. And he was cold; so cold." Amy's voice quivered, "Every mitch of him was frigid—colder than anything I've ever felt that was alive. It startled me. I, I, recoiled, and I saw the hurt that caused in his eyes and seeing that hurt made me weep. And he held me and whispered in my ear."

"What did he say?" Duke asked.

"He told me that we had to go to the farm and there we'd receive our orders . . . And that we were having a baby boy." Amy's voice broke as she said the words and tears streaked her cheeks. "He told me that we're to name him Noha."

Duke grasped her hand, brought it to his lips and kissed her knuckles. "We need to get to Samuel's farm." he said, "but I can't remember how to get there."

"I'll guide you." Amy replied, "In my dream, Samuel showed me exactly how we're to get there . . ."

Amy's voice trailed off as she gazed out the side window

of the Lux-roader. The bus ride home was the last thing she remembered and the world she'd known had changed radically. Maybe that was a good thing, she thought. Maybe there really was a future possible without the PCWO, the Inner Council, and DCCM thought monitoring. Even amongst all this death and destruction she felt suddenly a deep sense of calm as she rubbed her womb tenderly. She'd always known in her heart that in her lifetime, she'd see the Inner Council fall and the rights of the individual restored. If death and horror was necessary to bring about that brighter future, then so be it. That bright new world would need strong women and men to rebuild it. It would need leaders who resisted the temptation to seize absolute power. It was time for a future where leaders sought to extend power to others, rather than horde it all for themselves. This future would be free and just. Who cares if it was brought about by giggling undead cannibals.

"It's PrP6 that's causing this, isn't it?" She asked, "Just like they did to your father?"

Duke nodded his head in response. "I don't know how it happened, but it's PrP6 alright. The same lunatic infection that killed George—HON's first attempt to overthrow the Inner Council—'Eat all the people—giggle at the funny jokes . . .'"

"But didn't the Inner Council make sure PrP6 could never come back?" Amy asked with a hint of sarcasm in her voice that caused them both to snicker. "Well, I guess that wouldn't be the first time the Inner Council ficked something up beyond belief." She added.

"No, it wouldn't be . . ." Duke replied with a half chuckle, then became stern and silent suddenly. In the rearview mirror, he saw headlights from a black OFFROADER following them. He stomped down hard on the gas pedal and told Amy to tighten her seatbelt.

Amy looked back and saw the headlights gaining on them,

then reached across the center council and withdrew the Canik TP9SFX from the holster on Duke's hip. She pulled back the slide to visually confirm that a round was loaded in the chamber. "How long have they been tailing us?" She asked.

"I don't know, I just spotted them back there."

Duke cut the wheel in a hard right, bounded up over a curb, then splashed down in a giant puddle before ripping the wheel left down an alleyway. The Lux-roader launched over speedbumps and slammed dumpsters and garbage cans out of the way.

"Do you think we lost him?" Duke yelled over the roar of the engine.

Amy spotted the headlights in the alleyway behind them. "No!" she yelled, then opened her window and fired three warning shots into the sky.

CHAPTER 26

SANDMAN COMMETH

SANDMAN MADE HIS way down the gangway of Thomulous, the heels of his boots clicking like hooves over the metal grates. He stooped in a bow at the eye scanner and the door to his car opened in an exultation of pressurized gas and condensation. Blood pooled on the floor over which he strode as the wheezing wet sounds of Helton Quiver feasting on what remained of Nicolae filled the room. Her midsection bulged unevenly from the flesh she'd consumed, and her sluggishness was apparent when she hardly turned at all to face him. Sandman's long bionic arm clutched her wrist like a grappling hook, dragging her, flopping and thrashing, like a speared tuna across the deck of a ship. He secured her wrists and ankles again in the shackles, then left her there as she began hacking up bloody guts and bits of bone like a sick dog. Sandman clapped his hands, summoning the Clean-bots from the wall. Then, commanded them to clean the carpeting and remove the couch and dispose of Nicolae's remains.

The drones clicked out of the wall and began cleaning with white sudsy foam. Sandman went to his visiscreen and activated it using the chip in his mind. The screen pixilated out like ripples from a stone dropped into a still pond. As the screen spread, it separated into two-hundred-and-ninety-nine unique rectangles, each an emergency line to the surviving members of the Inner Council. One square—the three-hundredth—remained black.

Soon the wall was buzzing with hungover looking faces all twisted and irritated and demanding to know what was going on. Sandman clapped his hands as if to serve warning for quiet, then bellowed, "Silence!" He paused to ensure each stunned face had quieted before he continued. "I have summoned you here to discuss an important matter."

Behind him, Helton Quiver vomited intestines onto the floor, then giggled as she rattled at her chains. Sandman gestured back to her with his long bionic arm. "As you can see, the Supreme Chancellor has been stricken with the PrP6 super prion."

A gasp followed from each of the faces on the wall like a tidal wave passing over the screen. Cries of "Darwin!" and "What are we going to do?" followed, then the assembly devolved into a raucous and unintelligible gaggle of side conversations.

The Sandman's immense inverted cross necklace glimmered in the light of the visiscreen as he waited, annoyed, before demanding silence again. "Quiet!" his voice box rattled. Then he paused again to ensure his command was observed before he continued. "Members of the Inner Council," he said, "While you've all been sitting on your dumpers in your luxurious bunkers, I've been continuing our war effort against the Subversives. You all—for the first time in your miserable lives—have been kept in the dark about what's happening out here. Each of your heads are undoubtedly filled with questions about the PrP6 outbreak. Specifically, you're wondering how that mistake—which was supposed to have been destroyed—managed to return from extinction and become a bonafide global outbreak that now threatens to turn every citizen—both Bujee and Ujee alike—

into giggling cannibals, just like our *former* Supreme Chancellor back there." Sandman gestured back at Helton Quiver, who was staring at the Clean-bots with a thick strand of bloody drool running from the edge of her mouth to the floor.

"PrP6, as you are all well aware," Sandman continued, "was the first super prion created by HON. Prior to PrP6, all super prions had been created by Dr. Umur Tummel. But when the doctor's *friend* HON had surpassed his own intelligence, he allowed the AI the freedom to create a super prion that was tested on a group of PCWO Marines in an experiment. We all know how that experiment turned out. As we came to learn, HON was actively conspiring to overthrow the Inner Council and the entire Unified Global Government. PrP6 was HON's way of creating a global crisis that would distract us all while it implemented stage two of its plan—the extermination of the entire human race. Fortunately, HON wasn't quite as advanced as it is now, and we were able to stop it before it got very far.

Helton Quiver giggled wildly behind Sandman. He looked back at her, then shrugged and resumed speaking to the Inner Council. "Rather than shut down the DCCM program, you decided to have the PrP6 super prion strand discontinued, the PrP6 satellites deactivated, and safeguards were put in place to ensure HON could never attempt something like that again. Eventually, HON created PrP10 and all of the DCCM program, which is the bedrock of our civilization today—"

A member of the Inner Council, Cher Denimin, shouted, "Get to the ficking point, Sandman!"

Sandman's left eye began to tremble, and his mouth hardly concealed a growing snarl as he continued speaking, "Obviously, the PrP6 safeguards that were put in place were insufficient."

Dez Chevroy, a portly member of the Inner Council, bellowed, "We already know all this *Sandman*, you dunce! Get to the point—I have a massage scheduled!"

Sandman glared at his monitor, "Well then," he continued, "since you all have such important obligations to attend to, I'll get right to the point . . ." he paused, taunting Dez Chevroy by wasting precious cecs before he continued. "As you all know," Sandman said, "my father was a member of the Inner Council and I am his only direct lineal descendent. When I was very young, it was decided that because my mother was a whore, I would be disqualified from taking over his seat on the Inner Council when he died. *That* decision was made *despite* the fact that the Forbearer's bylaws *explicitly* state that a direct lineal descendent is to assume the seat of a deceased Inner Council member.

"Of course, back when my father died, you weren't able to game this system by having your consciousness downloaded onto a chip and plugged into the brain of a younger and more vibrant clone of yourself before you die. Back when my father died, direct lineal descendants actually assumed the seats of their dead relatives—which is exactly how some of you are in the position you are in today."

Sandman's eyes narrowed as he continued. He still couldn't stop his left eyeball from twitching. "I have studied the white papers written by the Forbearers and nowhere do they indicate that the 'son of a whore' is precluded from assuming the seat of his or her dead Inner Council parent! Which means, I have been cheated! All my life has been spent laboring on behalf of the Inner Council and I served you loyally and dutifully and consistently and successfully carried out your dirtiest of deeds. Yet you cheated me from my birthright—"

Clair Washington—the longest tenured member of the Inner Council—interrupted, "Sandman, you have no business addressing the Inner Council on this matter! You are totally out of line. If you continue speaking to us on this matter there will be serious repercussions!"

Sandman's strange flat smile spread as he replied, "Shut that sniveling hole in your face, Clair—the Sandman is speaking and from now on, when the Sandman speaks, each of you dunce piles of *trash* will listen carefully. Understood?"

A shocked wave of gasps swirled from the visiscreen. Sandman continued, "You see, I alone possess the answer to the question that's dancing around in your dunce aquatic brains. Because it was *I* who reactivated the PrP6 satellites. It was *I* who infected batches of Castaways and carried them aboard Thomulous, dumping them inside safe-zones all across the Unified Global Government like biological weapons—"

"Impossible!" Dez interrupted, "The only possible way to reactivate the PrP6 satellites was with Inner Council access privileges!"

The Sandman's strange flat smile spread until the creases of his uncolored lips seemed to touch his ears. "Have you all forgotten about your dear friend, Cameron Paddleton, already?" he asked as his left eye trembled wickedly, appearing as if it was trying to leap out of the Sandman's face. "Deceased Inner Council member Cameron Paddleton was discovered hanging in his closet with a belt around his neck and his donger in his hand . . . Certainly, you haven't forgotten your dear compatriot, Cameron, have you?" Sandman paused for a response, but none came. "Well, I suppose his indiscretions and the way they so poorly reflected upon the Inner Council would make me want to forget him as well . . . But as it is, I can never forget Cameron Paddleton."

Sandman's smile foreshadowed his knowledge of a great secret all knew, but none spoke of; a secret he'd soon put to word, thus, shattering their privileged lives with the truth of the horrors they tolerated amongst their ranks. "Did you all know that Cameron Paddleton had an island where he liked to hunt little children as though they were wild game? Oh, yes, it's true.

In fact, he routinely dispatched me to the Castaway villages to kidnap the children and bring them to his island. He had a great palace built atop the volcano there and he had cameras installed all across the island. He'd sit in that palace with floor to ceiling visiscreens and watch the children as they stumbled through the jungle, hungrily searching for a way to escape. He would do quite a bit of gak, as I remember it. Once the children had become rather weak, he'd don his hunting gear and take to the jungle, stalking them with pagan weapons of various sorts. He did this for yerts, and somehow, none of you were aware . . . Rather convenient, isn't it?"

Sandman paused with his scarred eyebrows raised as if to allow the question to ferment before he continued speaking. "I ordered one of my chipped soldiers to hack into the AI at Cameron Paddleton's island palace and stole all of the recordings he kept of himself hunting and butchering the children. One day—after dropping off a fresh batch of children to his island—I informed Cameron that I was in possession of the recordings and I was planning to hand them over to the Serfs. He knew, as I did, that despite the Inner Council's powerful control, the release of those recordings to the population would have inspired such anti-Inner Council subversive thoughts that half the population of the world would quickly accrue sufficient Subversion scores to place them into Level Nine. It would have destroyed the entire DCCM program! Needless to say, Cameron Paddleton was rather desperate to keep these recordings from falling into the hands of the Serfs. So, I offered him a proposition: in exchange for the recordings not being released, I'd give him eternal life in a consciousness chip and in exchange, he'd give me his eye—"

"Donald ficking Darwin!" a member of the Inner Council exclaimed, prompting Sandman's flat smile to spread further still. Sandman gazed at the visiscreen on his wall, soaking up with great pleasure this experience as it began to dawn on many members of the Inner Council what Sandman had done.

"Murderer!" one member shouted—"You'll ride that ficking cross of yours, Sandman, I swear it!" the member continued.

"Shut your odious mouth!" Sandman hissed in response, "I haven't finished speaking yet, you ficking dunce. If you keep on blabbering it will be *you* who rides my cross!" Sandman then continued recounting his story, "I had my left eyeball removed and had Cameron's surgically implanted in its place. Because you dunces failed to upgrade the security systems at the Skylark Medical Research facility, I was able to gain Inner Council level access to HON using Cameron Paddleton's eyeball to get through the scanners. With Inner Council access privileges, I was able to order HON to reactivate the PrP6 satellites and manufacture doses of the PrP6 super prion. I then created a custom encryption key over the PrP6 satellite control system and ordered HON to erase its memory of me ever being there ... It's rather amazing the access privileges you have granted yourselves with that powerful Superintelligence. The experience made me wonder what you all get up to when you're alone with HON."

"Impossible!" Tait Gled cried out from the bedroom of his bunker.

"Don't be a dunce, *Tait*." Sandman said, "You of all people should know that what I am telling you is absolutely possible and entirely true. Generations of total control and infinite power, now aided by the technological advancements that HON keeps creating for you, has turned the Inner Council into a lavish mob of dunce sloths who have no idea what's going on in the world they govern. All of you have become so dependent on your underlings—like myself and that stain on the floor behind me, Nicolae ... *We* ensured the Unified Global Government continued running smoothly. Because it was only us who knew what the fick was going on, *we* were able to throw a proverbial pagan wrench into the whole ficking thing—which is precisely what we've done!

"You ficks euchred me out of my patrimony and I decided I wasn't going to play nice any longer. I spread PrP6 throughout the Unified Global Government and I infected Helton Quiver with PrP6 at a lavish dinner party aboard Thomulous. I alone possess the encryption key to stop more from being infected. All I ask in return for doing so, is that you honor my birthright and grant me my father's seat upon the Inner Council . . .

"Oh, one more, *small* thing. After you have named me to the Inner Council, you will elect me Supreme Chancellor, replacing that dreadful dunce puking up behind me. Then, after I have deactivated the PrP6 satellites, you will inform the citizenry that it was me—Supreme Chancellor Sandman—who figured out how to stop the PrP6 outbreak. You will then place me into the Hall of the Eternal."

Each face on the Sandman's visiscreen held a silent, stunned countenance. The members of the Inner Council eyed the Sandman as one might eye a poisonous snake. Cameron Paddleton's eye trembled in the Sandman's skull, a skull more alloy than bone, and Sandman's lips curled up at the edges near the lines dangling from his eyes. Helton Quiver had begun giggling wildly again, but Sandman paid her little mind. He withdrew his pack of clove cigarettes from the pocket of his black leather PCWO jacket and with the long slender claws of his bionic arm, withdrew one and placed it between his grinning lips, then lit it with a blue flame that appeared mysteriously, as if produced out of thin air. Sandman took a long cool drag and exhaled the smoke through his nostrils, then cleared his throat and spoke, "Soon, my troops will launch an assault on Samuel Duke's farm. I've come to learn the location thanks to a message sent to him by the one, Dr. Umur Tummel, who I have come to learn, has been assisting the Serfs for over three-yerts now.

After I wipe Samuel Duke and the Serfs from existence, I expect that the Inner Council will have an answer for my demands . . ." Sandman took another drag from his cigarette, then continued, "I expect that your decision will be that you will allow me onto the Inner Council and elect me Supreme Chancellor. You have three days to render your decision. Goodbye."

Sandman's brain chip cut the communication feed and the visiscreen went dark. In the dark reflection on the wall, smoke curled from the Sandman's lips, like steam rising off dead bodies scattered along a black meridian.

FIND OUT WHAT HAPPENS NEXT
IN VOLUME II OF KILL AGAIN.

Follow the author @RDGreenfield1 on Twitter for updates
and please leave a review on Amazon.

ABOUT THE AUTHOR

R.D. GREENFIELD is the author of the science fiction series, "Kill Again." He's a futurist, free speech advocate, and enjoys exploring conspiracy theories. He lives in Chicago, Illinois, with his wife and daughter. When he's not working as an accountant, he's writing, reading, or cultivating new ideas. His stories are written for the thoughtful, disregarded, malcontents—those society ignores because their opinions are inconvenient for the bloviating blabbermouths. He hopes his art raises awareness about the dystopic future our world leaders appear hell-bent on creating. He admires all who defiantly refuse to relinquish their dreams.

Made in the USA
Lexington, KY
11 June 2018